The Samovar Murders

Also by Alexei Bayer

Murder at the Dacha

The Latchkey Murders

Murder and the Muse

THE SAMOVAR MURDERS

ALEXEI BAYER

russian life

ISBN 978-1-880100-69-1

Library of Congress Control Number: 2019951682

Russian Information Services, Inc.
PO Box 567
Montpelier, VT 05601-0567
www.russianlife.com
orders@russianlife.com
phone 802-223-4955

Cover image: Samovar photograph by Refat Mamutov

The propaganda effort never flagged. Red Army
troops were presented, effectively, with two wars
simultaneously. The first, the one that they alone
could know, was the war of the battlefield, the
screaming war of shells and smoke, the shameful
war of terror and retreat. But the other, whose shape
was crafted by writers, was a war that propaganda
created. Soldiers and civilians alike could learn about
it in the newspapers, the most popular of which, Red
Star, was read aloud to small groups at the front…
Fighting might seem to take place outside real time,
in horrifying moments that later defied recall, but
Stalin's official war unfolded with epic certainty, in
regular and well-planned episodes.

Catherine Merridale, *Ivan's War*

PROLOGUE

The soldier is battling sleep. His eyes have a life of their own. They repeatedly close in spite of his best efforts. His scrawny neck can no longer hold up his heavy head. It tilts helplessly onto his shoulder.

Sleep closes in like a soft white wall. Like the autumn fog that invades the flood meadows back home. It envelops you and clings to your body, leaving behind a sticky residue on your face and hands. The kolkhoz horses and beech trees silhouette against its white expanse. The horses whinny as he passes. He's almost home. His village is just beyond the ridge. The hill rises steeply, the footpath winds through wet clover.

He hears himself starting to snore and jolts awake, his heart racing. To be discovered napping on guard duty means certain court martial and a bullet in the back of the head. Wartime justice.

The vision of the fog, the horses and the hill has vanished. He briskly rubs the back of his neck and yawns. He'd better start thinking of something else, something that will keep him awake.

At night, it is always dark at the front, but never completely quiet. There are always noises. To the right and left, his comrades lay sprawled at the bottom of the trench; unseen, they snore and groan as they turn in their sleep, scratching the lice bites beneath their overcoats. There is the rumble of a tank engine in the distance, the hiss of a flare lighting up no-man's land, the burst of machine gun fire or the gunshot of a solitary sniper, all against the backdrop of a distant artillery bombardment. The sounds are so familiar that the ear ignores them. They are a part of the nighttime silence just as the momentary light of the flare is part of its darkness.

Wars are fought by large numbers of men. They are a clash of large male collectives. A wall of men in grey on one side and a wall of men in khaki on the other. Wall against wall. He is a small brick in one of the walls. There is nothing inevitable about being part of one wall or the other. Merely an accident of birth and geography. Of where the lines get drawn. Fog knows no borders, nor does rain and snow. Clover grows on flood meadows everywhere. Birds fly over borders and horses would travel across them if they weren't hobbled.

He had best not think of such things, of home things. Better to focus on the walls.

As things stand, he's mortared into *this* wall, the one on his side of the barbed wire divide.

His uniform is dirty and splattered with mud. It has turned from khaki to mud-brown, camouflaging him against the featureless mud-brown landscape and the mud-brown trench. His face and close-cropped hair are also mud-brown, and so is his helmet, rusting beneath a layer of chipped paint. His own mother would have trouble telling him apart from his mud-brown comrades.

He knows that in a war of very large numbers, the Workers' and Peasants' Red Army is invincible. Not only does Russia have millions and millions of mud-brown soldiers like him, but they are a true collective. Bricks in the wall. One just like the next. He has a will to live and a desire to survive, and he knows he is vulnerable. He has seen things happen to others – nasty things that make you tremble and throw up with fear. And those things – and even worse things – may yet befall him, but it does not make any difference. The mud, the uniform, the closely cropped hair make him like all the others. When his time comes, the next brick will slide snugly into his place.

He once heard Captain Makarov, their battalion commander, say to another officer: "Soldiers shouldn't have names. They should leave their names at home with their mammas when they're called up. They shouldn't even have numbers. They should be a mass, like a pile of coal that the fireman feeds into the furnace of a steam engine. Their only function is to make the great locomotive of the Red Army move forward."

Captain Makarov laughed as though it was a joke, and the other officer joined in.

"So, is it a mistake, then, for any soldier to think he'll survive?" the other officer asked.

"The pile of coal is there for one reason and one reason only," Makarov replied, "to end up in the furnace."

Captain Makarov is dead now, killed by a sniper bullet as he was getting out of his staff Studebaker to inspect their positions. The soldier saw it happen. He wasn't more than fifty paces away from Makarov when the man was hit.

Captain Makarov was replaced by Captain Malakhov. Captains are interchangeable, too. They too are bricks in the wall, just slightly larger ones. Or maybe they are the same size, just placed in more important sections of the wall, at the corners for example.

Captain Makarov was an old man by the standards of the war, twenty-eight or maybe even thirty. Captain Malakhov, however, is a kid, only a few months out of the officers' training school. In the war, you rise through the ranks quickly if you're a junior lieutenant and are lucky enough to stay alive for a few weeks. In the war, everyone aims at officers before they aim at soldiers. Captain Malakhov has been aging quickly, looking more and more like Captain Makarov with each passing day.

Theirs is a huge country. What was Hitler thinking when he invaded? Even if he had taken Moscow, which is anathema to think and would lead to a court-martial if you said it out loud, but still, even if he had taken Moscow, he wouldn't have won. There were more places like his village east and north of Moscow, with silky grass growing on the banks of no-name rivers and wooden houses perched on the ridge above. Their wall could have moved behind the Urals if need be, to the swamps and the taiga of Siberia, and they would have gone on fighting there, too.

Then the Fritzes with their tanks, mechanized howitzers and motorcycles would have been swallowed up by the swamps and the taiga.

He can almost see the German military gear sinking into the vast, impassable marsh that lies between his village and the town of Zakobyakino, twelve kilometers away.

Insidious thoughts of home are sneaking back into his head. They will make him nod off again. He must keep his mind on the war. The war keeps him awake.

His musings are interrupted by a dark shadow sliding noiselessly through the trench.

"Password," he shouts. Standing in the trench and peering in the darkness has made the soldier warm and stiff, and now that he has to turn around and face the shadow, pointing his rifle at it, the wet autumn air rushes into his threadbare overcoat.

"Sparrow," comes a hoarse reply.

The soldier relaxes.

"At ease, private."

The soldier recognizes the Jewish surgeon from the field hospital. What is he doing here, in the trenches? He's supposed to be with his wounded and the old ZIS-5 truck that transports them to the rear, its splintering wooden roof and doors emblazoned with red crosses.

The Doc sits down on the tree stump that serves their company as a chair and a table, depending on the need of the moment. He pulls out a cigarette. A real cigarette, and not the edge of a newspaper rolled into a tapered cone and filled with black, homegrown dust.

The Doc is a young man, too, not much older than the soldier. He has a boyish round face and closely cropped black hair. He is a Jew but not the kind the soldier has ever seen. He's tall and powerfully built. And supremely self-confident, of the kind that inspires confidence in others. A leader of men. If he is ever wounded, the soldier would like this guy to take care of him.

The soldier wants to score a cigarette off the Doc but doesn't dare ask. In any case, he is not permitted to smoke on duty. He breathes in, inhaling the dense cloud of tobacco smoke. He hasn't smoked since starting guard duty nearly three hours earlier. His head starts to spin.

"Take a cigarette, private," the Doc says, as if reading his mind. "Don't be shy, take a couple. Tomorrow is going to be a long day for us both."

ONE

The Boss has the largest office in our fortress-like headquarters that looms over the narrow lanes and shabby two- and three-story houses in this part of the city. To Muscovites, the building is known simply by its address: Petrovka 38, rather than by the agency it houses: Moscow Criminal Investigations, or MUR. The Boss's office is connected to the outside world by a reception area furnished with metal filing cabinets and presided over by the Boss's unsmiling secretary, Della.

The rest of the Boss's team are crammed into a few offices strung along a long narrow hallway on the opposite side of the landing that feeds the grand stairway and the elevator. When Della marches down to summon you to see the Boss, the walk to the Boss's office, with her marching a step behind as if you are under arrest, can seem long even if your conscience is clear, as mine was on that bright spring afternoon.

"What are you working on, Matyushkin?" the Boss inquired as soon as I came in and before I had time to click my heels.

This opening meant that whatever he had summoned me for was important. Because the Boss's usual practice is to leave a subordinate standing at attention, pickling in his own juices while he looks through a file or makes a phone call.

The Boss's office has a large window, with a panoramic view of Petrovsky Boulevard. Its ancient poplar trees were glinting silver in the light breeze, and the onion domes of the former St. Peter's Monastery rose behind them, gleaming like freshly polished copper samovars. And, this being a particularly clear spring day, I could also see the spiky towers of the Kremlin beyond, offering a vision of still more gleaming onion domes.

"What are you working on, Matyushkin?" the Boss repeated impatiently.

"What do you mean, Comrade Colonel?"

It wasn't that I didn't know what I was working on. I certainly did. But I wasn't ready to respond so quickly. I was sure I would have enough time to gather my wits while staring out his window.

"I asked you, what you were working on, Lieutenant. Is that such a difficult question?"

The Boss was notoriously quick-tempered. He could sour on you in a minute and hold a grudge for a long time. Our meeting was not starting on a good note.

"Senior Lieutenant Urumov and I are investigating an attempted robbery and assault on a salesgirl at Danilov Farmers Market, Comrade Colonel," I responded, trying not to get flustered by the Boss's grim stare. My brief hesitation did nothing to dispel his belief that all men under his command – and, especially, my partner Lenny Urumov and I – sat in our offices all day twiddling their thumbs. That could not have been farther from the truth: The Boss had assembled a remarkably hard-working, dedicated team of detectives.

"Ah, that one." The Boss waved his hand dismissively. "The one where a salesgirl got stabbed?"

"Yes, sir."

"How's she doing?" he asked, feigning concern.

There was no use reminding him that a week ago Urumov had reported to him that the young woman, who in addition to being stabbed had been hit in the face, was back home. The Boss never forgets anything you tell him. It was a trick question, and I knew exactly where he was going with it.

"She's out of the hospital," I replied. "They wired her broken jaw and she's resting at home. She had a concussion, too. The stabbing wound wasn't serious. Just a scratch."

"There we go," the Boss said, his voice dripping with sarcasm. "I like your attitude, Matyushkin." He mimicked me: "'Just a scratch,' he says. I suppose that's why you have been sitting on this case for more than three weeks. It's a simple case and I was sure you two would crack in a day or two. Perhaps I should have let the local boys handle it. At least they know their own hoodlums."

"It's not one of their hoodlums," I mumbled under my breath.

"What? What did you say? Speak up, man."

"I said it probably wasn't some local street thug trying to hit a market stall," I said. "It was some sort of a warning or settling of scores between organized crime groups."

"Well, even more reason for you to move quickly. I don't need to tell you that the longer a case remains unsolved, the less likely it is to be solved."

"Yes, sir," I said. "We are aware of that."

"In any case, both of you should not be wasting time on it. Your partner, whatever his name is, can do it on his own.

This was another one of the Boss's affectations: he liked pretending that he couldn't remember Lenny's name from one day to the next.

Until that moment, the Boss conducted the conversation in a decisive and even aggressive tone, but now he grew silent and shook his head pensively. His moustache drooped and he gave me a doleful look.

Because of that long, thick moustache, the Boss was known throughout Moscow Criminal Investigations as Budyonny, in honor of the Civil War Red Cavalry commander and the Marshal of the Soviet Union, Semyon Budyonny, who sported a similar moustache. But if the real Budyonny's moustache made him look fierce and warlike, the Boss's gave his face a permanent hang-dog expression.

"As for you, Matyushkin," he said at last, "I need you to do me a favor."

"Yes, sir," I said quickly, fearing that he was about to lapse into one of his long silences.

"It's about the Lumumba murder."

He turned toward the window. I stared at the back of his head, waiting for him to continue. He wore his hair short, revealing a fold running across his thick neck.

Patrice Lumumba had been a Congolese freedom fighter murdered some years back by the French. Naturally, it wasn't his killing Budyonny was referring to. Two days ago, Valentin Viktorovich Kotov, a famous poet and a war hero, had been stabbed to death at Moscow's Lumumba Friendship of Nations University. Kotov, who had been invited to read his poems during the Victory Day celebration, had been killed by one of the school's African students.

The murderer was caught red-handed, as they say in cheap crime novels. He didn't try to run or cover his tracks. There had been no quarrel and no apparent motive. The cops, who arrived ten minutes after the body was discovered, took the student into custody on the scene; he offered no resistance. There wasn't anything for us to do, and whatever loose ends there were would surely be tied up by the cops from the Southwest District, where the university was located.

Since Budyonny was not intent on continuing, I ventured to break the silence.

"It seems like it was an open and shut case—"

He pounced on me at once.

"Sure, Matyushkin, it may be an open and shut case in your professional judgement –" He took time to sneer and show how little he thought of my professional judgement. "But it involves a prominent literary figure. Valentin Kotov was a member of the Writers' Union. Not to mention the fact that his killer is a foreign national. A guy from the Central African Republic is not like a Frenchman or, god forbid, an American, but he's still a foreign national, no matter what color his skin happens to be. This requires us to keep an eye on what those clowns from the Southwest District are doing, to make sure they don't screw up too badly. It's not a typical murder case for them, where some guy cracks his neighbor over the head with a vodka bottle. They'll have to go strictly by the book. The world will be watching. So we, too, need to keep an eye on their investigation and be ready to pick up the pieces if they screw up. We could easily be told to come in at a moment's notice. I assume you know what I'm talking about, Lieutenant?"

I did. Budyonny was, in his own way, a brave man and an honest cop. But when it came to dealing with his own bosses, the Big Bosses at MUR, the Ministry of Internal Affairs, and elsewhere, his overriding priority was to cover his own ass. Doing so skillfully is how you survive in a high position.

"In short," the Boss concluded, "I want you to do me a favor. Drop whatever else you're doing and go pay a visit to the Southwest District headquarters. Don't be a jerk about it, don't try to butt in, and don't pick any fights. Just gather as much information as you can without ruffling feathers."

That last point was moot, because both of us knew that the moment a Petrovka detective darkened their doorway, local cops turned hostile and defensive and clammed up, refusing to offer any assistance. In such circumstances, when I was clearly coming in to second-guess them and to look over their shoulders, any attempt to mount a charm offensive would be doomed to failure. Worse, it would be seen as patronizing.

As I saluted and turned around, the Boss said, "Major Yegorov is in charge there. I've known him for years."

He hesitated briefly before adding, "He's a piece of work."

TWO

What I told Budyonny was true. The Danilov Market case was complicated because food and clothing markets are the only permitted form of private enterprise in the country. Everything else is owned and run by the state.

The market is a place where farmers can sell the produce, dairy and meat that comes from their private plots. The plots are small, and people are allowed to cultivate them only after they have finished their day's work on the collective farm. But they work hard on them, a lot harder than at their regular jobs. They charge higher prices, but you can't compare the quality and variety at the market with the paltry selections at state-owned stores.

Clothing and other items sold at such markets is more of a grey area, but the state turns a blind eye to any irregularities, as long as things don't get out of hand. Unfortunately, they always do. It becomes a black marketeer's paradise, where a lot of money is made and exchanged under the table. And, wherever there's a black market and a lot of money, you can be sure you will get crime. Organized crime to be precise.

One category of criminals sells clothing manufactured at underground sweatshops in the Caucasus, or popular items diverted from state stores. Another category of criminals – bigger fish, the

Thieves in the Law – run protection rackets, collecting a percentage of what the first category of criminals earn.

Everyone knows that we don't have much luck cracking such rings. Both categories break the law, so vendors don't go to the cops when they're shaken down.

The Boss is aware of the way things are, but he doesn't want to talk about it. He regards our inability to eradicate racketeering as a major failure. Racketeering was the reason he put Lenny and me on the Danilov Market case and didn't leave it to local cops. Local cops are likely to be on the take.

Indeed, the case reeked of racketeering. Everyone, including the injured salesgirl, Oksana Maltseva, claimed it was a robbery. Oksana said that money had been taken from the cash drawer, in the amount of 78 rubles and some change. But why attack her after taking the money, and why so viciously? The take ended up being too small and the robber got angry? But who would expect more from what was nominally a used clothing stall? Actually, the reported take was even a bit high for a weekday morning.

Another salesgirl working at a stall nearby confirmed Oksana's account. And yet, the cops responding to the call were unable to find a single shopper who had seen anything, even though the crime happened in broad daylight. And the descriptions of the perpetrator provided by the victim and the witness didn't quite match.

After reading the police reports and studying the statements, Lenny and I concluded that, first, there was more to the attack than Oksana had been willing to tell us and, second, whatever the robber looked like, he was probably didn't resemble the person either of them had described.

One reason my partner Lenny was such a good cop was because he hated all crime and all criminals and took the job of catching them personally. But he reserved his special hatred for criminals who preyed on the weak and the defenseless. The circumstances of this case made his blood boil. Assaulting a woman was bad enough but hitting her in the face and trying deliberately to disfigure her was the kind of thing that, as far as Lenny was concerned, had written the perpetrator out of the human race. As luck would have it, Oksana was also exceptionally pretty, which you could see even though her face was bruised and swollen. And her eyes, still bloodshot and reduced to slits, were of a rare violet color.

Lenny's problem was that he was highly susceptible to female beauty. Particularly if that beauty was in distress. And even more so if the distress had been caused by a crime, his direct line of work. He wanted to be a hero and that, naturally, made fall in love with Oksana.

They say that most people when they fall in love don't necessarily love the object of their affection but instead see themselves reflected in the eyes of their beloved. In Lenny's case, there was some truth in this. He saw himself as some sort of knight errant, a Don Quixote in the service of his beloved.

Lenny began visiting Oksana at the hospital. His excuse was, first, to determine whether she had recovered sufficiently to be questioned, and then questioning her. When it became clear that she would insist on her original version – of a robbery followed by a violent attack by a young kid whose appearance she no longer could describe accurately – Lenny declared that he wanted to get close to her in hopes that she would open up to him.

When we first started working the case, I told my girlfriend Tosya about Oksana. Tosya is very tough and prickly on the outside – she had to be, having grown up in an orphanage during the difficult postwar years – but she is tender and compassionate on the inside. She went to visit Oksana at the hospital, too, and they got along well. Tosya stopped by to see her a few more times, inevitably running into Lenny, who by that point was showing up with bouquets of flowers and boxes of chocolates. Tosya not only knew that Lenny was happily married and the father of two delightful little girls, but had become friendly with Lenny's wife, Raisa. So she would glare at him and then complain to me about my partner's unhealthy interest in Oksana, as if there was anything I could do about it.

Before long, Oksana's mother made it unpleasant for Lenny to come to the hospital, and Lenny had to flash his ID at hospital personnel in order to see Oksana at all, usually after visiting hours, when her mother was already gone.

He continued to lavish his attentions on Oksana after she had been sent home. In fact, his visits became more frequent and longer. Now Lenny spent several hours every day at her bedside. While Oksana's mother still disapproved of his visits, he had managed to strike up a friendship with Oksana's father.

"He's a war hero," Lenny told me. "Severely disabled. Completely blind and missing his left arm. And a few fingers on his right hand, too. Got blown up by an anti-personnel mine during the war."

Oksana's father was convinced that Lenny was stopping by daily for the sole purpose of answering his questions about the progress of our investigation and listening to his advice in the matter. They drank countless glasses of tea in the kitchen, which Lenny brewed under the blind man's supervision, and ate apple pie baked by Oksana's mother. She was a first-rate baker, Lenny assured me.

"The father, Stepan Sergeyich Maltsev, knows something about the attack on his daughter," Lenny declared after his first two visits. "I can sense it. Besides, they live far too well for someone who's receiving a veteran's pension. Others in his condition beg in the street, while he has an apartment in a new building. I feel I need to keep talking to the father as well as to the daughter."

But the sad truth was that, while Lenny was eating large quantities of first-rate apple pie and watching Oksana get better, and I was beating the bushes in and around Danilov Market, trying to find out something -- anything -- about Oksana and her used clothing stall, we were getting nowhere in our investigation.

Despite being married, overweight and having a head of thinning hair, Lenny had a magnetic effect on young women. But not this time. Perhaps Oksana was still suffering from trauma. Be that as it may, she was proving to be uncharacteristically indifferent. That made Lenny as melancholy as any unhappy lover, but it also made him all the more furious at the guy who had attacked her, and all the more eager to bring him to justice.

With this in mind, Lenny was not at all upset to hear that I was being reassigned, and that the Danilov Market case was henceforth his alone. All the glory would go to him and he would not have to share the spotlight with anyone.

"Let me know if you need my help on your case," Lenny offered magnanimously in parting, perhaps trying to make up for his evident joy at seeing me leave the field to him.

I'm not sure he took in what the Boss wanted me to do. He was mouthing the words but gazing dreamily out the window, at the spectacular blooming of spring outside. He seemed to have forgotten that he had not yet solved the case and whether he would depended on his ability to expose Oksana's lies and obfuscations. Which meant that, if he did solve the case, Oksana might not be at all grateful.

THREE

Orders are orders, even when they are couched as a request. That was why that same afternoon I found myself headed for the city's Southwest district.

Major Yegorov was a thick-set, paunchy man nearing retirement. He was one of those who had left their impoverished villages somewhere in the Russian North and moved to the city, usually after completing their military service. Becoming a cop is a natural career path. It comes with a uniform, a salary, and a room in a communal apartment. They marry early, because life can be lonely so far from home. They prefer to marry peasant girls, because city women are too independent for their taste and don't respect their husbands.

They cut their teeth patrolling some high-crime factory neighborhood on the outskirts. They make diligent cops, neither too smart nor too ambitious. Their climb up the career ladder is slow, but through sheer persistence they retire at the rank of senior lieutenant or captain. It's rare for them to make a leap all the way to a major, to wear a large star on their epaulets, but Yegorov had done it, and you had to take your hat off to him for that.

It didn't take a Sherlock Holmes to figure out all this about Yegorov. It was written all over his rough-hewn, dark-red face, in his small grey eyes, and on his massive plowman's hands, which still held the soil of his native region beneath his coarsely cut fingernails.

Yegorov sat sweating in the stuffy air of his office, eyeing me narrowly. To my request for a briefing on the Kotov investigation he gave an irritated reply, "Read the file if you've got so much time on your hands, Lieutenant."

He tossed a green folder in front of me. While I was reading it, he remained seated behind his desk, drumming his fingers on its dusty surface.

The folder was much thicker than I had expected. Yegorov's people had done their legwork. It confirmed the importance of the case and suggested that I was not the only one looking over his shoulder. There had to be some big bosses breathing down his neck, and I was soon to be given a demonstration exactly who they were.

The file contained a stack of highly detailed photographs of the crime scene, with one set showing the victim's body as it was found, slumped in an armchair. His arms were constrained by his jacket, which had been forcibly pulled down over his shoulders. His mouth was clamped over with black industrial tape. An enormous puddle of blood had spread at his feet and under his chair. It was thick, and dark as pitch in the black-and-white snapshots.

I am always shocked by how much blood can seep out of a human body.

Even before I read the medical examiner's report, I could see how Kotov had died. The wound had been inflicted with something like a very sharp lancet, a straight razor, or a thin knife. The man's stomach was cut dead center, opening him up groin to solar plexus. The intestines spilled out onto his blood-stained lap in a glistening tangle. His pre-knotted tie, hanging from an elastic strap over the front of his blood-soaked white shirt, looked like something that had also tumbled out of his abdominal cavity.

Another set of pictures, taken at the morgue, showed the body stripped naked and laid out on a granite slab. The intestines had been stuffed back inside, and the long wound traversing his pale hairless stomach hastily stitched together.

The scar was perfectly straight, as if drawn by a ruler. No sign of hesitation. Whoever carved him up must have had nerves of steel and a steady hand.

Next there was a stack of mug shots of the murderer. I pulled them out of their black paper envelope and set them aside.

Yegorov's croaking brought me back to reality.

"Hey, Lieutenant, if you intend to do all your reading here, keep in mind that this is my office and not a public library. I've got my own work to do. I'm not paid to watch you read."

Reluctantly, he offered me their large, shabby interrogation room. Everything he was going to do for me would be done with ill grace. I was ready for that. But I also knew he wouldn't go as far as to refuse my requests, as long as they were reasonable. He had to pretend to be cooperating.

I sat reading the file, and every time I lifted my head, I would see my own face reflected in a scuffed one-way mirror. While escorting me down the maze of narrow, dusty hallways strewn with cigarette butts and other trash, Yegorov had signaled to one of his uniformed cops to follow us. The man's faint outline was now visible in the mirror, behind my own reflection. The cop was watching me, perhaps to make sure I did not attempt to steal some important document out of the file.

The medical report confirmed that Kotov died from loss of blood and that his death was painful but relatively quick – it took between seven and ten minutes, according to the pathologist's estimate. The tape over his mouth prevented him from screaming. He had bit his lower lip hard and had tried to bite through the tape, too. He also tried to free himself, and would have succeeded, had it only been his jacket that was restraining his movements. However, there was also an elastic band tying his wrists together, which had cut deep into his skin.

Death doesn't change the way men look in life; it solidifies them and imprints the look of solemnity upon their lifeless features. But it rarely makes the dead look dignified.

The snapshots showed Kotov as a man of around fifty or fifty-five, muscular and powerfully built. It wouldn't have been easy to immobilize him, even if he had been taken by surprise. The police report, however, indicated that there was no sign of struggle in the room, which was relatively small. Any kind of struggle would have turned the place upside down.

Witnesses had been interrogated and their testimonies were typed up and attached to the file. It appeared that Kotov, a famous poet known largely for his patriotic war verses, had been invited to the Friendship of People's University on the occasion of the upcoming May 9 holiday, the anniversary of the Soviet victory over Nazi Germany. He was to read his poems to the student body, which consisted of foreigners from post-colonial countries as well as some Soviet students. The administration felt that his reading would do double duty: give foreign students an opportunity to hear Russian poetry, while also advancing their ideological indoctrination, which was part and parcel of getting a free education at a Soviet university.

Now I was ready to get acquainted with the murderer. He was a fifth-year engineering student from the Central African Republic named Joseph Kofunda. Set to graduate in less than a month, Kofunda had been in the audience during the reading and had spoken during the question-and-answer period, engaging Kotov in a discussion. Kotov's poetry apparently had a considerable effect on the young African, but by all accounts, a positive one. Kofunda too had been in a war in his native country, which he tried to express to Kotov in his flawed Russian. Far from being angry with Kotov or arguing with him, he admired Kotov's poetry, saying that he felt exactly the same way about war.

After the reading, two or three students approached Kotov on stage, but since the auditorium was about to be locked up, he invited them to continue the discussion in a small office adjacent to the auditorium, which was where his body was later found.

Kofunda didn't want to join the other students. He wanted to speak to the poet one-on-one. Kotov's seven-year-old son Oleg, whom he had brought along to the reading, also waited in the hallway, as did another student, a young woman from Argentina.

Little Oleg Kotov would later cause additional alarm, because after the murder he was nowhere be found, and everyone was worried that he too had been killed. He was subsequently discovered sleeping in the locked auditorium, woken up, questioned and delivered to his mother.

Despite his young age and severe shock, Oleg was a capable witness. He said that he and Kofunda had sat together while the Argentinian student had gone in to talk to Kotov. Kofunda was friendly but excited, waving his arms around and telling Oleg things that appeared to have something to do with shooting. The boy missed seeing the Argentinian leave the office, because he had gone down the hall in search of a bathroom. By the time he returned, Kofunda was no longer in the hallway: he had gone in to see Kotov.

Kofunda stayed in with Kotov for a long time. The boy could not be sure how long. He didn't have a watch, and, to a bored and hungry little kid, time must have seemed to pass extremely slowly. He did not hear any sounds from behind the closed door.

When the door finally opened and Kofunda emerged, Oleg knew at once that something had gone wrong. The African was shaken, unable to speak and tears were streaming down his face. He collapsed on the floor while several students passing in the hallway entered the office and raised the alarm.

Kofunda didn't move until the cops arrived. He allowed himself to be arrested, photographed, and taken to jail without offering any explanation as to why he had committed such an atrocity. He remained silent and only asked for a glass of water when they got to Butyrka Prison, whereupon he drank three in quick succession, his teeth rattling so much the arresting officers feared he would break the glass.

I took one of Kofunda's photographs from the pile. It was a standard mug shot, a double portrait, full-face and profile, showing a young, very dark-skinned African male. The flash used by the jail photographer reflected off his forehead and cheekbones. In profile, he had a flat nose, a prominent forehead, and an even more prominent

Adam's apple. He sported a long, curly goatee growing mostly under his chin. Written on the margins was his height, a tall one meter, eighty-nine centimeters. Under special marks, no tattoos were listed, but several scars on the suspect's chest and stomach were described as forming a pattern consistent with ritual tribal scarring practiced in some parts of Africa.

Another report, provided by the university's admissions office, identified Joseph Kofunda as a Negro male, place of birth the Central African Republic, holding a temporary travel document from the British Protectorate of Nyasaland, twenty-eight years of age. The report described him as a mediocre student, enthusiastic and eager to learn, but excitable and given to arguing with his teachers and other students, mostly about politics and European colonialism.

Ever since entering the university, he had lived in a dorm about half a mile from the university building, sharing a standard room with four roommates, all of them other Africans. There were complaints about them from the dorm manager, but that wasn't unusual: African students threw noisy parties and were incorrigible about smuggling in Russian girls as overnight guests.

Having finished, I headed back to Yegorov's office. Despite his claim to have work to do, he was still sitting in the same position I had left him in, still sweating and staring at the wall. Nothing had changed except his coat looked a bit more wrinkled and shabbier. It was not especially clean, either, and the collar of his blue shirt was frayed. His kind of old-timers don't care one bit about their appearance.

"Did you have a chat with this Kofunda character?" I asked.

The otherwise carefully put together case folder was missing any reference to an interrogation of the murder suspect.

The major shrugged, "We sure as hell tried."

Being laconic when answering questions is second nature for the likes of Major Yegorov. These long-serving types are not afraid to appear stupid or ill-informed, since this is what their bosses think of them anyway. They know that saying nothing is far safer than saying something that can later be used against you. Getting any information out of them is like pulling teeth.

"Does he speak Russian?"

"They all have to, at the university."

"Why hasn't he been interrogated then?"

"He won't talk. All he does is sob. Like a woman."

"Was he seen by a physician?"

"He's alright. The nurse gave him a shot to put him to sleep."

"When was that?"

"Last night. And the night before. Every night since the murder."

"He can't still be sleeping," I said, getting irritated.

"Even when he's up, he won't talk."

"Why is that?"

Yegorov shrugged.

"He just won't. But let me assure you, Lieutenant, you'll see his confession in this file before too long."

He winked at me. It wasn't a friendly wink. It was more like a keep-your-nose-out-of-my-business kind of wink.

"Easy, Major," I said. "He may be a French citizen or a British subject."

"Last I checked in the illustrated edition of the Great Soviet Encyclopedia, Lieutenant, the Brits seemed to me a bit whiter," he snapped, looking truculent. "And I don't need you telling me how to treat my suspects. I've been briefed by higher authorities then you stuck-up MUR detectives."

I nodded. I wasn't going to pick a fight with the good major.

Yegorov pulled out a cigarette and lit it thoughtfully. After a moment's hesitation he offered me his pack. I shook my head and he put it back into the front pocket of his uniform, visibly relieved. He smoked Dymoks, one of the cheapest, foulest brands on the market.

"There is nothing to worry about, in any case," Yegorov said suddenly, without being prompted, exhaling acrid smoke in my direction. "First off, as I said, the English Queen is not going to lose any sleep on account of some dark African subject. Second, those black guys can't stand the heat, even though they come from Africa. Half the time you don't even need to punch them. Just rub your fist into their snout and act like you're about to kill them. Mark my words, this one will break down if I so much as give him a hard look. Babies they are, not real men. We shouldn't be wasting our resources on trying to educate them. You can't knock any knowledge into their skulls no matter how you try, and even if they do learn something here, they'll forget it before they reach Africa."

I still had the file in my hand. I kept leafing through it, marveling at how the major had managed to acquire so much experience with people from Africa. In Moscow, an African is still such a rare sight that people turn their heads and stare whenever they see one walking down the street.

It was also amazing to see the quick change that had come over the major, transforming him from nasty and laconic to nasty and talkative.

There was something else missing in the file, but for the moment I couldn't put my finger on it. The major's racist patter irritated me and kept me from focusing.

"What about the murder weapon?" I asked, just to change the subject. "I didn't see anything about it having been recovered."

"That's because it wasn't," Yegorov said, shrugging. "If he didn't get rid of it, then one of the other Africans must have picked it up as a souvenir before my guys arrived. Their lot always fall for all kinds of shiny objects. Like magpies. It's their nature."

The door of his office suddenly swung open and two very young men in suits and ties marched in. They were all but twins: apple-cheeked, blonde, blue-eyed, clean-shaven and, in general, squeaky-clean. Both wore that ironic expression universally adopted by young men convinced of their absolute intellectual superiority, which is supplemented by an elevated social status. Yegorov gulped, hastily put out his stinky Dymok into a half-finished mug of cold tea and snapped to attention. He stood and waited, turning even redder and sweating even more profusely into the frayed collar of his shirt.

I stayed seated. To me they were a pair of civilian kids and just because they looked arrogant and Yegorov was deferential to them was no reason for me to jump up.

They approached Yegorov's desk and one of them jerked his chin in my direction. Yegorov said nothing. He was too intimidated to speak.

Having gotten nothing out of Yegorov, the young man turned to me.

"Who are you?"

I answered slowly, without getting up, "Senior Lieutenant Pavel Matyushkin."

A pause.

"Moscow Criminal Investigations."

"What is he doing here?" the other young man asked Yegorov.

Yegorov gave them a sheepish look. "He's making sure we're doing our job. They always pop up to offer us their help, whether we need it or not."

"Everything is under control," the first youth told me in a voice that brooked no disagreement. "You've got no business here, Lieutenant."

He turned once more to Yegorov, "It's been settled. Go ahead and charge him."

His voice was even colder and more contemptuous when he spoke to the old cop. It had not escaped Yegorov's attention.

"Milksops," he muttered when the intruders were gone, exiting as unceremoniously as they had entered.

He and I were silent for a moment. I didn't have anything to say.

"As you can see, you're not the only one poking your nose into this case," he said bitterly, breaking the uncomfortable silence. "They're the errand boys at the Ministry of Foreign Affairs, but when they come here, they act like they own the place."

He sighed.

"Well, as I was saying, the case is closed. You heard them. International relations and all that crap. He's not important enough. Just some damn African. Too bad for him."

"Meaning what?" I asked.

"Meaning my boys are now going to go to work on him. Those two whipper snappers say go ahead and charge him, but the prosecutor and the judge will want to see something more substantial. Well, don't worry about it. As I said, I'll have his confession on my desk in no time. I'll let you know when I do, Lieutenant."

"What if he's still not talking?"

"Look, Lieutenant, the bloodthirsty little savage is guilty. It's clear as day. He won't have to write anything. I can do it for him just as well. He may not be talking, but he'll sign."

"I'd like to question him."

Yegorov pulled out another Dymok.

"Once he signs his confession, he's all yours. I'll let you talk to him to your heart's content. But not before."

"There may be no one to talk to, once your boys are through with him."

"Come on, Lieutenant," he objected. "I told you there won't be much need for physical persuasion, trust me. We have a pretty good idea what happened. Why do you think he's been crying this whole time?"

"Yes, in fact," I said. "What do you think happened there, in that room? What's making him cry?"

"You guys like to complicate things, don't you? It's a simple case. For some queer reason, the savage went nuts and gutted Comrade Kotov."

"Why?"

"The devil only knows. A white man can never understand an African. We're all reason and they're all raw emotion. They're animals, if you ask me."

"I see," I said.

There was nothing more for me to do. I turned to go, and Yegorov waved goodbye to me sarcastically, sending me on my way.

I had felt bad for him when the Foreign Ministry boys were treating him like a nobody, talking to him like he was a servant. But now I was just plain angry.

What's wrong with these people? Whenever they feel humiliated or insulted, why do they look around for someone weaker to humiliate or insult in turn? Instead of being kinder and gentler toward their fellow men?

FOUR

Budyonny listened to my report without interrupting, just nodding his head gravely. I stuck to the facts, keeping my opinions to myself. He usually asked what I thought afterwards – except this time he didn't.

"I see," he said when I was done. "Dismissed."

The Boss was glad a suspect was going to be charged and the investigation wrapped up. That meant that we didn't have to get involved. But I could also see that the story about the two kids from the Ministry of Foreign Affairs had him worried. The Ministry far outranked our humble agency, MUR, in the government hierarchy. All the important decisions in this case would be made by them – but only the right ones. The wrong ones would be made by someone else, because the Ministry could never be blamed for anything. We could still become a scapegoat even if it was the Ministry that told us to stay out of this case. Staying out, in fact, would then become a serious lapse of judgement on our part. And, going down the line of blame allocation, it would also be decided that it was all my fault – since I was the one who was supposed to monitor this case.

"Lieutenant, what is the matter with you? I thought you were long gone."

It took Budyonny a few seconds to realize that I had not left his office and was still standing at attention.

"I want to take a closer look at this case, Comrade Colonel," I said. "There are several things that have not yet been made clear."

"Like what, for example?"

"To be honest, everything," I said. "Starting with the main question: why did Kofunda murder comrade Kotov, a man he had not met until an hour before the murder? What went on between the two of them in that room? If the killing wasn't premeditated, how come Kofunda went in with a knife and industrial tape and a rubber band to tie Kotov's hands? If it was premeditated, then why? What are we missing?"

"What do you propose?"

"I want to question the suspect."

"Isn't Major Yegorov going to do that?"

I shook my head.

"Yegorov has decided that Kofunda is guilty and that he knows exactly what happened. All he needs from Kofunda is a signed confession."

"Are you implying that the African is not guilty?"

"I don't know," I said, ignoring the ominous note in his voice. "Yegorov will write a confession for him and will probably get it signed. It may or may not be true, All I'm saying is that it has nothing to do with conducting an honest investigation."

"*Nyet*, Matyushkin. As far as we're concerned, the case is closed. People at the Ministry of Foreign Affairs think it is, and that's good enough for Major Yegorov and me. Go back to the Danilov Market case. Dismissed."

I continued to stand at attention, looking the Boss straight in the eye and steeling myself against the tempest that was sure to break out over my head.

"What do you want me to do, Matyushkin?"

Against expectations, the Boss didn't fly into a rage. Instead, his tone became more conciliatory. "Are you proposing we go out on a limb even though all you have done is read the file? Come on, you can't be serious."

I don't know what was making me so obstinate. The Boss was right. I had no proof. Major Yegorov was closer to the case, and if he was sure that Kofunda had gone mad and killed Kotov, I had no reason to doubt him. And yet I did. Was it because of the major's gut-level racism? Perhaps. We were taught in school that to hate a person because of the color of his skin or nationality is despicable. Yegorov was prejudiced against Kofunda because the man was an African, and that was the reason I was prejudiced against Yegorov. And then there were those two boys from the Ministry of Foreign Affairs. The Ministry had surely checked whether Kofunda was someone important, and if he had been, he'd be let go and some poor sucker would be put in the dock in his place. Whether Kofunda was guilty was the least of their concerns.

As I said before, Budyonny was a good, honest cop. He too wouldn't want an innocent man convicted, whether his skin color was black, white or purple. And my obstinacy, instead of making him mad, made him think.

"The Ministry of Foreign Affairs only cares whether Kofunda is someone important," I said. "They worry about the political fallout."

Budyonny said nothing and stared out the window. The weather in May is changeable and now a rain was falling steadily over the dark city. The dark windows of the tall apartment buildings along the boulevard reflected a dim yellow glow on the wet roofs of the older, smaller houses in front of them. The raindrops ran down the windowpane, distorting the view, showing us the smallpox-scarred face of rain.

"I know, Matyushkin," he said thoughtfully. "Believe me, I know."

Two Budyonnys were visibly struggling in front of me for the man's soul. Budyonny the cop was telling him that we had to get to the bottom of it, to investigate the crime properly. But the other Budyonny was a bureaucrat, a timeserver. And in that he was very much like Major Yegorov. The boss in him knew that the more you do, the more you get blamed. The entire system is amorphous and stagnant, and any poor sucker who tries to nudge it out of its apathy is viewed as a mortal enemy. Sure, inaction might get you in trouble, but taking initiative most certainly will. The choice is obvious.

The struggle was written plainly on his face, so I knew his decision the moment he made up his mind.

"*Nyet*, Lieutenant," he said firmly. "As far as we're concerned, the case is closed. Dismissed."

That was his final word. Arguing any further was pointless. I made an about-turn and headed for the door.

"If the Ministry says he should be charged," Budyonny added bitterly, "then there is no way the poor devil won't turn out to be the murderer. No matter whether he killed Kotov or not."

That was the honest cop side of him speaking. It was feeling guilty. I kept on going. It was Budyonny the Bureaucrat who had prevailed and had given me the final answer, and I wasn't going to respond to Budyonny the Cop just to make him feel better.

FIVE

In the beginning is the smell.

It overpowers you and for a time follows you everywhere you go, clinging to your hands, your scrubs, even your boots. Especially your boots. It's as though you have stepped in it and it is now stuck on your soles.

The smell intrudes on the food and you swallow it with every mouthful. It forces itself upon you until you give up and make it part of your being. Then you stop noticing it the same way you stop noticing the smell of your own body. You become the stench of disinfectant, blood, excrement and rotting flesh.

In the war you discover that smells not only attach themselves to material objects, but to sounds, too. Then they can be heard. The same smell is in the screams of the wounded and in the spasmodic breathing of the dying. You live in it as you do in your scrubs, once white, now blackened and stiff with dry blood.

The smell colors your dreams, too.

Sleep, like everything else, is in short supply. There are often shortages of bandages, gauze and cotton wool. The nurses use strips of bedsheets which they cut with scissors to bandage the wounded. There is no morphine, and often no chloroform. Only iodine solution, the ubiquitous viscous stuff staining everything dark yellow, the color of death. The dark yellow liquid that is the only thing standing between life and death.

His first task is to tell those who can be helped from those who can't, the living from the dead. The dead will be left to lie on stretchers where they were placed when they were first brought in. You want them to die quickly. You don't want to see them suffer and, besides, stretchers are in short supply, too.

You may think that by separating the living from the dead he plays god. But that isn't so. He's only god's humble assistant. He decides nothing. It's god who put those kids into the trenches and showered them with shrapnel. It's he who chased them out into the open, into the range of German machine guns. He dealt them their wounds, deciding who gets what, a jagged shard of an artillery shell in the stomach or a bullet in the left shoulder. It's god who plays god.

God is especially cruel to new recruits, mama's boys fresh from the school bench. They're the ones who fill hospital beds in disproportionate numbers. Their wounds tend to be the worst, too. More deadly. You come to hate the freshness of their faces, the blond fuzz on their cheeks, the youth that glows through the pallor of pain and the dying sweat. Those whom god grants a bit of life harden, thicken, grow old in the space of two or three weeks. Their eyes become dull and their faces turn brown, the color of the shattered landscape. They become hard to kill.

They live, but they're no longer god's children.

He does amputations – emergency work, before sepsis can set in. He doesn't count the number of body parts he saws off in the course of his workday. His patients flow past his eyes as a blood-soaked row of red meat. He doesn't even have to persuade himself that it is a dream, or rather a nightmare, that none of it is real. He knows it isn't.

When he has nothing to dull their pain with, he pours vodka down their throats and shoves a piece of vulcanized rubber between their clenched teeth, to give them something to bite down on. He's assisted by Polina, a squat, middle-aged woman from the Kostroma region who used to be a midwife in her small town. And by Nadezhda, a professional nurse from Voronezh.

Amputations are hard work. At the end of the day – and their day can last anywhere from fifteen to twenty-four hours at a stretch – all three are spent and drenched in sweat. There's no place to wash up and no clean clothes to change into. The sweat just dries into their uniforms and blood-spattered scrubs.

The survival rate among the wounded is low, but every life is precious.

The ones who live are sent to the division hospital for rehabilitation. They get their wounds cleaned for the last time and are loaded onto a beat-up ZIS-5 truck. Depending on how badly they have been maimed, some will return to fight another day, the ones without limbs will get their disability discharge. He often wonders how many of them there are, the amputees he is sending east. Sometimes he imagines crowds of them clogging the streets of all the cities behind the front lines, many thousands of one-legged men on crutches struggling to climb the steep ascent toward October Square in his hometown, marching four abreast.

His amputees. The macabre victory parade.

One time a front-line medical crew brought in a German they had picked up in no man's land. He had been badly burned by a flamethrower, and because his grey uniform was charred, they couldn't tell that he was an enemy. His face was burned too, but you could still see he was just a kid, another new recruit god had sent to the front lines to be killed. Nurse Nadezhda started to wash his burns with hydrogen peroxide but then he came to and began to babble in German. They couldn't waste time and supplies on him while their own wounded were waiting their turn. They put him outside and left him to die.

Then the medical crew got in trouble. They were questioned by SMERSH and nearly got court-martialed. Why did they try to save a German soldier, the SMERSH wanted to know.

Men and women on front line medical crews were the true heroes. They descended into hell several times a day to bring back the wounded, risking their own lives every minute. And half the time it was to no avail, because there was nothing he could do for those wounded except let them die. Perhaps there was a higher purpose in their heroism, one which he had trouble seeing. He felt guilty, ashamed before them for every soul they had saved, and he set free.

The best way to cope was to think that the wounded were created that way, with gaping wounds, bullet-ridden bodies or limbs hanging by the sinews and shards of bone sticking out of the red mess. That they were never whole, never had any previous existence. You just couldn't see them as boys and young men with strong, athletic bodies, with bulging muscles, as sons and fathers and husbands, as human beings created in the image of god. Of god who made them perfect and then sent them here, into this meat grinder, to go to waste.

He did not believe in god. God was a figure of speech.

You got so spent, your mind would start to wander, and strange thoughts would pop into your head. Thoughts of god, for example. Exhaustion was the best anesthesia. It cauterized you from the inside. It dulled your senses and made you deaf to the rest of the world. It blurred all sights. You could look at things you never imagined you'd see and shrug the vision off. Exhaustion made you apathetic, resigned to your fate. Exhaustion made the fate of others easier to accept, too.

Nadezhda means hope. He and Nadezhda made love whenever they got a break and a bit of privacy. Back home he had a wife. They had met at the medical college in Kiev. Most students at medical colleges were women, the few men that attended them specialized. They became surgeons and gynecologists and cardiologists. He was going to be a throat specialist and Dr. Katzelzon, a luminary in the field who had studied in Berlin with famous Edgar Opperman, once considered him his most promising pupil. God, how long ago that was. A lifetime.

Like most other female students at the medical college, his wife became a GP and worked in a district clinic.

Now his wife and their little girl were a mist, as though hidden behind a thick veil over his eyes. Especially their little girl. She had been born right as the war started, and he hadn't had enough time to get used to the idea of fatherhood.

He never felt guilty about betraying his wife. The notion of betrayal didn't enter his mind. War was separate from his life. Nothing that happened here could be brought back home. Life and war didn't mix. Life was the true opposite of war, not peace. Tolstoy should have called his great novel *War and Life*. To admit that he was betraying his wife with Nadezhda would have allowed war to intrude upon life.

When he is with Nadezhda, their sex is violent, mad, insatiable. It's as though the life that drained from the dying boys infused them with manic energy. They know they should rest and catch up on their sleep, but they can't help themselves. Four hours of sleep is not nearly enough. It won't make a dent in their exhaustion. They would need months and months of undisturbed sleep at a sanatorium somewhere on the shores of the Black Sea, away from the rumble of artillery fire and the screams of the wounded. Their violent sex is their vitality that needs an outlet.

It's as if they are the last people on Earth tasked with keeping the human race going. Or else the first man and the first woman, Adam and Eve, on a mission to populate Hell.

If their frantic lovemaking ever produced any offspring, he was certain they would be boys. That was how god works, filling the gaps made by man.

When they are in bed together, they are one being. At all other times they aren't just separate; they are strangers. She addresses him formally as Comrade Major even when they are alone, and there is no hint of irony in her voice. He calls her Nurse Volkova. He knows nothing about her, about her life or family, if she even has one, back in Voronezh, nor does she ever ask him about his. Life and war don't mix.

They are always on the move. The front-line changes all the time, moving this way and that but mostly forward, pushing westward toward the old borders of the Motherland, and they advance along with it. Yes, they advance toward ultimate victory of which there can no longer be any doubt, even though their advance is very slow.

Every day there are victories at the front, but it is always a defeat on his makeshift operating table. It is never good, whatever the outcome for the patient.

Their field hospital is always hastily rigged up. Sometimes it is a tent, at other times a barn or an abandoned manor house with windows shattered and holes in the roof. They were bombed many times and once, when he was at the regimental headquarters, the hospital took a direct hit. The Germans never paid much attention to their red crosses, nor did their side, to be frank – it was that kind of war – so half the time they never bothered to paint one on the roof of the building that housed their hospital. Several of the wounded were killed and so was Nurse Volkova.

Another nurse was sent over and almost immediately he began sleeping with her. She too was called Nadezhda, a common name in their generation of hope. Soon he couldn't honestly remember that she was a replacement for the first Nadezhda and would have been surprised if anyone had mentioned it.

SIX

Lenny was not as displeased to see me come back to the Danilov Market case as I had expected. Perhaps my absence, lasting as it did all of one day, was too brief for him to get comfortable. Besides, he had had a breakthrough that he was eager to share, and I was the only one who would be impressed.

"I think I've got something," he announced the moment I was back in the office.

Observing a self-satisfied smirk on his shiny round face I could tell that this something was going to be big. He sat me down in our cramped office and insisted on making us a cup of tea before starting to talk. He served the tea with a slice of lemon on the side and accompanied by his favorite oatmeal cookies. The elaborate preparations, which included arranging the cookies on a relatively clean plate rather than plopping the cardboard box on the desk between us – were meant to torment me with expectation.

"Yesterday afternoon I go to visit Oksana," Lenny finally said, after taking a sip of his tea and devouring a cookie. "The mother greets me at the door and tells me Oksana is not feeling well. That's fine, I know her mother doesn't care for me. But her father is a different story. He likes chatting with me. Not this time, however. This time he is not his usual self. He looks anxious, distracted, barely answers my questions. He clearly wants me to leave."

"In other words," I said, "you felt like you'd overstayed your welcome at the Maltsev household."

"Something like that. I sit in the kitchen with him a little while longer, try to tease a reaction out of him by mentioning some made-up gang of bank robbers we supposedly arrested – all in vain. He gets more impatient with every passing minute. Finally, I take pity on the poor invalid and say my goodbyes.

"But of course, I only pretend to leave. I get into my Moskvich and make a show of driving away – in case the mother or the daughter are watching me from the window. I turn the corner, stop and walk back. I have a hunch that I'm soon going to see someone walk through their front door and that person, whoever he might be, will be of interest to our investigation. The weather is nice, and I'm prepared to wait. My only concern is that I might not recognize who that person would be. Their building is big and has many apartments. How will I know that it's their visitor that I'm seeing?"

Lenny paused to take another sip of tea and eat another cookie. I had not touched my tea because it was still scolding hot. Nor had I taken any of the cookies. I don't love them as much as Lenny does, and even though he was generous enough to share them, I knew it would be an affront if I had actually put one in my mouth.

"After about twenty minutes, I get my reward," Lenny continued, talking through a full mouth. "It's not who walks in, it's who walks out. How do I know he's my guy? Because he isn't walking. He is rolling out of the building in a wheelchair. A big strapping lad of about fifty, very imposing-looking, despite missing both legs: a shock of black hair shot through with grey, a bushy salt-and-pepper beard, dark eyebrows hanging over dark eyes, broad shoulders and massive forearms. And pushing him is Stepan Sergeyich Maltsev, Oksana's Dad. How do you like the scene: A blind man pushing another guy in a wheelchair?"

"Does that mean he had been in the apartment all along?"

"It would seem so. And now Maltsev insists on personally pushing the wheelchair, even though his wife is by his side, helping him navigate by giving him all kinds of instructions – to the left, to the right, careful now, my dear, you're about to hit the door frame. I'm too far to hear what she says, but I can guess the gist. They go down to the curb and parked there is one of those motorized invalid carts for disabled veterans. The one with manual controls. The big guy pulls himself up and lowers his big body into the driver seat. It's a difficult maneuver, requiring considerable dexterity and upper arm strength. Maltsev's wife folds the wheelchair and places it in the back of the motorized cart. My new acquaintance drives off, spewing blue smoke into the fresh spring air, and the Maltsevs stand there waving until it gets out of sight, and only then do they go back. She has her arm in his and if you saw the two love birds walking together, you would never have guessed that Stepan Sergeyich was blind."

Lenny can be flippant about anything, including disabled war veterans.

I said, "I'm sorry if I don't share your enthusiasm. Two war invalids are friends and one comes over to visit the other. They didn't want a stranger to intrude, especially if he's a cop. What's so suspicious about that?"

"Well, to start with, the wheelchair," Lenny said. "The guy has the fanciest foreign-made wheelchair I've ever seen, with shiny nickel-plated parts and a leather seat. Very lightweight and folding flat. You can't get anything like that in this country, that's for sure."

I shrugged.

"So what? Fine, he has a nice, foreign-made wheelchair. Is that a crime?"

"I suppose it isn't." Lenny agreed. "Except I looked him up by checking out his tags. You know, they distribute them for free through the Association of War Veterans and they keep good records. Turns out it was given to one Arkady Matveyich Brunevsky."

I shrugged. The name meant nothing to me.

"A war veteran. Officially employed as a night watchman at the Gogol Metal Works in the town of Mazilov, outside Moscow. Which is also where he lives, Mayakovsky Avenue 22, apartment 5."

Lenny stopped talking and gave me a triumphant look as though this piece of information was some sort of clincher.

"What's so special about that?" I asked.

"I'll get to it in a second," he said, smiling mysteriously and shaking his head. "First listen to this, detective. I checked this war veteran's file in the Dungeon. Try to guess what I found out."

The Dungeon is the MUR archive housed deep in the basement of our Petrovka 38 headquarters. Hence its nickname, the Dungeon. And the woman who runs it is known, naturally enough, as *Vedma* – the Witch. The Dungeon contains not only files on most known criminals and criminal gangs, but also printed records of crimes committed anywhere in the Soviet Union, as well as newspaper clippings and police reports on unsolved murders, disappearances, kidnappings, suicides and various unexplained events and phenomena. It is probably the most complete trove of information on Soviet citizens anywhere, except for files kept on Lubyanka Square, at the headquarters of the Committee for State Security – which are off limits even to us.

After waiting in vain for me to try to guess what he had discovered, Lenny said, "I found out, my friend, that back in 1956 Comrade Brunevsky – who is indeed a war veteran and a double amputee with the highest level of disability – was charged with speculation. The cops had busted up a ring of speculators working at the market in Yaroslavl, selling items illegally obtained from a clothing factory in Tallinn. One of them fingered Brunevsky as their Moscow-based boss. Brunevsky was arrested and put on trial. By a strange coincidence, the guy who had ratted on him unexpectedly decided to take his own life in his jail cell, instead of testifying against Brunevsky. Must have had an attack of bad conscience, poor chump. And, bad luck for the prosecutor, none of the other defendants had ever set eyes on Brunevsky or even so much as heard his name. They all got between three and five years of hard labor. Brunevsky too was found guilty, despite the tragic absence of the only witness against him – you know our courts, they don't like to return not guilty verdicts – but got off lightly, only with a suspended sentence."

"Interesting," I admitted.

"I'd say. And this is by no means all. In fact, it appears to be the tip of the iceberg. That motorized cart he got from the Association of War Veterans is a kind of luxury item. They don't manufacture enough of them, and there is a five-year waiting list of amputees hoping to get one. Nevertheless, Brunevsky manages to get a new one every year. A nice perk, wouldn't you say?

I nodded.

"Despite being a night watchman, Brunevsky lives in a very nice place in Mazilov. The Gogol Metal Works recently built an apartment building for its senior managers and their families, and it turns out that a night watchman is so high up in their management structure that he got a two-bedroom apartment just for himself. Even though on the form he had filled out he claimed that he lived alone."

"It is not true either?" I asked.

Lenny laughed.

"Patience, buddy, I'm about to come to that. It is actually the most important part. As I said, his home is in Mazilov – does that ring any bells, detective?"

I shrugged. "Not really."

"Well, I've always known that you were not cut out to be a criminal investigator." Lenny paused, enjoying himself as I struggled to remember why the address did sound vaguely familiar.

"It's the same town where Gulya Aliyeva said she lives," Lenny said at last, taking pity on me. "The sole witness of the robbery and attack on our girl Oksana Maltseva."

Yes, of course. I had to slap myself on the forehead, and Lenny guffawed, thoroughly enjoying my humiliation.

"But that's not all," Lenny continued. "Aliyeva has provided the same street address, Mayakovsky 22, apartment 5."

SEVEN

Days lengthen rapidly this time of year. The languid stretch of a May evening feels almost endless after the gloom and the dark of a northern winter, but dusk was finally starting to settle in when Lenny and I rolled into Mazilov. The town was enveloped in lilac-colored shadows. Behind the grim cityscape of factory chimneys, high-voltage power lines, and concrete apartment blocks, the western sky still held the last brightness of the setting sun. A flock of small clouds stood out black and silver against the orange glow.

Even though it was a work trip, using one of the two canvas-topped utility vehicles assigned to our department was out of the question. Neither of us was willing to go to Budyonny with such a request. On the other hand, Lenny had recently acquired a creaky Moskvich 401 subcompact, which he drove everywhere, even to the corner kiosk to buy a pack of cigarettes. However, he refused to drive it on what he described as "the road to hell" that led to Mazilov. The Moskvich, for which Lenny had been saving for an eternity and yet, had to tap his in-laws for a loan, was the apple of his eye – on a par with his two daughters.

"You kidding me?" he exclaimed even though I knew better than to suggest anything so stupid as to take his precious car to Mazilov. "It's a river of mud out there, at least up to your waist. Why don't we take your motorbike?"

My war-booty Zundapp KS750 was half a ton of grey German steel propelled forward by twenty-six brutal horse powers. It was built in Nuremberg some time before the war, but whoever designed it must have had our Russian roads in mind. It could negotiate any rut or pothole, traverse a dirt road liberally seeded with boulders and overgrown with weeds, and plow through both mud and melting ice. All you had to do was keep a firm grip on the handlebars and not complain about your teeth chattering like a train car rattling on the approaches to the Moscow-Sorting Yards station. The Zundapp had a comfortable sidecar. It was reserved for Tosya when we travelled as a family, while her son Sevka sat in the passenger seat behind me, regularly reminded by his mother to hold on to my back and not wiggle, especially on the highway.

Lenny hated travelling by Zundapp, and so did his wife, Raisa, who thought all two-wheelers, including bicycles, were dangerous. For the trip to Mazilov, she equipped him with a wool blanket to keep him from catching cold, a leather helmet to protect his head in case we overturned, and a pair of aviator goggles, just in case.

"Why don't you get yourself a normal car and take this pile of Nazi junk to the scrap yard?" Lenny mumbled as I was trying to kick-start the engine. The Zundapp was temperamental, but Lenny's complaints were meant to cover his embarrassment over the quantity of protective gear he had brought along.

IN MAZILOV, GULYA Aliyeva answered her door wearing a thick wool sweater over a house dress and a pair of fur slippers. She was a tall young woman, with thick dark eyebrows and unsmiling brown eyes. She wore her jet-black hair braided and curled on the back of her head, a style that made her look older than she was.

She looked cozy and domestic. If our night-time visit had taken her by surprise, she didn't show it.

"We have a few additional questions to ask you, my dear," Lenny said.

Gulya shrugged and gave him a look that suggested that we could have easily chosen a more conventional time for calling on our witnesses. After a short hesitation, she stepped aside, inviting us in.

"Nice place," Lenny said, having taken a good look around.

Indeed, it was. War veteran Brunevsky's apartment looked like a sleek advertisement for the good life of the future, under communism: clean lines and lots of spare spaces. Imported furniture and bookcases made of light wood were filled with works of foreign authors in Russian translation. A floor lamp with an orange shade stood unlit next to the dining table. Another lamp, its twin, was glowing alongside a comfortable armchair. A checkered wool blanket and an open book lay in the circle of its yellow light. A brightly colored painting stood out sharply against the pale-green wallpaper. The television's rabbit ears reminded you of Sputnik, but a couple of hand-blown glass vases, decorated with a floral pattern, and a few antiques scattered around the room, intruded on the clean, functional lines of space-age modernity.

A tall house plant in a ceramic pot held the balcony door open, letting in a breeze that swayed the transparent tulle over the windows. Evenings outside the city were still chilly, and so the room was cold, which explained Gulya's winter sweater and wool blanket.

We surveyed the amazing elegance of the room for so long, it became embarrassing. Finally, Lenny asked, "How come you're living here?"

It was probably a stupid question, but, under the circumstances, it would have been difficult to come up with anything more intelligent.

She is the live-in housekeeper, Gulya explained. Her employer is a war invalid, a double amputee – missing both legs. He needs help. She's officially employed by him and legally registered as a resident in his apartment. She'll be happy to go and get her papers, in case we want to see them.

Lenny declined.

"But you still sell at the market?" he asked her.

Of course. Housekeepers' wages are a pittance, and she works for an invalid who himself barely manages to make ends meet on a night watchman's salary. She gets room and board, but almost no cash. Not that she's complaining. The place is beautiful, and her employer is a nice man, even though the work is difficult, understandably so, what with having to take care of a man who is effectively incapacitated. But she needs the money. Prices are high even in a small town like Mazilov, and she sends money to her family in Azerbaijan, to help support her elderly parents. That's why she has to work at the market on her days off. She used to work there full time, before she became Brunevsky's housekeeper.

"And I used to share a dorm room with three other girls from the market," she said. "It wasn't very comfortable."

She rattled all this off and stopped, staring at us. I had a distinct impression that she had been coached. She had been told what to say and to memorize it. You could almost hear a sigh of relief when she was done. She was a good student, the expression on her face seemed to suggest, but she didn't like being put to the test.

The apartment was remarkably clean. She was doing a great job keeping house for Brunevsky. A member of the Academy of Sciences would have been proud to live in such an apartment and pleased with an employee as conscientious as Gulya. The only sign that an invalid was living there was a folding wheelchair stashed discreetly in the hallway. It was an ordinary wheelchair, not the fancy foreign one Lenny had described.

"And your employer does what?" Lenny asked casually. It wasn't yet time to reveal that Brunevsky was the real reason for our after-hours visit.

"I think I told you. He's a night watchman at the Gogol Metal Works. If you look out of the kitchen window, you'll see the plant."

Her voice was matter of fact, as if there was no disconnect between his humble low-paying job and the domestic splendor that surrounded us.

"But I thought you wanted to ask me something," she said, changing the subject.

"Oh, yes, we did," Lenny said.

"I don't know," she said, shrugging and trying to look innocent. "I have told you everything I know about the robbery."

"I understand," Lenny said, slowly reaching into his briefcase and opening his notebook. "Let's see. Where were we? Oh, yes. Does Stepan Sergeyich Maltsev come here often?"

"Excuse me?"

Obviously, she had not expected Maltsev to be mentioned and couldn't help being thrown off by Lenny's question.

"You know," Lenny said, giving her a knowing smile, "Oksana's father."

It was only a momentary lapse and Gulya quickly regained her composure. But it was more than enough for us to see that she in fact knew exactly who Maltsev was. I felt we were getting somewhere, and in a hurry.

"Oh, him," she said, feigning indifference and waving her hand airily, as if to show that Stepan Sergeyich was a person of no consequence. "I didn't understand who you were talking about at first. He doesn't, considering his condition. But my boss and he have known each other for a while. They must have met through the War Veterans Association. Arkady Matveyich goes to see him now and again."

Lenny was in no hurry to ask the next question, letting a pregnant silence settle in. He looked like a school principal interrogating a wayward teen.

"So you do know Oksana's father well enough to know that he is blind," he said at last.

Gulya frowned.

"Yes, of course."

"Interesting," Lenny said slowly. "Because if you know Oksana's father, why did you tell us that you only knew Oksana by sight, as someone who worked at the next stall at the market, and that you had never spoken to her?"

Gulya shrugged.

"Do you want to tell us more?" I suggested in a kindly voice, playing an avuncular good cop to Lenny's nasty school principal.

Gulya didn't look perturbed.

"There is nothing to tell," she said. "How could I not know Stepan Sergeyich if until he retired last year, he had been deputy director of Danilov Market?"

Lenny gave me a quick glance. That was news to us – and a bad lapse on our part.

"It was Stepan Sergeyich who recommended me for this job," Gulya continued as we stared at each other, shaking our heads and shrugging our shoulders. "Arkady Matveyich was looking for a housekeeper, and Stepan Sergeyich asked me whether I would be interested. When I saw Oksana, I didn't connect her to her father. I only found out that later, when Arkady Matveyich told me."

"Is your employer at home?" Lenny asked. His voice was angry now. He was mostly mad at himself, but at Gulya too, because she was, in her subtle way, making fools out of the two of us.

"I don't think so," she said. Her face was impassive, but there was a mocking spark in her eyes. I rather liked her, but I suspected that Lenny didn't. Spunky young women who could talk back to him weren't his type.

"Where is he?" he asked.

"He doesn't report to me," she said. "But I assume he's at work. You can check with the Gogol plant. It's a twenty-minute walk from here."

"Don't worry, we will," Lenny said darkly. "And please make sure you call me at this number when he returns."

We had come to Mazilov expecting to use the information Lenny had dug up on Brunevsky to crack a simple-minded Azeri immigrant. I had even worried that she might break down and cry before telling us the truth about the Danilov Market incident. Instead, we were leaving with our tails between our legs – figuratively speaking, of course.

The Gogol Metal Works was visible from every vantage point in town. Its massive brick buildings and belching smokestacks, constructed at the dawn of the Industrial Age, dominated the skyline. It sprawled across a vast territory and was enclosed by a tall concrete fence. That was the main drawback of living in Mazilov: everywhere you go, even on the outskirts of the small town near the birch and pine woods where Brunevsky lived, the air had a distinct, acrid smell.

The second shift was over at midnight, which was when the night watchman's eight-hour stint began. Stopping by the shift foreman's office at around eleven thirty, we got our answer. Brunevsky was not going to show up for work tonight. Or the next night. He was on medical leave. Apparently, he got medical leaves often, considering his condition.

We were not surprised. We had expected something like that.

As we walked back to my Zundapp, shivering in the cold wind that had picked up late in the evening, dragging in its wake the thick clouds and heavy moisture of an imminent spring storm, Lenny said gloomily, "Guess what?"

"Yes, I know," I replied. "It's going to rain hard and we're going to get wet."

Lenny sneered. In the greenish light over the security booth of the Gogol plant his face was thoughtful.

"That too," he said. "But I was going to say something else. About the Danilov Market case."

"Go ahead."

"It's going to be far more complicated than we first thought."

It was a painfully obvious thing to say, but it had to be said, nonetheless.

EIGHT

When I opened my eyes the next morning, the sun was flooding the room through the half-drawn curtains, and particles of dust and poplar fuzz danced in its rays. Outside, the birds were doing their best to chirp and whistle, and kids' voices floated upward through the narrow courtyard.

Our trip back to Moscow in the blinding rain had been treacherous. I guided the bike slowly and cautiously through the darkness, bracing every time a car or a truck shone its headlights into my eyes, before showering us with a fresh dose of roadside bilge that stunk of diesel and motor oil.

Each time we stopped amid the logjam of trucks on their nighttime run to Moscow, I was forced to endure Lenny's unprintable tirades. He will never again ride with me. He's going to go to Budyonny first thing in the morning to ask for a different partner, and even demand to be transferred to the Moscow Metro law enforcement unit, because the kilometer-deep tunnels are always warm and dry.

Once, when we reached the city limits and stopped at a red light, he demonstratively unfurled a corner of his woolen blanket and wrung it out where I could watch him, baring his teeth and giving me a sidelong glance.

He kept saying I could drop him at the first metro station we came to, but by the time we reached the city it was well after one a.m., and the metro had stopped running. So, after enduring hours of abuse, I had to deliver my wet, cursing, thoroughly miserable partner to his place of residence. Raisa, his long-suffering wife, had been waiting for us by the window, awake and worried stiff. She came running downstairs as soon as she spotted the bright eye of my Zundapp turn down their street. She helped her husband out of the sidecar and all but physically carried him upstairs, as if he were a little baby.

I had to shake my head in wonder.

AFTER THE MISADVENTURES of the previous night I not only slept late but awoke with a bad cold. I was almost certainly running a fever, but could not verify this, since I had dropped my thermometer on the floor and shattered it. And I never found time to stop by the corner pharmacy to get a replacement.

When I finally decided to get up and knock on a neighbor's door, to ask to borrow their thermometer, I spotted a piece of paper lying on the floor that I had missed the previous night. It was a lined page from a school notebook, on which my neighbor Daria Filippovna had scribbled a message in her childish hand. Tosya had telephoned me at least four times. Seeing the note, I remembered that we had made a date to go to the movies, and that Tosya had asked her best friend Sveta, the one who worked at the prestigious Yeliseyev's Food Store on Gorky Street, to babysit Sevka.

It was a sensitive matter because even though she and Sveta were best friends going back to the orphanage, they had lately drifted apart. This made Tosya reluctant to ask Sveta to do her a favor and did so in this case only because she really wanted to see this movie, something called *July Rain*, which was some sort of love story. All Tosya's colleagues at the bookkeeping department of the Tryokhgorka Textile Plant had already seen it and had been reduced to tears by its sad ending. It was highly unusual for Tosya to be the last one not to have seen the latest tear-jerker.

For all these reasons it was an important date and it had completely slipped my mind. I felt guilty, but I also couldn't help thinking that my timing in getting a nasty cold could not have been better. Tosya would never hold a grudge against someone as ill as I felt myself to be – even if it was only a common cold.

I got back in bed. I had given up on the idea of taking my temperature – it wouldn't make any difference to get a confirmation that I was indeed running a fever. In my condition, it was better to forget about getting up and to go back to sleep instead.

I was awakened after what seemed like only a couple of minutes by a series of loud knocks on my door.

"Pavel? Are you there?" Daria Filippovna was shouting into the keyhole. "You're wanted on the phone again."

As I searched for my slippers beneath the bed and then hobbled down the hallway to our communal telephone, I was warmed by the thought that it was surely going to be Tosya, worried silly what happened to me and calling to see whether I was dead or alive. But what I heard on the other end was Budyonny's familiar rasping growl. It was even more grating than usual because of the poor quality of the line, into which snippets of other people's conversation kept intruding. And I found it difficult to concentrate, what with my head throbbing with the cold.

As was his custom, the Boss began by giving me a piece of his mind. Why wasn't I at work? Why had it taken me so long to come to the phone? Did I think he had nothing better to do but wait until I condescended to get on the line? And so on.

There was no need to explain anything. Nothing I could say would make any difference.

The phone was attached to the wall at the end of a long hallway, at the point where it came to a T. Another hallway running at a right angle led to the communal kitchen at one end and the bathroom at the other. A string was attached to the black body of the telephone, and a dull stub of a pencil dangled on it. A piece of yellowed paper pinned to the wall was covered with a palimpsest of words and numbers scribbled by a couple of generations of neighbors, with quite a few of the scrawls spilling beyond the margins and onto the cracking plaster. The wall had once been decorated with a stenciled design of gilded roses, which had mostly faded.

To kill time while the Boss vented his exasperation with my laziness and incompetence, I stared at the writing, trying to make out some of the notes – a few of them undoubtedly written by me over the years – through the thicket of scratches, erasures and overwriting. I had a bad headache and a sore throat.

Suddenly, Budyonny changed the subject. "Did you know that the African confessed, Lieutenant?"

It took me a moment to figure out what he was talking about.

"I did not," I croaked, suppressing a cough. "I followed your orders, Comrade Colonel. You took me off that case."

I had prepared myself to be chewed out some more, but Budyonny surprised me a second time.

"Good," he said almost gently. "What do you make of this case? Open and shut?"

Based on my conversation with Major Yegorov the fact that Joseph Kofunda had confessed meant absolutely nothing. I had no reason to doubt that Yegorov's guys at the Southwestern District police headquarters knew how to knock a confession out of a suspect.

Sure, things in the case didn't quite add up. But, was it my irritation with Yegorov, his methods of obtaining confessions and his racist prejudice that had affected my judgment and kept me from accepting Kofunda's guilt? Because, objectively speaking, Kofunda was the only likely perpetrator.

To look at it another way, who would have wanted to kill a well-known poet? I didn't know anything about Kotov, but even if he had an enemy or a deadly rival, surely, they could have found a better venue to settle the score than a crowded university in the middle of an afternoon? And why kill him with such savagery? It certainly looked like a murder committed in the heat of the moment, in a paroxysm of rage, by a mentally unbalanced individual.

Perhaps something had set Joseph Kofunda off during the poetry reading. There were witnesses who confirmed that he had become emotional in the auditorium. He asked Kotov a question and then wanted to talk to him one-on-one. Why? What was he going to talk to him about? Just to express his opinion about the man's poems? How important could it have been? Yet he waited a long time to see Kotov, perhaps steaming inside about whatever had bothered him. He might have concealed his agitation from Kotov's son, but then again, a seven-year-old would not be the best judge of a man's state of mind.

So, finally Kofunda gets Kotov alone. They argue. The African becomes even more enraged and stabs Kotov. He had clearly come prepared, with a knife, tape, and a rubber band. What if Kofunda had snapped long ago, harbored some homicidal design and Kotov merely provided a pretext for the madman to act?

Still, this version of events was not airtight, either. If there had been an argument, it couldn't have been one-sided, and if they had been arguing, Kotov would not have been taken unawares. He was a strong man and, being a war hero, unquestionably brave. He wouldn't have allowed himself to be stabbed without a struggle. Yet, the room was in perfect order.

But even if something didn't completely add up, it wasn't a big deal. The truth is never airtight. There are always things that don't match or don't fit, always a bunch of unanswered questions. You have got to focus on the big picture and not sweat the details. And the big picture, diligently assembled by Yegorov's men, made psychological sense.

Budyonny was showing uncharacteristic patience as he waited for me to think it all through, even if in reality it only took a few moments.

"I think Joseph Kofunda is guilty, Comrade Colonel," I said at last.

"Come on, Matyushkin. Be serious. I don't give a damn whether he's guilty or not. What I want to know is whether this case is going blow up in our faces, which by the way all cases involving foreigners do, sooner or later."

That was a different matter, and if I hadn't been so sick, I would have realized more quickly that the Boss was only interested in covering his own ass. And I should be thinking of covering my own, too, because I would be first in line if, or rather when, blame allocation began.

I needed to take another look at this case and the Boss agreed. After hanging up with him, I dialed the Southwestern District headquarters and, after considerable delay, was put through to Major Yegorov.

"Did you get your confession?"

"Oh, it's you, detective," the major drawled slowly in his exaggerated Volga accent, rounding his Os. "I didn't recognize you at first. You know what the old wives say. If someone doesn't recognize you, it means you'll get rich."

He giggled and then fell silent.

"So?" I asked. "Did you, or didn't you?"

"I told you there would be no difficulties, didn't I?" He chuckled. "You never trust us rank-and-file men. You think we're stupid and don't know what we're talking about. And yet we got his confession and even earlier than I had expected. You may think of us as laggards, but when push comes to shove, we're Stakhanovites. Live and learn, Lieutenant."

"Is he talking again?"

"Why don't you come and find out for yourself," he suggested. "You seem to be itching to see him. I told you before and I don't mind repeating it: you'll be wasting your time. But you, Petrovka 38 types, never take a no for an answer. That's because you don't trust us, ordinary cops. Well, come and talk to him and see whether you find out something we haven't."

Having started the conversation in a good mood he was working himself up into a lather. I was in no condition to argue. Nor was I going to tell him that my purpose was to make sure he had got it right, not to prove him wrong.

On my way back to my room, I ran into Daria Filippovna. She leaned against the wall to let me pass and then remarked in a worried whisper.

"You look awful. You should be in bed. Let me call the doctor."

I shook my head.

"Thank you, Daria Filippovna. I need to go to work."

"Oh my god, you need to get better first. Work can always wait."

"Not my kind of work."

She flailed her arms in despair: "At least let me make you some hot tea."

She made me a glass of very strong black tea and served it with homemade raspberry preserves – her answer to all ailments. She insisted that I sit and drink it in the kitchen, in her presence. I swallowed it in large mouthfuls, burning my lips and tongue on the boiling brew. I had my doubts as to whether this torture was going to do me any good.

"Bundle up, will you!" Daria Filippovna shouted down the stairwell as I hurried downstairs without waiting for the elevator. "And for god's sake don't get on that stupid motorcycle of yours."

She didn't have to admonish me. The thought of riding the Zundapp in my condition was abhorrent. In the crowded metro car, I sneezed and sniveled while the other passengers shot me nasty looks and covered their faces. Muscovites fear infections, and nobody wants to get sick during the May holidays, when everybody gets time off work.

NINE

I hate Butyrka Prison. It is a barrack-like pile of red brick, located in the northern part of the city and blackened grime and soot. The white highlights over the rows of arched windows and the round Pugachev Tower on the corner add a touch of macabre frivolity. Constructed in the time of Empress Catherine and made famous by Yemelyan Pugachev, the tower famously held the Cossack rebel during his inquiry and trial, and up until his execution. The complex looks like an early 1900s factory, and in some ways it is, because our penal system has always functioned like a production line.

Even though I had studied his mug shot and read his physical description, Joseph Kofunda was taller and skinnier than I had expected. He was also taller and skinnier than the average Russian *z/k*, or prisoner. The standard-issue prison garb was both too big and too short for him. It hung like a potato sack on his gaunt figure, and his wrists stuck several inches out of its sleeves. He had a chiseled face with prominent cheekbones and small, reddish eyes. His goatee had been shaved off by the prison barber. He fidgeted a great deal, but I could sense a kind of dignity and deep-seated sense of self-worth beneath his nervousness. It showed when he took control of himself. His dark skin glistened in the relentless light of the overhead light bulb.

"Who are you?" he asked in a heavily accented sing-song Russian when the door slammed behind me. A guard stepped into the shadows against the wall.

I introduced myself. The interrogation room was too hot. I was sweating and shivering at the same time. My fever must have gotten worse, and the black man in front of me in his ill-fitting prison uniform, the lurid light, and the brick walls painted dark brown were like a scene from a nightmare. I had to summon all my strength just to concentrate on questioning him.

"Did my Embassy send you?"

"No," I said wearily. "I'm from Moscow Criminal Investigations. I'm a detective."

He waved his hand impatiently. He had long, elegant fingers with light fingernails. His palms were almost white, too, with dark lines etched in the skin.

"I have already talked to the cops. What do you want?"

"I'm from a different agency," I said. "I need to ask you a few questions."

"So many agencies," he said angrily. "I have complained to my consular officials about my treatment here. They laugh in my face because my family is no longer in power in my country. But I thought they would extend me the courtesy of relaying my complaints to the prison administration."

"I don't know anything about that," I said.

"I reported to my consulate that I'm being harassed and called all kinds of racist names. Not only by imprisoned criminals, but by the guards as well. We were taught at Lumumba University that you are against colonialism and racism, but it's not true. You people are even more disgusting than the English."

"I'll see what I can do," I said. "I'm sorry about your treatment."

"I don't believe you. The white man is the same everywhere."

He smiled bitterly, baring large, yellow teeth.

"I'd like to talk to you about Comrade Kotov's murder," I said.

He shuddered and turned away quickly. The muscles on his neck flexed and an artery began to throb on his throat.

"What do you want to know?"

"I see you signed a confession," I said, pushing a few sheets of typewritten paper toward him, a carbon copy that Major Yegorov had given me earlier in the day, when I stopped by his office.

Kofunda strained to read the upside-down, pale text in a foreign language.

"Oh, that," he said, dismissing the paper with another princely wave. "They told me it's a mere formality, something that they need in order to put me before the judge."

"Who told you that?"

"The consular official from my country. Once I'm brought before the judge, I will be able to plead my case. I'll tell him exactly what happened."

I shook my head in amazement. Shaking my head was painful.

"Is it not true?" he asked anxiously, inferring from my silence that he had done something wrong. "They told me it is regular procedure during criminal investigations in the Soviet Union. Two individuals drawn from the ranks of workers and peasants assist the judge in reaching a correct verdict. They question everyone thoroughly in order to arrive at the truth. It seems like a just process. Better than having the police investigate. The police often make mistakes, and they can be prejudiced."

While he talked, I was trying hard to think through my pounding headache. So, that was how they got him to sign a confession, by telling him a blatant lie. And I couldn't blame Major Yegorov. It went well beyond him. It was a fix on a much larger scale, involving not only our Foreign Ministry, but also the embassy of a foreign power. I knew I needed to tread carefully.

"Did the people at your Embassy send you a lawyer?" I asked.

"They said there is no need for one. But now I'm worried they didn't tell me the truth. We're no longer in power back home. The president doesn't like my father."

Apparently, the president didn't like the son either.

"Tell me what you were going to tell the judge. What happened after the poetry reading? Why was Comrade Kotov killed?"

"I don't know," he replied heatedly. "That's the thing: I don't know. Nothing happened. It's all a lie, believe me. They have no right to keep me here. I'm completely innocent."

"But Comrade Kotov ended up dead. It had to happen somehow."

"I didn't kill him."

"Who did then?"

Kofunda looked exasperated.

"I don't know. All I know it wasn't me. I just walked into the room and there he was."

"Already dead?"

"Yes, dead and covered with blood. But I didn't kill him. I was only talking to him."

"So he was still alive when you went in?"

He was sweating now. We both were, except I was the only one who had a fever. He was getting more and more agitated, and I was afraid he'd have another nervous breakdown. I took a close look at him. Although gaunt and skinny, he was physically strong, a powerfully built individual. In excellent shape, too. His strong hands and long fingers could strangle a man. I would be no match for him if he attacked me – even though I would certainly put up more of a fight than poor Comrade Kotov did. All of a sudden, I was glad there was a guard present, leaning on the wall behind me.

"Let's backtrack a little," I said, easing off. "Were you at the reading and why did you go there?"

Kofunda took a deep breath. I lit a cigarette and offered him one, which he refused.

"I went along with everyone else," he said. "They told us to go and listen to a famous poet reading his works. They said it was going to be good for our Russian comprehension, and for understanding the mentality of the Soviet people. I see what kind of mentality it is, here in this jail."

"I'm sorry," I said. "This place is full of criminals. You can't expect decent behavior from them."

"No," he objected. "It's the guards, too. And senior staff. They say they've got no bananas in the kitchen and then they laugh at their own stupid, bigoted joke. They say the same thing every day and it is always as funny to them as the first time. They're just like the English who don't think that you're human if you're black. Except the English don't think you're human if you're Russian, either."

"Let's get back to Comrade Kotov," I said. "Did you like his poems?"

"I did. I liked them very much. They were extraordinary. I didn't understand everything he said, but what I did understand rang true. That's why I wanted to talk to him afterwards. I know exactly what it is to be in the war."

"Can you handle weapons?" I asked.

"I never tried," he said.

I raised my eyebrows: "I thought you said you were in the war."

"No, I didn't. I said I know how the war feels because it's in my blood. Personally, I never actually fought. But I have seen others fight."

"That doesn't mean being in a war," I objected.

He pulled himself up on the uncomfortable low metal stool and suddenly, he cut a remarkably aristocratic figure.

"It absolutely does," he declared, giving me a supercilious sneer. "You don't need to experience it to know it in your bones. I have seen people killed in the war. My own brother—"

He broke off.

"Did Comrade Kotov's description of the war upset you?" I asked. "Given that it was so vivid and true to life?"

"It didn't," he replied. "But seeing him dead did."

"Let's not get ahead of ourselves," I said. "You stayed behind to talk to Comrade Kotov. Were there any other people?"

"Yes, there was a group of students, I believe they were Cubans. And a woman from Latin America. She went in after the Cubans left and ahead of me."

That must have been the Argentinian student Oleg had mentioned. I didn't remember seeing any testimony by her in the Kotov file, but I might have overlooked it. She was probably the last person to see Kotov alive, aside from Kofunda.

"What was her name?" I asked.

"I don't know. I had never seen her before. It's a big school."

"How long was she in with him?"

"I don't know. I was talking to the boy. Maybe twenty minutes. Maybe a lot less, because I didn't see her leave."

"What do you mean? Didn't you go in after she left?""

"No. It wasn't like that. I've been telling it to them, but nobody will listen. It was taking her a long time, and when the boy went to the bathroom, I knocked on the door to ask how much longer she was going to be. There was no answer. I hesitated, because you don't go in when a man and a woman are alone without getting permission first."

"Yet you did open the door and go in?"

He nodded. "The room was empty. Except—"

He shuddered. I looked up and saw how sweaty he was. His dark face had grown pale, if you can say that about a very dark-skinned African. He was shaking all over.

"Are you unwell?"

He didn't answer. His teeth were chattering audibly, and his full lips were moving.

"He was dead," I finally heard him say in a whisper.

When you're dealing with someone hysterical, you need to be firm. The best thing is to slap their face lightly, but you can't do that to a prisoner, especially if he is a foreigner.

"Calm down," I said. I picked up a dusty glass and poured out the yellowish dregs of water from the decanter. He drank greedily, tapping a rapid tattoo against the edge of the glass whenever his teeth touched it. "Get a hold of yourself. Take as long as you need."

I waited a few minutes for him to calm down.

"Now describe exactly what you saw," I said.

"I can't. I think I passed out. I saw him sitting in an armchair, and I knew that he was dead."

"What did you do?"

"I don't remember. I don't know."

"But you were there for a long time, Kotov's son says. What were you doing all that time?"

"I don't know."

"Did you pass out when you saw that Kotov was dead or while he was still alive?" I asked.

"I don't know."

"That won't do," I said tersely. "You must realize that the judge will never believe you unless you tell the truth. What did you do in the room when you were alone with Comrade Kotov? Why didn't you raise the alarm sooner? It looks very suspicious."

Tears welled up in Kofunda's eyes and he began to sob.

"I didn't want to do it," he said at last.

He hid his face in his hands. All I could hear through the sobbing was "I didn't want to—"

So Kofunda was confessing after all...

I nodded.

"I know you didn't mean to do it," I said softly, patting him on the shoulder and offering him my handkerchief. "It happens sometimes even when we don't want it to happen. You argued and you got angry and you did it."

"I was seven years old," I heard him whisper through tears. "My older brother, Junior, my father's first born. They made me kill him."

"Who did?" I asked.

"My father's enemies. They tied him to a chair, and they made me stab him through the heart. The same way. I didn't want to do it. But they said they'd kill me like they had killed my mother. I was scared, but I didn't want to do it. It was not my fault."

He was bawling now.

"They were soldiers," he resumed, sobbing. "They were from a different tribe, they were our enemies. They tied him to a chair, and they told me to kill him. The same way."

"What was Comrade Kotov killed with?" I asked.

"I don't know."

I grabbed him by the shoulders. I shook him hard and made him raise his head. He was forced to look at me and when our eyes met, I fixed him with a hard, unblinking stare.

"Did you kill Comrade Kotov?" I asked, and when he didn't reply shook him again, harder.

He looked away.

"That's the thing," he began to babble, mixing Russian with his own language. I couldn't make out everything he was saying, except this: "It was not my fault. I passed out. All I know is that he was dead, just like Junior had been dead, the same way, sitting in a chair. And there was blood all over the place, on his uniform, on the floor, on my hands. I couldn't take it. It was not my fault. I had to do it to save my own life…"

TEN

I felt bad for Kofunda. There was no denying that the young man was emotionally disturbed, troubled, his psyche severely affected by his childhood experience. That must have been what made him stab Comrade Kotov, whose poems brought back his traumatic memories. How it happened, what ticked him off and what was going through his head when he stabbed Comrade Kotov was for psychiatrists to figure out. It was not my job. If they wanted to get to the bottom of it, they could put him through a psychiatric evaluation. My job was to make sure that Kofunda was guilty, and that Major Yegorov's men had not committed blatant errors in the course of their investigation. I felt that I had done it to everyone's satisfaction.

And yet…

I chased away all those nagging doubts.

Visiting Butyrka drained me of my remaining strength and made my cold worse. All I wanted to do was to go home and get back under the covers. Another glass of hot tea, prepared by the solicitous Daria Filippovna, was what I desperately needed at the moment. But I still had to go to the office to report on the results of my interrogation.

"Are we in the clear?" he asked, squinting at me from beneath his bushy eyebrows. "Or is there going to be a nasty surprise at the end of the tunnel?"

The Boss is an Armenian. He was born in Armenia and he lived there until the age of eighteen, when he was drafted in the Soviet Army at the start of the war. His Russian was fluent, but he still got his idioms wrong now and again.

"Yes, Comrade Colonel," I replied, sounding as confident as I could. "We should be in the clear."

"Very well, Matyushkin. If you say so. Dismissed."

I turned around and started to walk out, trying to hold myself upright and suppressing a cough. That was the moment when I decided to track down the Argentinian student, the last person to see Comrade Kotov alive – even if her testimony was unlikely to add anything substantial to the case.

I must have looked awful, because even the Boss had noticed it. As I was walking out of his office, he added as an afterthought:

"Go home, Lieutenant. Get in bed."

However, coming out of the elevator on the first floor, I ran into my partner Lenny. I suppose I should have been glad to see that he had emerged unscathed from our nighttime ride through the rain. On the contrary, he looked the picture of robust good health.

"There you are, buddy," he exclaimed, putting a heavy hand on my shoulder and squeezing it with his chubby, hairy-knuckled fingers. "I've been looking for you."

"I have a nasty cold," I said. "And yet I had to drag myself to Butyrka to wrap up the case the Boss put me on."

"Ah, the Kotov murder. Did you manage to solve it?"

"Someone else already had," I replied, shaking his hand off my shoulder. "I'm telling you, I've got a cold. I want to go home."

"Come on, buddy. Come hear what I've learned."

It was useless to resist. I let him drag me upstairs, to our undersized, stuffy office. It is a peculiar feature of Moscow offices that they often get quite cold in the dead of winter, but the moment spring arrives and the weather turns nice and warm, the heat comes on full force, so that you can literally burn yourself if you inadvertently touch the radiator.

In the end, Lenny had nothing substantial to report. He had wasted time looking for me, he declared, giving me a reproachful look. He called my apartment and was told by a neighbor that I had just left for work. He then waited for me to appear at the office and, since I didn't appear, went to see Oksana and her invalid father on his own – to try his luck with them after we had failed so miserably with Gulya Aliyeva.

Oksana's jaw was still wired shut, and she could only nod or shake her head in response to his questions.

"I asked her first whether she knew a guy named Brunevsky," Lenny said. "To this she nodded vigorously. It was not a big surprise, because Gulya no doubt had already told Oksana and her Dad about our visit. Did she know that Gulya, the only witness of the attack on her, was Brunevsky's live-in housekeeper? Negative. Did she think it was kind of surprising? A shrug, meaning, coincidences happen, it's a small world. Even if her father actually recommended her for the job? Another shrug. Did she ever see Brunevsky at Danilov Market? She gave it some thought, hesitated, and in the end decided to shake her head. Negative.

"After about twenty minutes of this exercise in futility, Oksana discovered that she was getting tired and needed a rest," Lenny concluded.

I needed a rest too. I was feeling miserable, but I had no hope that Lenny would let me go.

"Her father was even more difficult," Lenny continued. "You know, when I first met him, I thought he was a kind of simple soul, asking me about the progress of our investigation, listening to my true crime stories, and giving me all kinds of amateur sleuthing advice about what we at Criminal Investigations should be doing to be more successful. But he may not be such a simpleton after all. Or else he's been nicely coached by that guy Brunevsky."

Of course, he knew Brunevsky, he told Lenny. They had so much in common, both being war invalids. They were members of the War Veterans Association, and of course they bonded right away when they first met. They had been through hell: the war, the wounds, the hospital, the amputations. Life was no bowl of cherries for injured warriors in the postwar years. What with the poverty, the hunger, the reconstruction. Even today it can be hard, and they need to stick together. Yes, Brunevsky was visiting them a couple of days ago when Lenny dropped by. No, Brunevsky wasn't hiding from Lenny, he has no reason to hide from anyone. But Brunevsky lost both legs in the war, he's a wheelchair-bound invalid. It is a hard reality to deal with for a strong, intensely proud man. It makes him exceptionally private. He feels uncomfortable meeting new people, he is painfully conscious of getting those pitying looks; people are horrified when they see amputees, they are even disgusted sometimes, and certainly no one wants to see compassion in people's eyes. It may be unreasonable, but this is how Brunevsky feels and you have got to respect his feelings.

"I'm blind," Maltsev had concluded, "and perhaps that is why I don't mind people staring at me. I'm proud of my wounds. I got them while fighting for the Motherland."

No, Maltsev had no idea where Brunevsky lived, somewhere out of town, near the place where he worked as a night watchman. The Association assists war invalids in finding jobs they are able to perform, because their pensions are not large, and they need to supplement them with extra income. For example, he, Maltsev, for many years had held a job at Danilov Market, where he worked as deputy director.

"That was the next question I was going to ask," Lenny said in disgust. "About his job at the market. He gave me that smart look, as though he knew he had taken it off the tip of my tongue."

It turned out that Stepan Sergeyich had never liked his job.

"It's bad business when a soldier starts trading," he told Lenny with a sigh. "Perhaps I shouldn't have taken it."

Maltsev wasn't surprised when Lenny told him that Brunevsky was on medical leave.

"I supposed he might be," he replied. "Many veterans get upset ahead of the Victory Day commemoration. Some of us can't even work."

Lenny then tried a different tack. Did Stepan Sergeyich know anything about Brunevsky's conviction for speculation? No, and even after Lenny had told him about it, he was not going to think any worse of his friend. Life was hard for war invalids after the war, and some of them possibly made mistakes. To err is human, and certainly someone like Brunevsky had proven his patriotism and dedication to the country. He, Maltsev, had complete confidence in Brunevsky, in his honesty and integrity.

Did Stepan Sergeyich ever have any dealings with Brunevsky in his capacity as deputy director of Danilov Market? Never. They saw each other socially, never for work.

"In any case, let's be sensible, comrade detective," Maltsev had said to Lenny. "What kind of dealings could a deputy director at a collective farmers' market have with a night watchman at a metals plant?"

Lenny's impressions of Oksana's father were so sharp and realistic that I couldn't help laughing, even though the laughter promptly brought on a painful fit of coughing.

"What indeed," Lenny said. He liked it when people laughed at his jokes and his impressions. "What kind of dealings could these two have had? That's the question I've been asking myself ever since I saw Brunevsky leave their apartment."

When I finally got home, I dialed Tosya's number. I should have walked across the courtyard to her place to apologize in person, but I had no strength left.

I waited while a neighbor went to fetch her, listening to the static on the line, and what sounded like the shuffling of well-worn felt slippers on the parquet. A long time passed.

Finally, the neighbor returned to the line.

"She's not at home," she said.

Her irritated voice was the last thing I remembered before sinking into oblivion. I had no recollection of how I got back to my room and tumbled into bed.

ELEVEN

The Patrice Lumumba Friendship of the Peoples University is our anticolonialist project. The official line is that its mission is to support the struggle of the subjugated peoples of Asia, Africa, Latin America and wherever else there are vestiges of colonial rule. That's why it bears the name of Patrice Lumumba – the first prime minister of independent Congo.

Once the oppressed nations succeed in throwing off the yoke of colonial rule – which is where history seems to be headed, anyway, and eventually most colonies will probably be free – we help them create their own educated classes. We want them to develop their own industries, along with their own industrial proletariat, and then build communism – which is also where history seems to be headed. The young men – and a smattering of young women, too, since we believe in the equality of the sexes, which is yet another path history seems to be taking – get their degrees at Lumumba University and return home with the skills they have acquired here and a lot of goodwill toward the Soviet Union. Or at least that is the idea.

The ugly racism of Major Yegorov and the insults hurled at Joseph Kofunda by Butyrka prison guards were sabotaging the foreign policy of the Soviet Union. That was what I kept saying to myself while walking the halls of the university. All around me thronged exotically dressed foreign students. They were laughing and chatting animatedly in variously accented Russian. Young people are resilient. Looking at them, you could never tell that a brutal murder had been committed here only a few days ago. The place was brimming with energy and joy, and it couldn't have been more different from the Southwestern District headquarters or Butyrka.

A full night's sleep had done me a world of good. My cold was mostly gone and, having gotten up early, I set out in search of the Argentinian student.

But first I wanted to see the auditorium where Kotov had read his poems. Trying several sets of double doors, I found at last one that was unlocked. Behind it was a vast space with rows of linked armchairs descending steeply toward the stage. The seats angled upright between the armrests were upholstered in red velvet. Looming over the stage was a red banner bearing a quote from one of Lenin's speeches. It was printed in gold letters in the original Russian as well as in English, French and Spanish, the languages of the most egregious of the colonial powers. A plaster bust of Lenin atop a square pedestal loomed blindingly white in the background.

Lenin's dictum was straightforward enough, one that is hard to disagree with: "Study, Study and Once Again Study!" It was presumably why the students were there in the first place. There was a little too much red in that auditorium, and it was of a saturated purplish hue that made you think of the color of congealed blood. Perhaps it was the red, along with Comrade Kotov's martial poetry, that made Kofunda lose his mind.

"The place is closed, comrade."

I had not noticed a short woman standing foursquare by the stage, wearing a blue cleaner's uniform and leaning on the handle of a mop.

"Geschlossen, Geschlossen," she repeated in German, and, since I continued to walk down the steps toward the stage, added in an exasperated Russian: "No one is allowed in, you dumb foreign idiot, how many times do I have to tell you?"

"I'm with Criminal Investigations."

I had to repeat it a couple of times, and to show my ID, because she was both hard of hearing and extremely distrustful.

"At least you're one of us, sonny," she said at last, smiling broadly. "I get tired of chasing those Mohammedans out of here. None of them understands any human language. It's not my job to run after them. If they don't want any of them Mohammedans in here, they should post a guard at the door."

She sat down in a the front row, stretched out her short legs and began fanning herself. She had a broad face, round as a pancake, and with what in the countryside they call a potato nose. Her eyes were narrow, watery blue, watchful, and framed by a web of tiny wrinkles.

"My name is Klava," she introduced herself.

"I want to ask you a few questions about the murder, Comrade Klava," I said.

In my experience, a cleaning woman can be more observant than a professor, a student, or any other kind of intellectual.

"Oh, it's about time," she exclaimed, perking up. "I thought you boys would never get around to it. You only asked me about it once."

"And once wasn't enough?"

"You kidding me, sonny? For a horrible thing like that? You need to keep asking. Every time I start telling the story, it comes out different."

"Well, then, let's hear it one more time," I said, suppressing a chuckle.

"What's that?" she asked seeing that I had taken out a notebook. "No, don't write anything down. If you keep scribbling you get distracted. You should listen and memorize everything I say, sonny."

Her tale turned out to be long and focused on how she had felt before Kotov's reading. It turned out she had had a strong premonition that the event wouldn't turn out well. In fact, her stomach had started to churn with fear when Kotov told those who wanted to see him after the reading to go to the adjoining office.

However, when it came to important details, her story didn't differ from what I had learned by reading the case file.

"Do you remember who wanted to see Comrade Kotov?" I asked.

"I don't know them by name," she said. "I have my own nicknames for them, like the Cubans who have bushy beards and long hair, and the black Africans, and the Asians. There was a bunch of them that afternoon. But if you want the truth, all those Mohammedans look alike, only a different color. Except the murderer. I remember him well. He sat in the hallway for a good long time, chatting with a little kid like he wasn't intending to go in and kill his Daddy. He was dark and looked scary as hell, I can vouch for that. I went all numb with fear the moment I took one look at him. When I saw him sitting there, I said to myself: 'This man is up to no good.' And sure enough—"

I asked her to let me into the office where Kotov had been killed.

"Oh, I don't like going in there."

She crossed herself furtively.

"Did it get cleaned up?"

"Of course, it did. They told me to clean it up right away. My knees are still shaking when I think of all the blood on the floor. They had to get rid of the armchair. A nice armchair it was, too, as good as new, but they couldn't keep it because of all that blood it was soiled with."

She kept telling me how scared she was while unlocking the door, but then went into the room showing no sign of fear. On the contrary, she was as eager to prattle as ever, and to show where the armchair had stood and how the dead man had been slumped over, and where his blood was still staining the floor and the carpet if you looked closely

"Lots of blood," she declared. "The water in my bucket turned blood red. I couldn't believe my eyes. It was like some kind of a miracle."

She crossed herself again.

It was a narrow office used by speakers and lecturers to gather their thoughts before taking the podium. It had a desk, a couple of chairs, an old overstuffed couch, and a full-length mirror on the wall. The ubiquitous carafe of yellowish water stood on the desk, with a glass placed upside down over the stopper.

"And there was so much poplar fuzz on the floor, like you wouldn't believe. Even in the blood on the floor some poplar fuzz was floating, and all around the edges of the puddle. You can't get away from that stuff this time of year"

The office had two doors – one leading to the auditorium, which Klava had unlocked, and another, to the hallway, where Kofunda had waited to see Kotov.

"You can't use that door," Klava said. "It's been sealed by the cops."

That was typical of how Major Yegorov's people worked – seal one door but neglect the other.

"What about female students?" I asked. "Was there a young woman waiting to see Comrade Kotov as well?"

"Don't ask me, sonny. They all look the same to me. Except for Cubans. Cubans are very noisy. They don't know how to behave in public. All the Muhammadans are noisy, except for the Asians. The Asians are quiet and polite. The Africans scream and shout and laugh all the time."

"So, there was no young woman?" I asked, interrupting her before she could begin working through a list of the member states of the United Nations.

She shrugged: "Of course there was one. I remember her, but I remember the murderer even better. He was as scary as a dozen devils."

"If you saw that young woman again, would you be able to recognize her?" I asked.

"Of course I would."

She tried to sound confident, but I was far from being reassured.

TWELVE

Getting past two receptionists, a typist in a short skirt and high heels, and a personal assistant took up the rest of my morning and parts of the early afternoon. Quite a challenge just to see the rector of Lumumba Friendship of the Peoples University. I was told that I needed to state the purpose of my visit in writing and request an appointment at least three weeks in advance. It was that kind of an institution.

"Oh no," the typist told me, interrupting her rapid-fire typing of a document titled Order No. 678 just long enough to wag a long forefinger tipped with a blood-red fingernail. "Comrade Rector is too busy to help you look for some Argentinian student. You need the Dean of Students for that."

Eventually, however, Comrade Rector's assorted support staff figured out that they would not be able to pawn me off on some minor functionary. I was ushered into a large corner office behind a gold nameplate listing the titles of its occupant, which included Honored Scientific Worker, Doctor and Professor.

The man behind the polished desk wore a bespoke three-piece suit made by a London or Paris tailor rather than some underpaid hack at one of Moscow's *ateliers*. He had thinning blond hair. A pair of tinted eyeglasses straddled the bridge of his long sharp nose. He was clean-shaven and smelled of an expensive aftershave. It all made him look less like Comrade Rector and Distinguished People's Educator and more like an unctuous CIA operative from an old spy movie.

The similarity was enhanced when he reached into a black attaché case and pulled out two different packs of American cigarettes. In the movies, CIA recruiters always try to lead Soviet citizens astray by offering them Marlboro or Kent cigarettes. It came as no surprise that those were the exact brands he tossed on his desk.

I decided not to fall for this transparent ruse and pulled out my own brand, filtered Red Presnyas. Seeing them Comrade Rector made a face.

"If you like these, I strongly recommend you try smoking Kent." He pushed the white pack toward me. "I prefer Marlboro myself, except at the end of a long day. Then I often feel like smoking something milder, something to soothe my throat."

I helped myself to one of his cigarettes, more because I didn't want to argue than because of any real desire to try a foreign brand. Comrade Rector flicked a shiny foreign lighter and held it out for me before lighting his own Marlboro.

"Do you like it?" he inquired after a minute. The cigarette did taste good. The tobacco was of much better quality than Red Presnya's.

With these preliminaries out of the way, he picked up my Criminal Investigations ID and made a show of studying it.

"I thought that the investigation into Comrade Kotov's murder has been wrapped up," he said, arching an eyebrow over his tinted eyewear. "It's unfortunate that such a tragedy should happen at our institution. And on such an occasion – the anniversary of the Great Victory."

He shook his head sorrowfully.

"Some people up there think that it was our fault." He raised his finger to indicate that by "up there" he meant somewhere in the upper reaches of the government. "They say that we should have been able to spot a student with a mental problem. I honestly don't think we could have. There had been no signals. We were as surprised as everyone else when the tragedy occurred. Perhaps even more."

"Are you convinced, then, that Joseph Kofunda is guilty?"

"Why?" he asked promptly. "Is there any doubt? New evidence?"

I shook my head.

"Not really. I just wanted to hear your opinion. You know your students well. Is he capable of such a brutal murder?"

Comrade Rector relaxed and pulled on his Marlboro.

"I don't know how to answer this question. Joseph was a difficult student from what I hear. Personally, I didn't have much contact with him. But those who knew him were decidedly not impressed."

He drew on his Marlboro.

"But not to the extent that it should have given us an indication of a real problem," he added promptly. "I hope you understand the difference between a student who is not especially bright and someone who's capable of such brutality. Not every mediocre student—"

He blew the smoke toward the open window.

The rector spoke about Kofunda as though he was already dead, even though the man had not even been convicted.

"Several witnesses claim that a young woman, a student from Argentina, was the last person to see the victim before Kofunda," I said. "I wonder if I could have a word with her."

"What is her name?"

"That's the problem," I said. "No one seems to know. That's why I need your help."

The Rector shook his head, visibly distressed by the evident shortcomings in my work. He picked up the receiver of one of the instruments on his desk. He sounded annoyed.

"Get me the student files. No, by country. No, just the first one. The letter A."

While we waited for his secretary to bring in a metal box brimming with index cards, the rector lit another Marlboro and said: "As far as I recall, we have no female students from Argentina. But I may be mistaken. We'll know soon enough."

It took us less than a minute to prove him right. They had only three Argentinians, all of them men.

"As you can see, we have a more substantial group from Algeria and Afghanistan," he explained. "Also mostly men, although there are some women, too. Your student must be from some other college in the city. I'm sorry that I can't be of greater assistance."

He signaled to his secretary to remove the box.

"What about other Latin American students?" I asked, ignoring his outstretched hand which was meant to show that the audience was over. "Surely you have women from Cuba, Mexico, Venezuela?"

"Yes, of course. And from Peru, Uruguay and Chile as well. Especially Chile. A large number. Surely you are not going to try to interview them all?"

I thought I detected a note of sarcasm in his voice.

"It's not a bad idea," I said. "How long will it take for you to have them assembled in the auditorium?"

Lumumba University proved remarkably efficient. About two dozen young women – most of them very pretty, with beautiful dark eyes, black hair and olive skin – were sitting in the auditorium three quarters of an hour later, talking seemingly all at once in their throaty Spanish. They were shrugging their shoulders, probably wondering why they had been pulled out of their classrooms with such urgency.

While they were being assembled, I stayed in the adjacent office by myself, examining it at my leisure and without Comrade Klava's running commentary.

The office had a window that was narrow and long, stretching the entire length of the wall behind the drawn curtains. I pulled the curtains apart, letting a wedge of spring sunshine into the room. There were several potted plants on the windowsill, but only a cactus had managed to survive winter darkness and institutional neglect. Another, very large ceramic pot contained desiccated remains of something else that could have once been a geranium. It was supported by a metal peg stuck into the bone-dry soil.

I pushed the flowerpots to the side and undid the lock on the widow. The gust of fresh air made me realize how stuffy and airless the room had been. I often find that rooms in which a person was murdered smell persistently of corpses, although it is probably my imagination playing its tricks on me.

The street below had a busy pedestrian traffic. Some of the people on the sidewalk were Lumumba students. The Africans especially seemed to have a spring in their step, enjoying the sunshine and the warmth after a never-ending Russian winter. The bright colors of their clothes made them stand out in the drab, grey-and-brown mass of our own citizens, many of whom were still wearing winter coats and fur hats.

I leaned out and examined the outer wall. Built into the rough concrete was a decorative aluminum cornice running parallel to the ground about three feet below the window. There were no other windows to my right, where the auditorium was located, and a row of similar long narrow windows on the left. Those were classrooms.

You could probably climb out of the adjoining window using the rough concrete surface of the wall and clinging to the cornice – but you would have to be a circus acrobat of considerable skill. And then you would surely be reported to the cops by a passerby or a tenant in the surrounding buildings.

"You keep looking for some alternative version of the murder," I said to myself. "You should stop. There clearly is none."

The office was quickly filling with poplar fuzz. I pulled the window shut and then thought of something Klava had said earlier that day.

Yes, of course. She had mentioned poplar fuzz being all over the room.

The case was closed but questions about it continued to accumulate.

When the Latin Americans had been assembled, Klava circled the auditorium several times, eyeing each of them in turn. After a minute or two they noticed her; the cacophony of their voices died down and an uneasy silence settled in. Two dozen pairs of dark eyes were now glued to the cleaning woman.

"I know which one it is," she announced breathlessly in a conspiratorial whisper, rushing into the adjoining office. "Over in the second row."

The student in question was tall and had long hair and thick eyebrows joined over the bridge of her nose. But when I asked Klava twice whether she was quite certain, she hesitated, circled the auditorium once more and declared that she had made a mistake. According to her, a student in the middle of the first row, also quite tall and dark, but with her long dark hair braided, looked more like the elusive Argentinian.

At that point I ended the experiment and went out to greet the young women. I asked them whether any of them had been to see Kotov after the poetry reading. They stared, suddenly uncharacteristically quiet. At last one of them, broke the silence to tell me what I already knew: a group of her compatriots, male students from Cuba, had gone to talk to him. The were older than most other Lumumba students, she explained. They had been with Fidel at Sierra Maestra and were now studying literature, because they wanted to write novels about their revolutionary struggle.

"Like Papa Ernesto Hemingway," she added.

None knew of any female student from Argentina studying at the university.

"We know a Venezuelan," one of them shouted to peels of raucous laughter and embarrassed giggles. "He's a guy, but he spends so much time in the girls' dorm he might as well be a girl himself. His first name happens to be Ilyich, just like Lenin's patronymic."

Klava was mad at me. Fine, if I didn't want her help, she wasn't going to give me any. To my question whether the office window had been open or closed when Kotov's body was found, she responded that she didn't remember. I couldn't get anything further out of her.

Before leaving I stopped at the Rector's office once more.

"Please thank Comrade Rector for his assistance," I told the typist. "Also, could he please send us the snapshots of all your female students? This way we won't have to bother you anymore."

The door behind the titled plaque opened and Comrade Rector bent his head around the door jamb.

"We will definitely do that, Lieutenant. All the snapshots. Please rest assured. We definitely will."

The sarcasm in his voice was so thick you could cut it with a knife.

I had to stop at the office and spend a few hours doing paperwork. By the time I got home it was once again too late to call Tosya. I felt I was screwing up. My apologies, and therefore our reconciliation, were being pushed back from one day to the next, the quarrel was stretching out unreasonably, and we were not seeing each other. And it was all my fault.

I was starting to miss her very much.

THIRTEEN

The doctor surprised Nadezhda and Lieutenant Panin in a shed in the back of the wooden house used as a makeshift field hospital.

He had gone out for a smoke, heard strange sounds coming from the shed and discovered the two of them on a bed of fresh straw.

A chill was in the autumn air and they had not taken off their clothes. Nadezhda was too absorbed to see him, but Panin lifted his head, locked his gaze in his and went on thrusting between Nadezhda's upraised legs. He was like some kind of a machine, a locomotive with only the lower half of his body as a moving part.

The doctor didn't stay to watch. He shrugged and walked away.

They had a lull on their stretch of the front. Their workload was light, and he didn't see Nadezhda for the rest of the day. Late at night she slipped into his bed, in her usual spot at his side. She was naked and had become chilled running down the hallway. He recoiled from her touch, pressing his back against the wall.

"I couldn't resist him," she whispered. "He forced himself on me."

She stayed long enough to get warm. She gave him a kiss on the forehead before leaving again. Silent, he patted her on the shoulder.

Panin was only a lieutenant and he, a major, was three ranks his senior. But Panin was SMERSH, the dreaded *Smert' Shpionam*, or

Death to Spies. SMERSH were on a scale of their own. He had seen tank corps generals defer to SMERSH lieutenants.

Lieutenant Panin seemed older than his twenty-five years, but he was old in a different way from the raw recruits who aged quickly on the front lines. His was an institutional maturity, ageless and implacable.

The doctor knew when he first clapped his eyes on Panin that the man was trouble. He hadn't been badly wounded. The open-top Jeep in which he had been travelling took a wrong turn and came under German fire. The driver and another SMERSH officer riding in the front were killed, but Panin got a scratch on a forearm, a few bruises, a gash on his skull, and a concussion when the jeep overturned in the ditch. An army lieutenant would have been bandaged up and sent back to the front the same day. Lieutenant Panin stayed on "to recuperate."

The doctor was nearly a full head taller and physically stronger than Panin, more intelligent and better educated. He was a senior officer. He objectively was doing more for the war effort, saving lives and patching up the wounded. And yet he had no authority over Panin. Rather, the other way around.

The war was still raging elsewhere, far away, on other sections of the unfathomably long front that stretched from the snow-capped Caucasus mountains of and the palm trees around the Black Sea, to the northern ocean, brutally cold and choked with ice floes. But for a rare spell, theirs was a quiet life, almost bucolic, almost reminiscent of peacetime.,

The doctor confronted Panin the following morning on the second floor of the house, where he had allotted a private room to the SMERSH lieutenant.

"I believe your wounds have healed," he said. "It's time for you to return to your unit."

"I'm on assignment here, Doc," Panin replied.

"What kind of assignment?" he asked, trying to ignore the man's insolent stare.

"SMERSH business. Top secret investigation."

"Into what?"

"Very well then. I'll explain if you insist. I'm trying to determine if after getting a kike dick up her ass your nurse still prefers a real Russian one."

The doctor didn't have time to think.

He had promised himself he would not rise to the bait. No matter what the creepy Lieutenant Panin said or did, he would stay calm and remain polite. No mention of Nadezhda. He would stick to his professional medical opinion and insist that Panin leave the hospital to make room for those who needed a bed.

But the man's anti-Semitism scrambled his intentions. The rage blew up red and hot over his eyes like a hand grenade. The goddamn punk was a fascist, no better than a German Nazi who picked Jews out of a lineup of prisoners and hung them on the spot, with a placard reading Jew around their necks.

The rage blinded him, took control of his brain. No longer knowing what he was doing he struck Punin in the face.

The doctor was a big man, with broad shoulders and massive forearms. The long line of kosher butchers from which he descended had passed their powerful physic on to him. He used to box in high school, making it onto the first team of his local Army, Navy and Air Force Volunteer Association. He could really step into a punch, putting his entire weight behind it – and in this case he did.

Panin reeled, falling backwards, hitting the wall and sliding down. His face went blank. Blood squirted from his nostrils and dribbled in two thin red splotches onto his chin. Exhaling through his mouth, he blew a red bubble. He leaned over, spitting more blood and broken teeth. Then he threw up.

The doctor's rage dissipated as suddenly as it had come upon him. He was a medical professional once more. He leaned over the supine Panin to assess the damage. The lieutenant, mistaking his motion for more aggression, twisted out of the doctor's grasp with remarkable agility, jumped up and trundled down the shaky wooden steps.

The doctor was arrested the next morning, at dawn. They arrived in three vehicles. A company of SMERSH troops in smart uniforms, armed with brand-new submachine guns, surrounded the field hospital as though they were about to storm it. They pulled him out of bed and made him strip naked. He stood shivering by the plywood-covered window while they ransacked his room, throwing his belongings on the floor and trampling over them with their boots. They took all written materials, all his papers – books, newspapers, letters from home, his diary, family snapshots. They detached the wall map on which he had marked the progress of the Red Army based on Informburo reports, folded it and added it to the pile.

Lieutenant Panin was there too. His face was swollen, and a red and blue bruise was starting to spread down the sides of his broken nose.

At first, he paid no attention to the doctor, pretending to be absorbed in the search. But toward the end, he came up close to him and said softly: "What I really want to do is to give you a nice, hard kick in the balls. But I can wait. Pleasure deferred is pleasure enhanced."

They took him away. Two armed guards with the NKVD's blue visor caps squeezed him between them in the back of a ZIS truck. He was still naked. The early morning wind was cold, and he was getting splinters in his backside from sitting on the rough pine boards.

Those splinters would get infected and bother him over the next few weeks. But, considering all the other pain and humiliations he suffered, it would be a minor inconvenience.

They took away Nadezhda too, placing her in the back of a black Studebaker.

One time – when the war was over, in 1949 or 1950, he thought he glimpsed her in a busy crowd in the city of Kostroma. He was aware of someone staring at him and turned just in time for their eyes to meet. Then she hastily looked away. He thought he recognized her, but everything was different by then. He had changed in so many ways, and her life was probably different, too.

SMERSH weren't especially sophisticated in torturing him. Just sleep deprivation, lots of beatings, and, in between the beatings, standing on his feet for hours at a stretch. Whenever he passed out, they would kick him in the kidneys until he got up. If that didn't work, they'd poor ice water over him.

Also, hunger. And thirst. They gave him salty fish to eat and no water to drink.

It wasn't sophisticated, but it was effective. Lieutenant Panin, the swelling on his face gradually receding and his contusion changing color and healing, would take him out in the courtyard every couple of days and make him crawl through frozen mud, kicking him in his privates with his heavy jackboots. Just for fun, not as part of the interrogation.

They told him that he was the mastermind of a conspiracy to treat wounded Germans and smuggle them back across the lines, so that they could continue to fight. They wanted him to identify other traitors who were in league with him, the more the better, so that they too could be brought to justice. In the end, when he had lost his will to live, he signed a piece of paper incriminating the two medics who had mistakenly picked up the wounded German several months before. With the remnants of his mind he hoped that they had long before been killed. Frontline medics didn't have a long life expectancy.

After that, the beatings stopped, and he was able to stretch out on the bunk in an overcrowded cell where soldiers and officers arrested for various ideological crimes and transgressions awaited their fate. One or two were taken out every night to be shot.

That was when he was brought in to see Lieutenant Panin for the last time.

"The two medics you've fingered have been executed," Panin told him with a nasty smile on his prematurely aged face, baring two rows of chipped and broken teeth. "Their families back home have been arrested too. But your medics were lucky. It's a quick and painless death. As for you, the military tribunal decided to take into account your service as a surgeon. You'll be demoted to private and sent to a penal unit. A *shtrafbat*. You'll be given an opportunity to wash away your treason with your filthy Jewish blood."

What a difference a few weeks had made. Panin's anti-Semitism no longer bothered him. Now, he couldn't care less.

FOURTEEN

Next morning, I rushed past the security desk on the first floor, flipping my pass at Sidor, the stocky man of undetermined age with greasy gray hair and a red, perfectly square face who was guarding the entrance of the Moscow Criminal Investigations building ever since I started working there, and probably for several decades before that.

Usually, Sidor gives me one of his unsmiling nods, reserving progressively warmer greetings for the bosses, in strict accordance with their rank and position. Whenever someone from the Ministry or, god forbid, the Central Committee graces us with their presence, his face spreads in a broad smile, regaling the high and mighty with the dull glow of his metal teeth.

This time, however, Sidor flagged me and, without saying a word, pointed to a young man standing behind his desk. The young man nodded, whereupon Sidor gave him a kind of half-smile, leaving me guessing as to the visitor's rank. Surely not a general, but no ordinary whipper-snapper civilian in a suit, either.

"Senior Lieutenant Matyushkin?" the young man inquired politely.

"At your service," I replied, keeping up the well-mannered conversation.

The sharp tips of his orange cowboy boots stuck out from beneath the cuffs of his fashionably tight pants. Now, cowboy boots may be fine for an American official somewhere in Washington, but they are unquestionably an aberration in the Soviet context. It's not only that you have to be able to find cowboy boots in Moscow, which is next to impossible, but your bosses have to allow you to wear them. Budyonny for one would have had a fit if any of us had showed up for work sporting something like that.

"Follow me, please." The young man ordered me curtly and, not giving me another look, headed for the exit. When he pushed his way out through the revolving door, he had to stop, since he found him alone in the street while I was standing exactly where he had left me.

He waited to see whether I would finally grasp the meaning of his instructions, but in the end had to retrace his steps, which made him look rather foolish. Whether or not Sidor approved of the young man's cowboy boots, he certainly didn't think much of my ornery behavior, turning around and shaking his head at me.

"What's the matter with you, Lieutenant? Didn't you hear what I said?"

"I would like a little more information," I said. "You know my name and rank, but I don't know yours, and I have a few things to do at the office this morning."

"We have cleared it with your boss, Lieutenant. He knows you'll be late. You don't need to know my name; all I'm doing is acting on my instructions. I'll explain where we're going when we're outside."

My Criminal Investigations colleagues were streaming past security and gathering by the elevator. Some were starting to turn their heads in our direction, to see what kind of new trouble Senior Lieutenant Matyushkin had managed to get himself in.

Reluctantly, I followed the young man out of the building.

A black Volga was waiting for us outside. Its shiny black flanks reflected the red banners decorating the facade of our building for the May holidays.

"Get in, please," the young man said.

He pointed to the back seat and got in next to the driver. The car took off, diving skillfully into the middle of the heavy traffic on Petrovka

Street, changing lanes to get onto the median, reserved for black limousines carrying high government officials, and swiftly reached the intersection with the Garden Ring. The traffic cop manning the round glass booth on the crosswalk nodded to the driver and stopped the flow of cars to let us through.

"You're being summoned to the Ministry of Foreign Affairs," the young man explained, half-turning in his seat. "You'll be told the reason for this when you arrive."

The Ministry of Foreign Affairs used to be located near where I live, on the corner of Dzherzhinsky Street and Kuznetsky Most, kitty-corner with the headquarters of the KGB. But the old building – once the sprawling Hotel Angleterre – wasn't grand enough for them. About a decade ago, the Ministry had been moved to a newly built, granite skyscraper on Garden Ring, with a huge Soviet Union emblem on its facade.

We were driven to the main entrance, where a security pass was waiting for me. The young man accompanied me as far as the elevator, saying nothing. Other young men, looking very much like my escort – minus the cowboy boots which were apparently a rarity even here –scurried around the lobby, carrying files, folders and briefcases. The lobby was busy, with a lot of people shuttling to and fro, but remarkably quiet, as if all those young men had taken the vow of silence. No sounds reached my ears except their muffled footfalls on the stone floor and the hum of the descending elevator.

If it wasn't the Minister I was going to see, it must have been someone quite high up their hierarchy. The glass nameplate on his door identified the occupant as Eduard Vasilyevich Sumarokov. Unlike the nameplate of Lumumba University's rector, this one gave no title. But, then again, if you had business with someone so high up, you probably already knew what their title would be. Since I wasn't in that line of work, and since I rarely read the newspapers, the name Sumarokov meant nothing to me. But the view out of his window was spectacular. All of Moscow in the palm of your hand.

"I see you're admiring the view," Comrade Sumarokov said.

I nodded. "Very impressive."

"Now, please stop. Looking out the window is a distraction. I'm a busy man and I would like to get to the point right away, if you don't mind. Why are you interested in Comrade Kotov's murder?"

You didn't have to be a rocket scientist to have connected this sudden summons with the Kotov case, but the high level of officialdom involved took me aback.

"It's not a routine investigation," I responded slowly, choosing my words carefully. "It's a murder case in which a member of the Writer's Union was killed and for which a foreign national has been arrested. We at Moscow Criminal Investigations naturally want to make sure that the investigation is being conducted properly, that procedures are being followed correctly, and so on."

"You don't trust Major Yegorov then? You don't believe his men are professional enough?"

"On the contrary. We have full confidence in Major Yegorov, which is why he has been in charge, but another pair of eyes can never hurt."

"Are you certain then that Joseph Kofunda is guilty?"

"Based on what I have seen in his file and on my personal conversation with him – yes, pretty much."

"But not entirely?"

"Well, there are some loose ends in the investigation—" I started to say, but the man behind the desk interrupted me.

"The case is closed," he declared. "Joseph Kofunda is guilty."

The pleasant diplomatic baritone suddenly had a bit of ice in it.

"—and those loose ends need to be tied up," I finished my sentence, ignoring the interruption.

"Enough said, Lieutenant. Let me give you a bit of the international background. I don't have to, but you look like an intelligent person, and I think you should understand what is going on. Mr. Kofunda, Senior, was defense minister in the government of the Central African Republic until six months ago. Although only a minister of defense, he was running the entire show. He was very well disposed toward the Soviet Union. Exceptionally so. A true friend of our country. It didn't hurt that we were educating his only surviving son – the rest of his family had been killed during the civil war in which the Kofundas' tribe, and Mr. Kofunda's party, the National Liberation Front, came out on top. To cement this mutually beneficial relationship, we were periodically depositing various sums into Mr. Kofunda's dollar-denominated Swiss bank account. But those Africans are incompetent. Mr. Kofunda was asleep at the switch and allowed some two-bit sergeant to stage a coup, machine-gun the presidential guard along with the president and install himself as the new national savior. We gave as much support to the National Liberation Front as we could, but in the end, he had to flee to Paris and we had to cut our losses. Unfortunately, the sergeant who replaced him turned out to be a clever son of a bitch. He didn't break with us, but at the same time he started flirting with Uncle Sam, France and Britain. When Mr. Kofunda was in government, he awarded us a contract to build an international airport in the capital, which would be strictly for civilian traffic but could sometimes be used by the military. The sergeant keeps hinting that he might cancel it, making public declarations that negotiations with the Americans are underway. We need something to pull him our way, and the criminal case involving Joseph Kofunda is something we would have had to invent if it hadn't so conveniently fallen into our lap."

I nodded.

"You see how important it is, Lieutenant?" he concluded. "Joseph Kofunda is going to jail. You can put your doubts to rest or not, it's entirely your affair – as long as you don't try to meddle."

I did not get a ride back. I didn't mind that. I wanted to spend some time alone. I walked back to the office thinking the situation over. The meaning of Comrade Rector's sarcasm the other day, when I was at his university, was now clear. He knew all along that the Ministry was going to pull me off this case.

I wondered what I should do about it.

FIFTEEN

There were two distinct aspects to this case. The political one strongly suggested that Joseph Kofunda will go to jail. Whether he murdered Valentin Kotov or not, too much was stacked against him. The criminal aspect had to do with whether Kofunda was actually guilty, and that aspect still interested me very much.

Truth will out, I kept telling myself. The time may yet come when the real culprit will need to be produced – assuming of course that it wasn't Kofunda.

I can't say that I didn't take seriously the warning from the Ministry of Foreign Affairs. Eduard Vasilyevich Sumarokov, whatever his official title, was not a man to be trifled with.

The result of my deliberations on my walk back to the office was to ask Lenny to introduce himself to Comrade Kotov's widow. After all, Sumarokov had said nothing about Lenny not being allowed to carry on the investigation, and therefore we would not be technically in violation of the letter of his instructions. As to their spirit – well, we would cross that bridge when we got to it.

Valentin Kotov was an established poet, a member of the Writers' Union well-liked by the authorities. Hardly a year went by when he didn't publish a book of new poems or a selection of recent works, a retrospective or greatest hits. The print runs were always impressive, reaching into the tens of thousands, regardless of whether they were purchased by the reading public or remaindered. He was, in a manner of speaking, a Soviet literary classic. No one else but a vetted and approved poet would have been invited to read his works at Lumumba University.

Such literary figures, pampered by the authorities and receiving major accolades, tended to live exceptionally well. However, right from the start Lenny was surprised by the Kotovs' modest digs. The widow received him in a small room at a communal apartment, off an unlit corridor hung with other people's laundry, which dripped onto Lenny's police uniform while he waited for his knock to be answered. Before Kotov was murdered, the three of them lived in that one room, sharing the bathroom and the kitchen with five other families.

Mrs. Kotov's name was Malvina. She almost seemed too young to be a mother of a seven-year-old. She would have been more convincing as Kotov's daughter than his widow.

She was ashamed of the way they lived: "Valentin Viktorovich was a very generous man. He had a big heart. It took him a very long time to leave his other family, his first wife and children. Oleg was already five when someone sent his wife an anonymous letter, opening her eyes on the fact that he had me and Oleg. Then and only then did he finally decide to come to live with us, because his first wife had made his life a living hell."

Lenny was quoting her verbatim and even sounded like a pouting young woman. Lenny was a first-rate mimic.

"Valentin Viktorovich left everything he owned to his first wife, his wonderful apartment, his Volga car, his dacha in the writers' village of Peredelkino. She insisted on it and he was a very generous man, he never thought about money or creature comforts. He had been in the war, and wartime experiences colored his entire life. Here he is with his unit. A group portrait."

Lenny pulled out an old black-and-white photograph. It showed a military unit, several young kids in uniform and a lieutenant, recognizable as a much younger, fresh-faced Comrade Kotov.

"I figured I borrow it from her, and she said she had other copies," Lenny said before going back to recounting Malvina's sad tale:

"That African monster murdered him in cold blood. I don't understand why we're wasting money educating them. What can they ever understand about Tolstoy? Or Pushkin? Or Valentin Viktorovich's poetry, for god's sake? Nothing but trouble comes from foreigners. Valentin Viktorovich was like Pushkin, who was also killed by a foreigner. And Valentin Viktorovich was more generous than Pushkin. He left his apartment to his first wife. We were lucky to get even this lousy place. Oleg's half-brothers have always lived in the lap of luxury, they had everything their hearts desired while they were growing up. And now Oleg is in shock. He had been talking to his father's murderer moments before Valentin Viktorovich was killed. Nothing good has ever come out of Africa."

"I had to chuckle at that," Lenny said, interrupting his account again. "I wondered if someone had ever told her that Pushkin's great-grandfather was African."

I laughed.

"I'm surprised you didn't remind her of that."

She met Kotov just as she started at the Gorky Literary Institute, one of the few young women admitted to the poetry faculty. No, she didn't graduate, and she doesn't write poetry any more. She got pregnant with Oleg and withdrew after the first year.

Kotov was the first professor she met, teaching her first seminar at the Gorky. It was love at first sight. They were meant for each other.

"You know, Lieutenant," she told Lenny, "there is an old legend. When god created people, he split everyone in half and sent each half into the world by itself. And now we are looking for our other half, but only the fortunate few find it. I've often had a feeling that, once upon a time, Valentin Viktorovich and I were the same person, despite our age difference. It was my luck to have found my other half when I was still practically a child, but Valentin Viktorovich spent a good part of his life living with a woman he didn't love and looking for me. His life before we met had been trial and error."

Lenny was a hopeless romantic in his own way. He could fall in love with a waitress at a railway station bar and build her up in his imagination into a Juliet. But that was only when it came to his own love life. Other people's relationships he could analyze with a sober, clinical eye, pinpoint their follies, and make fun of them.

He was a top-notch detective, too. Once he was done with the widow, he had a talk with some of her neighbors. Neighbors in communal apartments make it their business to know what happens in other people's rooms. They also tend to dislike each other – especially if the new arrivals happen to be fancy people like famous poets and their young second wives. Walls have ears in communal apartments – and whatever those ears pick up becomes grist for the gossip mill in the kitchen and the courtyard.

In other words, everybody knows everything about everybody else.

"Turns out the peace and harmony were rare guests in the Kotovs' love nest," Lenny reported. "They were squabbling most of the time. The second Mrs. Kotov is no angel. She resented all that gentlemanly stuff about leaving the apartment, the Volga, and the dacha to the old sponge, as she called the first Mrs. Kotov. The little fortune hunter must have thought that she had ensnared the old man and will live in his big apartment and be driven around in his Volga. It turned out differently, to put it mildly. The first Mrs. Kotov fought hard for what was hers and won."

Lenny was a ladies' man. He loved many individual women – often several of them at the same time – and tended to fall in love frequently. But, like many other ladies' men, he had a strong misogynist streak. He actually didn't like women all that much.

"What about the kid?" I asked. "Did you see him?"

"A clever little tyke. His mother told me he's crazy about animals. They used to take him to the zoo every Sunday, to a class where they teach kids how to take care of animals. I should take my girls there, too, they'll love it. Naturally, he's in shock about his Dad. Imagine going into that office and seeing your father eviscerated? It's not something you'd wish on any kid. It took me a while to break the ice, but in the end he and I got to be friends."

Lenny had a way of making children and animals like him. It easy to see why they did. It was his success with women that always left me dumbfounded.

"I'd like to get him alone some time and ask him what it was he saw," I said. "You may have to do it for me. That might be better in any case, since you're so good with kids."

"By the way," Lenny said. "The current Mrs. Kotov was not the poet's first attraction. I checked. Kotov was infamous at Gorky for scouring the incoming classes for pretty faces. Students used to laugh at him and his old-goat ways, but he usually got his prey. He was a celebrity, after all, and fame attracts women – as does everything else that glitters. In other words, the late lamented Comrade Kotov had his share of fun on this earth."

"Until he stumbled upon the second Mrs. Kotov," I added.

"Not so fast, brother," Lenny said. "A student at Gorky told me that he had seen Professor Kotov with a young woman recently. Or rather a young woman was waiting for him after class."

You've got to hand it to Lenny. When he conducted an investigation, he did it thoroughly.

I had a sudden inspiration. Or rather, I took shot in the dark.

"Tall?" I asked quickly. "Dark? With long black hair?"

Lenny's face fell. He likes taking me by surprise and he often does, and in such cases his childlike joy is boundless.

"Oh, so you already knew," he muttered.

"*Nyet*," I said. "A lucky guess."

I was about to tell him about the Argentinian student, but at the last moment I changed my mind. Lenny gave me a suspicious look. "A lucky guess, eh?" he repeated after me, and shrugged.

"One other thing," he said, his voice terse now. "You ignored that picture I showed you, but it is well worth taking a closer look. Kotov was in the war and had a bunch of shiny medals to prove it, but the truth is that, judging by this picture, he was in the NKVD. And you know what kind of war those guys had."

He didn't have to tell me. Everyone heard tales of NKVD detachments stationed behind the lines, shooting those of our own who wouldn't advance under deadly machine gun fire or clear mine fields with their bodies. Or NKVD troops sent to deal with war widows protesting at home – women who couldn't stand watching their kids starve while party hacks stuffed their fat faces.

As a result of Lenny's detective work, my opinion of Comrade Kotov came down a few notches, while my view of the importance of the elusive Argentinian student surged. I don't know why I had that hunch, but the descriptions tallied, and it was too much of a coincidence. She existed – if not, perhaps, as a student at Lumumba – and she already knew Kotov when she went in to see him after the reading.

If she was his mistress, why did she come forward after the murder? Was she also married?

Discounting Klava, the Lumumba cleaning woman, who was not a very reliable witness, of the two people who had seen the Argentinian at a close range, one was in Butyrka, accused of murder, and the other a little kid of seven, the son of the victim. I had no chance of interviewing the one in Butyrka again. It was therefore crucial that I had a chat with the kid. While Lenny was better at getting along with kids, I would have to do it myself.

SIXTEEN

The Soviet Union and its Western allies fought two different wars. They are even called by different names. Ours was the Great Patriotic War and theirs World War II. Ours started in June 1941, when Germany attacked our country. By then the British had been fighting Hitler for nearly two years and we were his allies. On the other hand, we fought the Germans one day longer. Our Victory Day is celebrated on May 9, while VE Day in the rest of the world is marked on May 8.

In the early years after the war, the celebrations were subdued. People were happy that the war was over and that the invaders had been expelled from our soil, but the terrible price that the country had paid for it was still fresh in everyone's memory.

My sister Natashka was born a few months after we got an official form in the mail, a half-sheet of cheap grey paper preprinted with words IN THE BATTLE FOR THE SOCIALIST FATHERLAND, FAITHFUL TO THE MILITARY OATH AND DEMONSTRATING HEROISM AND COURAGE, into which my Dad's name and address had been inserted in a hurried, careless hand. On the next line, the choice was KILLED/WOUNDED/DIED OF WOUNDS. The first word had been emphatically underlined.

One Victory Day when Natashka was six she snuck into Mom's armoire and found that sheet of paper and Dad's military decorations.

She picked a few early May dandelions sprouting along the rail spur near the factory where Mom worked and placed them in a glass.

Mom came home – at the time, May 9 was still a regular workday and not an official holiday. She saw Natashka's display on the dining table, the dandelions already starting to sag, replaced Dad's death notice and military decorations in their box, tossed the dandelions out the window and said:

"Come, Natasha, help me make supper."

Over the years, official celebrations became bigger and more lavish. Radio broadcasts hailed the patriotism of the Soviet people and their heroic struggle and kept reminding the rest of the world that it had been the Red Army that delivered it from the evil Brown Plague. There was less sadness and more self-congratulations. It wasn't that people who went through war were starting to forget – they weren't. But younger people, too young to remember, were doing the celebrating. May 9 was declared a national holiday, parades were held, and medals were minted and awarded indiscriminately to everyone.

Tosya's eight-year-old Sevka called me on the evening of May 8 to say that he had been delegated by his second-grade class to greet war veterans in Red Square. His mother was going – she wouldn't miss an occasion like this, when she could be proud of her son – and he wanted me to be there too.

I would have gone with them in any case, but now I literally jumped at the opportunity. The truth was that I had not yet managed to speak to Tosya after that missed date two weeks before. Not that I didn't try. I knew I had been at fault and I needed to apologize. But a couple of my attempts to reach her by phone had been rebuffed and then my work got too busy. Every day I was getting home too late to call her. Besides, my cold, which had passed quickly, transformed itself into bronchitis. I still had occasional debilitating coughing fits, which refused to respond to Daria Filippovna's linden blossom tea, raspberry preserves, and other home remedies.

It was a beautiful morning when we met at the passageway connecting our courtyard to Kirov Street. I arrived well in advance of the appointed time. I wanted to make sure the two of them would not have to wait for me. Sevka was wearing his Young Octobrist five-point star, an aluminum pin with Baby Lenin's curly head in its center. Sevka's white shirt was freshly laundered and ironed, his hair washed and combed.

Seeing Tosya made me realize how much I had missed her – physically, too.

She greeted me formally, saying "Good morning, Pavel," and quickly looked away. I wanted to start apologizing immediately, but Sevka preempted me.

"Let's go quickly," he shouted, running ahead. "We need to be at the meeting point in half an hour. They'll be distributing the bouquets. I don't want to be late."

The meeting point was only a ten-minute walk from our house, and we had plenty of time, but you couldn't reason with Sevka in his current state of excitement.

Kirov Street, where we live, is one of the great thoroughfares, running from Dzherzhinsky Square in close proximity to the Kremlin to the Three Stations Square, from where long-distance trains depart to the North, Northwest and Southeast. We live at Kirov Gate, just inside Boulevard Ring. It's a nice place to live because it is central and because the boulevards are planted with trees and have gravel paths and benches.

The usually busy Kirov Street was closed to traffic for the holiday. Lots of red flags and flowers lined the sidewalks, giving the city a festive air. A kid in a peasant outfit played the accordion, and half-dozen girls were dancing to it. Their boyfriends stood around grinning stupidly, too self-conscious to join in. The girls were wearing wartime khakis, but they looked too young and fresh-faced to have been in the war. In any war, thank god.

Sevka ran well ahead of us and we had to pick up the pace in order not to lose sight of him in the crowd. We were a little out of breath and walking – or rather half-jogging, sidestepping celebrants on the roadway – side by side and in silence. Casting an eye at Tosya now and again I could see that she was still angry with me.

The flower ceremony took place in Red Square. A military band played uplifting martial music. There were lots of kids with bouquets, all dressed in white shirts and blue pants and skirts, with their Young Octobrist stars gleaming on their chests. Looking like a flock of oversized seagulls, they rushed a small group of veterans huddling in the shadow of Lenin's Tomb and literally buried them under a mass of tulips, daffodils and blood-red carnations. The veterans – hoary old men in military jackets that had seen better days and were much too big for their shrunken frames – were festooned with so many medals they were in danger of topping over.

The Young Octobrists, supervised by imperious women who looked like gym teachers, were herded into a kind of parade formation to perform a song. A boy and a girl recited a poem and gave thanks to the veterans. The entire group of tykes then swore that they would sacrifice their own lives in defense of the Fatherland in the next war, whenever it came. Tosya didn't like that part.

Press photographers kept snapping pictures, and there was a television crew on hand to record the proceedings.

The ceremony took no more than half an hour, but a lot more time had been consumed setting it up. By the afternoon, the sun had turned hot. Standing on the polished flagstones of Red Square, Tosya and I got tired of doing nothing. Silence still weighed heavily between us.

On the way back, adrenalin was still coursing through Sevka's veins.

"Were you in the war, Uncle Pavel?"

I laughed and shook my head: "I was about your age when the war started."

"So what? I'd run away from home if there's a war and join a fighting unit at the front."

"They didn't allow that during the war," I said. "Kids were not supposed to fight. That was men's job. Kids were supposed to go to school and study hard."

"I wish there was a war now," Sevka said, a wistful note in his voice. "Not with the Germans, though, we've given them a sound beating and I bet they'll think twice next time when they think of invading us. But maybe with the Americans this time."

Tosya stepped in to interrupt his musings:

"Don't talk nonsense," he said sternly.

Sevka fell silent, insulted. He held a grudge for a minute or two, but couldn't stay quiet for long.

"Was your Dad in the war?"

I nodded. I wasn't in the mood to talk about my Dad.

"My grandfather was in the war," he said. "And my grandmother. They might have been killed in action, but we don't know that for sure, right, Mommy?"

Tosya nodded, saying nothing. Tosya grew up in an orphanage, like so many kids after the war. She didn't remember her parents and had no idea what happened to them.

"I don't know whether my own Dad was in the war," Sevka said.

"Oh, shut up, you little fool," Tosya shouted, suddenly shaking with rage.

Sevka bit his tongue and pulled his head in. Tosya could be scary when she got angry.

Sevka's father was an older man Tosya met soon after leaving the orphanage. When they came of age, students at the orphanage were supposed to get a job and live on their own. They were still kids of sixteen and seventeen and had no experience of the big world outside. The man kept giving her flowers and cheap jewelry and finally sweet-talked her into his bed. Except he had a family and he promptly dropped her when she got pregnant. Tosya hated all references to that period of her life: she felt humiliated because she had been played for a sucker. She was also determined not to make the same mistake twice, which was why she kept her guard up even with me.

We walked the rest of the way in silence.

That night she came to my room after midnight, having put Sevka to bed.

"I'm sorry about our date the other day," I began the moment I opened the front door. She didn't let me finish, placing her lips over mine and starting to take off my shirt.

We were still in the hallway and a door could have been opened by a neighbor at any time. My god, we could have been seen making out. That was a highly unusual behavior for my girlfriend.

"I missed you so much, you have no idea," I whispered.

"I think I missed you more," she replied, not smiling.

Later, as we were lying side by side and I was smoking a cigarette, Tosya said, "He was never at the front."

It took me a few seconds to realize that she was talking about Sevka's father.

"He was some kind of Party boss," she continued. "He spent the war well behind the front lines, sleeping with the wives of the guys who were fighting."

There was real anger in her voice.

"What are you thinking about?" she asked after a while.

"Nothing," I replied.

But I had been thinking about my mother. Was she ever unfaithful to my Dad while he was away at the front? I didn't know. Life was hard in the town over in the East where we had been evacuated. There was no food for the two of us, and no coal to heat our place during the harsh Urals winter. And the party hacks and NKVD officers who controlled the distribution of food and coal were well-fed men in sleek uniforms, with oily eyes and lascivious smiles on their lips. I was old enough to remember that.

SEVENTEEN

War veterans marked the anniversary of the end of the war in their own way. Without pomp and circumstance, and as far from Red Square as you could get. Many went to Belarus Station from where trains depart in the Western direction and where for so many of them the war had started. For them it was a private event, away from the brass band marches and the self-congratulatory speeches. It was a melancholy occasion when they drank to the memory of their fallen comrades. They gathered in small groups if they were lucky enough to have living comrades, or in the company of strangers, lonely veterans like themselves. They drank vodka, of course, nothing else would do but grain spirits, and never clinking their glasses. And since each had so many fallen comrades to commemorate, at the end of the day they would be drunk out of their wits.

Good cops are a cynical lot. Nothing is sacred to a good cop in the course of an investigation. Suspecting that he could ferret Brunevsky out during his so-called medical leave, Lenny once again took up a position outside the Maltsevs' apartment building early on May 9, and stayed put all morning. His Moskvich, in case he needed it, was parked half a block away.

There was no way a war veteran was going to spend that day at home.

Accordingly, around midday a young kid arrived in a taxicab. He was short, lithe and dark. Even from a distance, watching him as he told the cab driver to wait and then crossed to the building, Lenny could tell he was a thug. The kid had the body language and the loose-limbed gait of a member of a prison gang.

After a short while, he came out again, helping Maltsev down the stairs and showing him signs of deference of the kind junior gangsters reserve for their authoritative senior comrades.

By the time the cab took off – suddenly and at speed, scattering a group of girls playing hopscotch on the road – Lenny had written down its license plate number. His mission accomplished, he got into his car and drove home.

Although eager to find out where Maltsev had gone to mark Victory Day, Lenny spent the afternoon with Raisa and the girls. They had a picnic lunch and took a walk in the park.

Later in the evening, Lenny was back at his observation post, moving closer under the cover of thickening darkness. This time he had to wait much longer, keeping watch well after the fireworks had finished lighting the northern corner of the sky and the boys who had found their way onto the roofs of the surrounding buildings had stopped shouting Hurray. Finally, another cab pulled up. It unloaded Stepan Sergeyich, who was so drunk, he could barely stand on his feet. Only then did Lenny spot Oksana standing on the sidewalk in front of the building. He had almost given himself away.

Maltsev gesticulated and tried to say something to his daughter. He kept exclaiming "Wait a minute," stopping and pressing his remaining hand to his chest.

Oksana and the young thug, who had also come back with Maltsev, were supporting him. Lenny was struck that while the thug was still highly deferential toward her father, even in the man's inebriated state, Oksana was, in turn, almost obsequious to the kid. She kept whispering in his ear, leaning close to make sure Maltsev wouldn't hear her. The thug made an angry reply and waved at her as though he was chasing away a fly. She wouldn't stop, and at last he stomped his foot in annoyance.

That was so obvious that even Stepan Sergeyich's noticed. He stopped and shook his head.

Now Lenny had the choice of two taxis – to check one against the other, fill in possible holes, and have something in reserve in case one of the drivers would not cooperate.

After that, Lenny went straight to the garage where the first cabbie worked and got the man's home address. It was early morning by then, but that didn't stop Lenny from driving to some outlying bedroom district beyond Sokolniki Park and drag the unfortunate driver out of bed.

"The guy was sleeping off the quarter liter he'd celebrated Victory Day with," Lenny told me as he summarized the results of his day's work. "I hope he hadn't imbibed it while behind the wheel. But he sure sobered up when I told him what I was after. That kid must have scared him half to death. For a good long time he pretended to have no memory of any of it. Not the ride, nor the passengers – and certainly not their destination. I had to scare him at least as much before his brain cleared up and he started talking."

Lenny was a decent human being and a loving father, but if he wanted to scare someone, he knew how to get it done.

Their first stop, of all places, was Botkin Hospital, where the little thug got out, talked to the guard at the gate and got him to let the taxi through – which was strictly against the rules. They stopped in front of the oncology ward. The cabbie happened to know it well, because his mother-in-law had died of pancreatic cancer a year and a half before. The blind guy on the front seat and the cabbie waited while the thug went in.

"I asked him whether he and the blind guy talked much," Lenny said. "Maltsev is a talkative type when he wants to be. But this time they sat in silence for half an hour exchanging perhaps half a dozen words. The cabbie was bored, and he wished Stepan Sergeyich a happy Victory Day in the hope of drawing him into a conversation, but to no avail."

Eventually, two burly nurse's assistants brought out what the cabbie at first mistook for a package. But then it turned out to be a Samovar.

"Like a copper samovar?" I asked stupidly.

"*Nyet*," Lenny said. "A person. That's what quadruple amputees are called. Guys who lost their arms and legs in the war."

The Samovar was missing both legs and both his hands had been amputated to the elbows. He was in fairly bad shape, in terms of health. He was sweating and panting so heavily, you would have thought it was he who had carried the nurse's assistants to the cab and not the other way around.

They placed the Samovar on the back seat and the thug then gave the cabbie a weird address not far from Peace Avenue, in the old Meshchansky District. The cabbie had never heard of the street, and the kid had to show him the way while they drove. They ended up down a no-name dead-end with walls on both sides and a steel gate topped by coils of barbed wire.

"The young thug told the driver to stop in front of the gate" Lenny said. "He rang the bell, the gate slid open and who do you think welcomed the two invalids? Correct. A guy in a wheelchair, a big guy with a bushy black beard and no legs."

"Brunevsky?"

"I would guess one and the same," Lenny said. "But that's not all. Helping them unload their precious cargo was a young female. Also going by the cabbie's description, I take her to be our old friend Gulya Aliyeva."

"What a gathering of old friends," I said. "A veritable witches' sabbath."

I hoped my voice expressed all the admiration I felt for Lenny's sleuthing.

The girl and the thug helped the blind guy out and then took out the Samovar. They closed the gate again and the thug came out to pay the driver. The meter showed almost twenty rubles, by far the biggest fare of the day if not of the year, and the thug gave him a red bill on top of that."

"A tenner?" I exclaimed. "No kidding."

Red is the color of the ten-ruble bill. Thirty rubles is about one-third of the cabbie's monthly pay.

"You got it," Lenny confirmed grimly. "But it came with strings attached. The thug told him to forget everything he had seen, especially that address near Peace Avenue."

Lenny laughed.

"Then it was my turn to tell him to forget about my visit. The man is going to need a good dose of memory loss to survive between the rock and the hard place."

"As long as he still remembers where Brunevsky has been spending his medical leave," I said.

"He can forget it now," Lenny said patting himself on the forehead. "I have it memorized."

EIGHTEEN

The flowering of black poplars throughout Moscow is like a blizzard in May. The fibers they shed are weightless, and the slightest breeze grabs them by the handful, gets them airborne and spins a wispy cloud trailing on the sidewalk. They dance in the warm sunlight like myriad snowflakes, never melting, but turning golden in the glow of the evening and gathering into drifts along the curbs.

It is a warm-weather mockery of the long Russian winter, spring thumbing its nose at Grandfather Frost from a safe distance, while the ground is still heavy with melted snow and April showers, and when it seems that the cold and the bone-chilling wind will never return. But, as the white cotton gathers on flower beds around the slim stems of tulips in their first bloom, the sight can send shivers down your spine. The green buds look so vulnerable, so much like they're about to freeze. You know it is only poplar fuzz, but the joke is not funny.

Recent plantings form regular rows along the muddy paths on Boulevard Ring, but thick old poplars grow wild in the maze of courtyards and narrow lanes in the old part of town, reaching over patched-up fences and towering above the roofs of old houses. Their new leaves are shiny, yellow, and sticky with sap. They emit a resinous odor that everyone who grows up in Moscow associates with spring.

The Latin name of black poplars is *Populus nigra*, which can also mean black people. Craggy old poplars often assume the human form, not necessarily of Africans. But then again, all trees resemble human beings. Some, like the ancient olive trees in the hills of Abkhazia – the ones that were there when Athenian ships sailed past their shores – more than others.

Perhaps god didn't create man in his image after all, but in the image of the olive tree.

Trees are living beings, just like us. The root system is their heart, it is buried deep underground. The trunk is their body, and the branches are their eyes, ears and mouths. They breathe with their leaves and reproduce with their flowers. Trees can move and they can dance. Their dance is fluid and graceful and sometimes fast and wild, but their time is slower than ours. To us, living as we do on our time, their trunks and limbs look like frozen motion.

A snapshot is also motion, frozen in time.

Destroying the roots will kill the tree, whereas if the branches are amputated the tree can survive and grow new ones. Even when the trunk is cut down, the heart of the tree often keeps beating and may sprout new shoots.

Trees can feel pain and cry or laugh and express happiness. Perhaps someday we'll learn to measure their pain and their happiness. Learn to hear them speak to each other and to understand what they say. Then we'll feel respect for them the way we have learned to respect other humans who are different from us. Like black Africans for example.

Trees can look threatening, too, as they stand with their limbs raised as if in anger. Because their time is slower than ours, they can't harm us, but we can harm them. He who is faster wins. They can't run from us. Their heart roots them to the spot.

But just because we can harm them, we shouldn't.

There are tens of thousands of black poplars in the city, growing on its boulevards, in its parks and courtyards, and on its vacant lots. It's a great nuisance when they shed their fluff all at once. There is no hiding from it. You can't avoid the soft, cottony fibers that land in your hair and on your clothing. If you leave a window open even a crack, they drift into the room.

And if there is a puddle of blood on the floor, the white fluff will get caught in it. It will soak up the congealing liquid and sink, or else cling to the edges like mold.

NINETEEN

The Drummer's Fate is a children's novel written in the nineteen thirties. Its author, a famous writer of books for kids and young adults, was killed in the early months of the war. It may not seem right that a writer of children's books should be fighting in a war, but it was a strange war. Some writers of children's books were even sent to gas chambers, along with the kids for whom they had written their books.

The Drummer's Fate is a book about spies and about people going to jail. So you might think it's a strange children's book, too. But it's a good book. I read it three times when I was growing up, and I lent my dog-eared copy to all my friends.

It's about a kid whose father goes to jail for embezzlement, and whose stepmother goes to the Black Sea with some other guy, leaving the boy alone in their Moscow apartment. He falls in with some small-time hoodlums and, sure enough, a spy soon appears on his doorstep, pretending to be his stepmother's brother and hoodwinking him with tall tales.

The spy is in cahoots with a thug, because that's the company spies typically keep, but that is beside the point.

There's a scene in the book in which the spy asks the kid to befriend another boy at the park, so that the spy can become friendly with the boy's father and steal important military secrets. The other boy's father is an engineer working on a miracle weapon for the Red Army, which is what engineers always do.

I still had my old copy and I got Sevka to read it. Sevka liked it, even though he was a little too young for it.

"Let's play a game, Sevka," I said to him next Sunday morning as I took him to the Help Us Care for Our Animals class at the zoo. "I'll pretend to be a spy and you'll pretend to befriend a boy in the class so that I could chat with his Mom?"

Sevka liked the idea at first, but then his suspicions were aroused: "But you're still one of the good guys, Uncle Pavel? Right? Not a spy or a thug?"

I had to reassure him that I was certainly not a spy – to start with, I didn't know any foreign languages except three words of German I had retained from my school days – and I was still working for Moscow Criminal Investigations, where my job was to catch bad guys while trying not to become one myself. Which probably made me a good guy.

Tosya was very happy when I first suggested that I take Sevka to the zoo. To start with, she loved it when the two of us spent time together. She felt that Sevka badly needed a father figure in his life and should spend more time in the company of grown men. Besides, a visit to the zoo was not all fun and games like an outing to the stadium to see a soccer match. It was educational, especially since I had expressed an intention of signing him up for a class.

She would have killed me if she knew that I was planning to enlist Sevka's help in a criminal investigation. Her recent anger about a missed date would have been nothing compared to the hurricane that would break over my head. But I had to take risks if I wanted to get to the bottom of the Kotov murder. How else could I get to know Malvina Kotova and her boy without violating the Foreign Ministry's orders? Only by making the encounter a chance one.

Lenny's verbal portrait of the second Mrs. Kotova was not entirely accurate. He may be a good mimic, but he is a poor judge of character, especially where a young woman was concerned. Misjudging character is a prerequisite for falling in love, and if you misjudge character in a positive direction, imagining the object of your affection to be an angel, you can just as easily err in the opposite direction.

In the case of Malvina Kotova, Lenny had exaggerated her negative qualities. In other words, he had presented me with a caricature. In real life she was just an ordinary young woman, a mother, and someone who had very recently lived through a shocking tragedy. She was lost and scared. Like many women married to older men at a young age, she had gone straight from her mother's house to her husband's, who treated her more like a daughter than an equal partner. Now she felt abandoned and helpless. She couldn't see the way forward and didn't know where to turn.

Her son was traumatized, too, having seen his father's dead body. She needed to figure out how to help him.

She felt vulnerable and was eager to share her problems with anyone, even a stranger, another parent whose son was also enrolled in a class at the zoo.

Sevka did a super job befriending Oleg. The drummer in that old children's book acting on behalf of his fake uncle couldn't have done it better.

"Is this your boy?" I asked Kotova, who was sitting on a park bench while the kids were gathered around the Java rhino's cage, watching the attendant mop the floor and feed the pachyderm, who looked more like a young bullock than a rhino. Oleg and Sevka were having an animated discussion, with Oleg explaining something to Sevka with an air of absolute authority.

She nodded.

"He looks like young Charles Darwin," I said. "Except he needs to grow a beard."

"A beard? Why?"

You could tell she was one of those humorless types. Or else she was not in the mood for my feeble attempts at humor. In any case, making jokes was clearly not the way to go.

I introduced myself and she told me her name. Two minutes later we too were having a conversation and after another two minutes she grew sad and told me about Oleg's father having been murdered.

"My son is in shock. But I decided to take him to the zoo anyway. As it is, we missed last Sunday's class and he was quite upset about it. His doctor says he should keep to his usual routine as much as possible. He loves animals. They help him forget the tragedy, at least for a time. He's a very sensitive boy."

"He seems very bright," I said.

She gave me a grateful smile.

Then she changed the subject and began to complain about Kotov leaving everything to his first wife and their children, just as Lenny had warned she would. Except the story was a little different. The first Mrs. Kotova took poor Valentin Viktorovich to the cleaners. He was a Party member and the Party was a serious organization. It frowned upon all kinds of hanky-panky. It didn't like it when card-carrying party members left their perfectly good old wives for young ones. It was not a moral thing to do and it set a bad example for the younger generation. Kotov's first wife threatened Kotov with a huge scandal unless he left her all his worldly possessions.

"Oleg's half-brothers have a dog and two cats. Oleg would love a dog, too, but we can't have one. The people we're renting the room from won't allow it. My husband's other family, they have a housekeeper who walks the dog whenever it's cold or it's raining, or when the kids don't feel like it. It's so unfair. Naturally, we don't have a housekeeper. Oleg had to make do with a fishbowl."

She sighed.

"Thankfully, he is just as happy with goldfish as with a dog. As long as they don't die on him too quickly. He loves all kinds of animals. If it's a living and breathing thing, he loves it."

The class moved on to the pool where a bunch of seals were luxuriating in the gentle May breeze, rubbing their fat backs on the rocks. They started to bark the moment they saw the attendant approach, carrying two buckets, one in each hand. The buckets were filled with fish. With their bushy moustaches, the seals struck me as looking very much like the Boss, except their heads were bald, whereas Budyonny proudly sported a head of black hair.

The attendant started tossing the fish in the water. The seals were back in the pool in no time. Watching them dive for the fish, the kids screamed with delight.

"Before he got killed, my husband promised Oleg to take him to the swimming pool and teach him to swim," Malvina said. "At the open-air Moskva pool. Oleg was very much looking forward to it."

"What a coincidence," I said quickly. "I was going to take Sevka to the pool too. Maybe we could start going together."

"That would be great," she said. "Oleg will be very excited when I tell him."

The kids were now coming out of the monkey house. The class was at an end.

"Is he your only child? she asked.

"He is not even mine," I said. "He's my girlfriend's boy."

I felt myself blush. For some reason, admitting that Sevka was not my own – and not even my stepson, for that matter – always made me feel embarrassed. Malvina didn't like it either. She gave me a suspicious look and when the boys joined us, she didn't mention anything about swimming lessons.

"I'd like an ice cream," Oleg said.

"Me too," Sevka echoed him.

"No, son, we're going home," Malvina said. "You haven't even started your homework."

We walked out the main gate together. Malvina and I were walking in silence while Oleg and Sevka, a few paces ahead, were still talking. Or rather Oleg was talking and Sevka was listening.

"See you next week," I said. "Sevka and I are going to take the metro."

She gestured to a beat-up car parked at the curb.

"At least Valentin Viktorovich bought a car before he was murdered," she said.

And, as coincidence would have it, she had just gotten her driver's license. She liked driving and, apparently, was good at it. Even her instructor had been impressed by how fast she learned.

"It's not such a great car, and Valentin Viktorovich wasn't happy with the price," she added. "He thought he was taken advantage of."

"Who did he buy it from?" I asked quickly.

"He got it from a man named Rubashkin. Everybody who wants to get a used car goes to this Rubashkin character, apparently. And yet he's not supposed to be a very honest man."

I certainly remembered Rubashkin well. No, he was not a very honest man. He was not a very good man, either.

"It wasn't just a game, Uncle Pavel?" Sevka asked me on our way home.

"Eh? What?"

I was not paying attention. I was thinking about Rubashkin, and about an old investigation during which our paths crossed.

"I said that it wasn't just a game," Sevka repeated. "Me becoming friends with Oleg. Is that right?"

"It depends how you look at it," I said. "If you like Oleg and the two of you become good friends, it's not a game. Friendship is always serious. You have to be loyal to your friends, Sevka."

There must have been something in my voice that made Sevka look up. Despite his young age, he could tell when people tried to sell him a bill of goods. In this respect, he was very much his mother's son.

I couldn't help feeling ashamed of myself.

TWENTY

Last time I came across Rubashkin was in Potapovsky Lane, a narrow side street running almost the entire length of Clear Ponds Boulevard. The lane is lined with eighteenth-century mansion which were once private but had become decrepit over time and were now divided into crowded communal apartments. That old investigation also involved a car, which had always been Rubashkin's line of business. And it wasn't Rubashkin himself that I encountered, but rather his handiwork.

It was the most important case since I started at Moscow Criminal Investigations – and in some ways the most important case ever in the history of our agency – and it certainly was not going well. Kids were being murdered in their apartments and we couldn't find the bastard who was doing it, The Boss's entire team was working on it, and every officer had his own theory. I did too, and I had been involved in the investigation from the start, pursuing leads and interviewing witnesses. Except my theories were dismissed by my colleagues as wrong and harmful to the investigation. Since I persisted, I was eventually accused of sabotaging other detectives' work and even of leaking information to the killer – whether maliciously or because of professional incompetence, it remained to be determined.

Finally, the Boss took me off the case and suspended me from the force, to make sure I would not do the investigation any more harm.

That was bad enough, but worse was that my main accuser was my partner and best friend Lenny Urumov. We had nearly come to blows arguing about the case. We had different ideas about the best course of action, and that wasn't unusual – except Lenny decided that my ideas were not just wrong, but maliciously wrong, designed to mislead the investigation. We were all under a lot of pressure and that was the only way I could explain what happened between us. It took me a long time to get over it, but in the end I forgave him — and I'm glad I did.

While my colleagues were conducting the investigation, I stayed at home, fuming, doing nothing all day and fully expecting criminal charges to be filed against me. So it came as a surprise when early one morning I got a call from Lenny. The Boss had instructed him to escort me to the scene of a new crime, Lenny told me. Naturally, I assumed that another child had been murdered, and I was going to have my face rubbed into it.

Potapovsky Lane is very close to my house. It starts behind the Main Post Office which sits across the street from my apartment building. Lenny took me to a vacant lot on Potapovsky, where an old house had been demolished. It was a strangely warm day in the middle of a January thaw. The melting snow had soaked the orange clay under the rubble, and it had been all churned up by police boots. There were plenty of people at the scene – uniformed cops as well as men and women in white scrubs who were part of our forensics unit – or Criminal Investigations' forensics unit to be exact, since I was no longer part of Criminal Investigations.

A body was lying among the puddles. It wasn't another dead child. It was my friend Nastya. She had been beaten to death with a heavy object – a metal pipe or a brick. Her face had lost its contours and had been turned into a palimpsest of blood, sinews and chips of bone. Her disfigured mouth had been stuffed with mud and debris, which in the language of the criminal fraternity to which Nastya belonged meant that she had squealed.

She had never talked to any cops other than me, and she had never been my informant. She had given me Rubashkin's name when I was looking for a certain automobile, but she hadn't betrayed him in any way. Still, he had Nastya brutally murdered – or even did it himself – to set an example to others who might think of befriending a cop. There was no anger, no emotion in the way she had been worked over – just calculated, murderous cruelty.

Nastya was my friend. She was also a criminal, and perhaps there could never be a friendship between a cop and a robber.

She and I had met soon after I joined Moscow Criminal Investigations. She was a teenager, enrolled at a vocational school but not attending classes and working Central Market as a pickpocket.

She had grown up across Tsvetnoy Boulevard from the market, in the mean alleyways and labyrinths of the Sretenka neighborhood, with children of hard-drinking parents and large, dirt-poor Tatar families. It was Sretenka that reliably provided fodder for Butyrka and for convict transports further East, to labor camps in Mordovia and Siberia. Sretenka had taught Nastya to pick pockets and it was the only marketable skill she ever had.

I caught her pulling a wallet from a customer's purse. I was an idealist back then, believing that everyone could be saved and that the world could be improved one Nastya at a time. I offered her a deal: I would let her go if she quit stealing, went back to school and learned an honest trade. She turned it down; she had no interest in becoming a house painter or a typist. She was up-front about it, not like other petty criminals who would lie and cheat to get out of being arrested and brag afterwards about how clever they were in abusing the trust of a credulous fool.

She was a thief born and bred, she declared proudly. Besides, her friends, the ones who had put time and effort into her training, weren't going to let her go so easily. I offered to take care of her friends, too, if she let us. She just sneered. She was a thief, she repeated, and thieves don't snitch.

In her own way, she too was naive and had a romantic view of the criminal underworld. But the point is, she was not an informer.

I let her go, but it wasn't the last time I heard from her. After that first meeting, she fell in love with me and began to pester me with her attentions.

I have no illusions about being especially attractive to women. It's just that I happened to be the first man who was nice to Nastya without wanting anything in return. I took her seriously and showed concern for her. Her Dad drank, like most men of his kind on Sretenka, and beat up her and her mother. Her friends – tough guys who had had a brush or two with the law – used her. She was just a number for them – the quantity of rubles she brought in at the end of the day. If she got caught and went to jail, why, there were dozens of other girls just like her coming of age in the teeming Sretenka tenements that could be trained to pick pockets.

Small wonder she fell for someone different, even if it was a cop.

There was nothing I could do to stop her. Her courtship included flowers ripped off from flower beds on the boulevard early in the morning, before gardeners arrived for work, and gifts for my birthday that she claimed were not hot items but purchased with her own money – earned by picking pockets, of course. She also spied on me and reported to me gleefully what she knew about my movements. My inability to spot her when she was tailing me drove me mad. I was angry as much at myself as at her.

It all ended abruptly when she was arrested and sent away.

She came out a year and a half later. The jail had also made her even more determined to have me.

She tried it one night at the same vacant lot where her body would be dumped ten months later. It was a hot summer night, the ground was overgrown with weeds and littered with trash. A section of the building wall was still standing, blocking the view from the street. She lured me in with some cock-and-bull tale and tried to seduce me by taking off her clothes.

I thought that once I had rebuffed her advances her love for me would be over and might even turn to hatred. She was nothing if not fiercely proud. But I was wrong yet again. She found a way of justifying my rejection: apparently, I had been turned off by the prison tattoos now covering her breasts and shoulders. She gave up pursuing me, but we remained friends.

Yes, she was my friend. We had a kind of grudging respect for each other. We were friends even though she stayed loyal to her criminal fraternity. Or was it a sorority? I never asked her to betray other thieves, to inform on anyone. I knew better than to do that.

Seeing her body on that lot off Potapovsky made me physically ill. As I stood there, retching and wiping sleaze off my mouth, I swore to get back at Rubashkin. But promises made in the heat of the moment are rarely fulfilled. Rubashkin lay low for a while, and there were rumors in the Moscow underworld – probably spread by Rubashkin himself – that he'd got out of the car business, or even quit the criminal fraternity altogether. Of course, it wasn't true, and he had become even more careful. I kept an eye on his activities and knew his whereabouts. But he never did anything blatantly illegal, and I was sure that if I decided to look into his transaction with Kotov, I would find that it was on the up and up. All the papers would be in order.

TWENTY-ONE

Lenny and I had no illusions: Arkady Matveyich Brunevsky would be a tough nut to crack. If his live-in housekeeper knew how to answer our questions, despite being surprised by a late-night visit, it meant that she had been coached well – and, after meeting Brunevsky, we had a pretty good idea by whom.

As expected, talking to him was a waste of time – until the very end.

The Danilov Market investigation was mostly carried out by Lenny. That was true even before my involvement with the Kotov murder, and when I returned to that case my heart was no longer in it. I was thinking more about Joseph Kofunda and the Argentinian student than about Oksana, her father and his war invalid friends. To give Lenny his due, all the progress in the Danilov Market case was achieved by him. The question was how much real progress there had been.

The truthful answer was, not much. Sure, Lenny had discovered Brunevsky and had made a connection between him and Gyula, the only witness of the assault on Oksana. This confirmed our earlier suspicion that there might have been more to that attack than Oksana had admitted. Tying Brunevsky, a man once arrested for black market activities and a night watchman who was clearly living well beyond his modest means, to the attack on Oksana was a sure sign that organized crime was involved. The viciousness of the assault and the paltry sum taken suggested that the whole thing had been meant as a warning.

The question was to whom and by whom. The most likely answer was to Brunevsky and not to Oksana or her father, because Maltsev had been retired for some time. But why was Oksana chosen as a target? Wasn't Gulya more likely, considering that she was Brunevsky's live-in housekeeper? Then, the warning *was* meant for Maltsev; he may be retired from Danilov market but not from the black market. What was the relationship between the two invalids? They surely seemed to be the best of friends, but you can never tell what goes on below the surface in criminal gangs. When push comes to shove, it's every man for himself there.

Keeping Brunevsky's no-name dead-end street under observation, Lenny discovered another interesting tidbit. On Sunday night, he watched a taxicab pull up to the gate and saw Oksana get out. The gate opened just wide enough for her to slip through and was promptly shut again.

"Think of it, man," Lenny said shaking his head. "The moment she's feeling well enough to go out, she grabs a cab and goes to see this Brunevsky character."

Lenny sounded outraged. There might have been more than a touch of jealousy in his voice. Oksana had been completely indifferent to his advances and now had gone to an older man and an invalid. But beneath his outrage there was also a sense of pride: he had managed to surprise me with yet another discovery.

"Did she stay the night?" I asked.

"No. She came out maybe an hour later. As she was walking toward me, where I had my observation post at a window on the stairwell of an apartment building, I could tell that there was something wrong. The streetlight there is very dim, so I couldn't see what it was. But then I figured it out. She was crying."

"Really crying? Are you certain?"

"Definitely crying. Looking disconsolate. I wondered what he had done to her."

"And why," I added.

While Lenny had uncovered much interesting information and we had a variety of leads to pursue, none of it was arranging itself into a coherent narrative. The case remained a bunch of disjointed, random pieces of a puzzle. There was a lot of work still to be done.

"What about that Samovar?" I asked. "What do we know about him? Anything interesting?"

Lenny shook his head. "*Nyet*. Nothing there. He's known as Andryukha Samovar. Not his real name, of course. His real name is Andrei Nikolin. I checked his background. There's nothing that would interest us, and this stands to reason: what kind of crime a human doughnut like him would be able to commit? Anyway, now, in addition to all his other troubles, the guy is dying of cancer. He's not long for this world, his doctor assured me."

With all this in mind, it was time for us to pay a visit to Brunevsky. I had heard him described by Lenny, and I was curious to meet him in person.

We had been expected. Lenny had parked his Moskvich some distance away, next to the Durov Menagerie, and we covered the rest of the distance on foot. Aside from his gate – tall, painted blue, and sporting a large lock, a coil of barbed wire on top, and a sign – "Beware of an Attack Dog" – there were no other residences or offices in the blind alley. It had been forgotten by municipal authorities and was still paved with rutted cobblestones, left over from before the age of the automobile.

There must have been a tripwire or some other device alerting the inhabitants of our approach. As soon as Lenny pressed the bell button, rousing the attack dog on the other side of the fence, the gate was opened a crack. A hostile, dark eye peered out.

"What do you want?"

"Moscow Criminal Investigations," Lenny said, pushing his lips close to the crack. "We're here to see Comrade Brunevsky."

The gate slammed shut. Lenny and I looked at each other, not knowing what to make of it. The voice on the other side ordered the dog to be quiet. There was the sound of an iron chain being dragged on the ground, its links clinking. We shrugged and decided to wait.

The wait lasted a long time. Finally, the gate was opened again – only a little wider this time, but enough for us to squeeze through. We walked past the dog who looked like it should have been cast in a starring role in a screen adaptation of *The Hound of the Baskervilles.* It watched us attentively, in apparent anticipation of being sicked on us by its master.

Standing by the gate and letting us in was a stocky young man with dark complexion and short black hair. He nodded to us and led the way across the paved courtyard to the house. A brand-new invalid cart was parked under an improvised car port, rigged up from a piece of tarp stretched over four vertical poles.

Lenny winked at me, pointing to the back of the dark-haired young man and then the invalid cart as if to say "I told you about them."

"Brush off your feet," the kid commanded as we entered the house. He had a low voice and just a touch of an accent.

Once we made a show of cleaning our feet on the doormat, he ushered us into the living room, which was vast and, unlike Brunevsky's place in Mazilov, furnished with heavy, antique furniture. There were paintings on the walls – portraits of men and women in old-fashioned dress and modern paintings in which one could not make out the subject, just a bunch of color splotches and shapes, as if a five-year-old had painted them. There, too, were bookcases overflowing with well-thumbed volumes. A Persian rug was spread on the floor. A wheelchair was parked in its thick nap.

The man in the wheelchair was massive. Missing both legs made him seem even larger than he was, because that huge torso of his sat low, only a couple of feet off the ground. His features were heavy, and among them the flat nose of a prize fighter was dominant, flanked by a pair of wide-open, watchful eyes. Not a good-looking face by any standard, it was further marred by scars over the cheeks and the forehead. The face was framed by a tangle of unruly hair that formed a kind of halo on top of his head and transitioned seamlessly into a curly beard. Even though the man was well into in his fifties, his mane was still mostly black, with only a few grey strands mixed in here and there. Black hair grew thick on his forearms, too, which he was leaning heavily on the dining table.

He gave an impression of strength and power. The two hollow pant legs, carefully pressed and folded onto themselves on the leather seat of the wheelchair, did nothing to dispel it.

Our visit could not have been a surprise. Gulya had most certainly told him about our conversation and had reported our interest in him. True, we didn't know where to find him, but he couldn't have hoped that his whereabouts would not be discovered by Moscow Criminal Investigations sooner or later.

"Arkady Matveyich Brunevsky?" Lenny asked formally, checking his notebook as though he needed to jolt his memory.

"What can I do for you, Comrades?"

"We would like to ask you a few questions," Lenny said.

Brunevsky smiled, baring a row of shiny gold teeth.

"I'm at your service. Please ask away, Comrades."

He didn't invite us to sit down, but Lenny was not one to stand on ceremony. He pulled out one of the chairs and placed his notebook on the dining table. I looked over my shoulder and saw that Brunevsky's thuggish factotum was still in the room. Shooting us a sullen look that reminded me of the attack dog waiting for us in the courtyard, he stationed himself behind our backs, leaning against the door as though determined not to let anyone else in. His demeanor suggested that, if anyone attempted to harm Brunevsky, they would have to deal with him first. However, the man in the wheelchair looked perfectly capable of taking care of himself, too.

"Do we need witnesses?" I asked, jerking my head in the direction of Brunevsky's thug.

"Shamil is my manservant," Brunevsky said, using an old-fashioned term that was no longer in use in the Soviet Union, where all manservants, lackeys, butlers, maids, valets, gentlemen's gentlemen and others of the serving classes had been abolished – at least on paper.

"Meaning what?" Lenny asked quickly. "That he's not human?"

Brunevsky kept smiling: "No, you must have misunderstood me, Comrades. What I meant was that he knows everything there is to know about me, my activities and my whereabouts. It is the unfortunate part of caring for an invalid. There isn't a question you can come up with to ask me that he would not be able to answer."

"Oh yeah?" Lenny was already getting irritated by the man's supercilious tone and the irony in his voice. He was making it clear that he thought of us as two dumb cops involved in a pretty dumb business. "Fine, let him stay, then. We'll start from the beginning. Is this your residence?"

"It's a house of a friend. He is currently very ill. While he is at the hospital, he has graciously let me use his place. I too am on a medical leave from my place of employment."

"What is your friend's name?"

Of course, it was Andrei Nikolin, a.k.a. Andryukha Samovar. It had to be.

"What's wrong with you, that you're on medical leave?" Lenny asked.

It wasn't a good question. Brunevsky pointed to his hollow pant legs.

"When one has sustained this sort of injury," he said slowly, "too many other health problems develop, stemming both directly and indirectly from one's condition. Believe me, I know what I'm talking about. I'm a disabled war veteran and it pains me that a Moscow Criminal Investigations officer should be accusing me of malingering just days after the country marked Victory Day and the government pledged to make the lives of all veterans prosperous and comfortable."

The conversation went downhill from there. Brunevsky had an answer for every question Lenny threw at him. Everything he was involved in appeared innocent and above board. His answers matched what we already knew. Yes, Stepan Sergeyich Maltsev was a friend. Absolutely nothing surprising there, they were fellow veterans, after all. No, they didn't know each other in the war, they met not long after it was over. But it's the experience that they shared, and they liked talking about it, reminiscing about the war and remembering their fallen comrades. Time goes by. There are fewer and fewer real combat veterans left, especially disabled ones, for they tend to die young.

Brunevsky let the sentence hang.

No, he didn't know a whole lot about the assault on Oksana, even though his friend Maltsev had, naturally, told him about it. Crime is rampant in the city; it's getting worse with every passing day. It's a disgrace, really. Fortunately, Stepan's girl wasn't badly hurt. It could have been much worse.

No, he didn't have any professional dealings with Comrade Maltsev. First of all, Stepan Sergeyich is retired, but, even if he weren't, what kind of professional dealings could the deputy director of a market have with a night watchman? Let's be serious, Comrades.

This was, almost verbatim, what Maltsev had said to us, his exact words. Brunevsky smiled and I could swear he shot us a tiny, barely perceptible wink.

"Not even during the time you were caught up in that criminal case?" Lenny asked.

"What criminal case? Oh, you must be talking about my arrest. It happened so long ago, I had forgotten about it." Brunevsky sighed. "Yes, I was once charged with a crime. But it was nonsense, Comrades. After the war, when I was discharged from the hospital, I spent some time begging at flea markets and going from city to city on trains. I'm not proud of that chapter in my life, it's so much more respectable to earn one's living by the sweat of one's brow. Personally, I prefer being a humble night watchmen to begging and relying on the kindness of strangers, but you've got to take the good with the bad. Besides, after the war I could not do the work for which I had been trained, and there were no other jobs for a double amputee."

He sighed again.

"Naturally, during the years of my vagabondage, I came across some unsavory characters. When they got caught, they tried to save their own skins by making a show of cooperating with the cops. They started naming everyone they could think of as accomplices in their vile crimes. It was all a patent lie. Investigators saw right through it, but in those days, they wanted to be safe rather than sorry, and I was given a suspended sentence. Since then, the conviction has been rescinded and I no longer have a criminal record. You're welcome to check into it, Comrades."

He was making fun of us, and enjoying himself in the process.

"What a shame your accuser hung himself in a cell. He must have regretted bitterly smearing your good name, and his bad conscience drove him to suicide."

Brunevsky raised an eyebrow: "Did he really? I didn't know that he died. Good riddance to bad rubbish, I say. I've seen so many good men die, you'll forgive me if I don't feel sorry for a scoundrel."

Has he been to Danilov Market recently? No, not even not so recently. The prices there are so steep that a guy working as a night watchman can't afford to buy even a couple of potatoes and a carrot.

And so on. We were not getting very far at all with Brunevsky.

"When you came to visit Stepan Sergeyich the other day," Lenny asked. "Did you visit his daughter?"

"Naturally, I asked her how she was doing. I picked up a bunch of flowers for her. I was glad to see she was getting better."

"So much better than she came to see you last night," Lenny said, lightning fast.

But Brunevsky wasn't put out by the question.

"I see you've done your homework. That's to be expected. What detective nowadays goes to see a suspect without first watching his home for a few days?"

"Yes, but apparently you know Oksana Maltseva rather well, not merely as the daughter of a friend," I said.

"You're funny guys, Comrades." Brunevsky gave us a mirthless smile and shook his head. "I understand that it is your job to peep into law-abiding citizens' windows, tap their phones, and pick through their dirty laundry in case one of us decides to commit a crime. But surely you can't expect me to discuss Oksana Stepanovna with you or to answer questions about the nature of our relationship."

"So, it is a romantic involvement?" Lenny asked.

Brunevsky didn't respond and Lenny too fell silent, looking as though he had run out of questions.

"If this is all you wanted to know," Brunevsky said after a minute, still pretending to be offended, "then you should get going. If you come up with any other questions, you know where to find me. I'll be staying here for a while, but I believe you know my home address as well."

We got up and headed for the door. The surly manservant detached himself from it and began undoing the lock to let us out.

"By the way," Lenny asked casually looking over his shoulder. "Is it purely a coincidence that the three of you – Stepan Sergeyich Maltsev, Andrei Nikolin and you – all served in penal battalions, the *shtrafbat*, which is also where all of you suffered your injuries?"

I gave Lenny a quick look. He had kept this information to himself and saved the best question for last. Brunevsky's face suddenly grew red. If it were not an impossibility, I would have said that he rose up in his wheelchair. He certainly grew larger, placing his ham-like fists on the table. His eyes flashed and his Biblical beard bristled.

"Get the hell out of here," he said softly, almost in a whisper.

I have seen many scary people in my life – some working themselves up into a jailhouse fit of hysteria, others genuinely enraged. I have rarely seen anyone as scary as that middle-aged invalid hissing at us from his wheelchair.

It was good. Lenny hit the mark. He managed to rattle Brunevsky, and Brunevsky revealed where his vulnerabilities lay.

As we left the house, a question nagged at me.

"He mentioned his profession," I said to Lenny. "He said that, because of his injuries, he no longer could do the work for which he had been trained."

Lenny nodded.

"That's right."

"Do you know what it was?"

"He was a doctor. A throat specialist, I believe. But when the war started he volunteered and became a surgeon."

"Before being sent to a *shtrafbat?*"

"Before being sent to a *shtrafbat,*"

TWENTY-TWO

It begins right after *artpodgotovka* – the softening of the enemy lines by artillery fire. *Artpodgotovka* can go on for hours in order to suppress enemy machine gun nests, tear openings in the barbed wire, and deafen enemy fighters in their trenches. But usually it ends much sooner. Artillery shells are costlier than soldiers' lives.

But even a short *artpodgotovka* can be effective.

When it is over, the silence falls abruptly over the battered trenches. In the first few minutes it stuns, because the ear has grown used to the roar of shells and the whine of Katyusha rockets. It is thick, almost palpable. Enemy soldiers, half-buried in the mixture of snow and mud, begin to stir in their trenches. They raise their heads and adjust their helmets and pat themselves, reassuring themselves that they're alive and intact. They sniff the air that stinks of trotyl, freshly churned soil, and violated human flesh. They look around to see whether the men next to them in the line, to their left and to their right, are still there, and, if they are, exchange curt, relieved nods. They call over medical personnel to evacuate the wounded.

They think of checking their *karabiner*, because, having survived the shelling, they will need their guns to go on living.

The silence presses heavily against their ears, isolates them from the world.

Then it comes. It originates below ground, somewhere in the deep entrails of the snow-bound earth on which they lie and bounces off the low clouds overhead. The steppe hums and vibrates with this strange a cappella death dirge.

It starts tentatively at first, as if trying to break through, to reach out from under the layer of ice, but even its first half-formed sounds are threatening in a gut-level, primal way. It gains strength quickly, thickens, and begins echoing and building in intensity until it reaches a thunderous crescendo:

"Hooraaaaaaaaaaaaaaaay!"

It is like a distant thunder – but prolonged, continuous, never pausing. Its long single note suddenly sucks the air out of the German lines.

The barren wintry steppe comes alive with the collective roar. New voices join in, drunken and savage, weaving their way into the initial chorus. It is as though all the accents of the enormous Empire are braided into one. It is the *shtrafbat*, the penal battalions, the units formed of those who had transgressed against the Soviet State and Comrade Stalin personally, because what is the Soviet State if not Comrade Stalin, of those who should have been shot in the back of their heads but were not, and now have been given a chance to wash away their guilt. They will, with their own blood and with the blood of others.

They have no chance of surviving, but if they push forward and die honorably their families back home won't suffer. Or they will suffer less. Or suffer the full wrath of Soviet justice anyway, but their sons, husbands or fathers will be dead by then and won't know it, and what you don't know can't hurt you.

The *shtrafbat* are positioned closest to the German lines, having been brought under guard by NKVD soldiers in cattle cars, kept waiting all night in the numbing cold, and then unloaded and marched into a nearby woods. They were moved in position under the cover of artillery fire and given double rations of foul third-rate vodka to stiffen their resolve. The lines of regular troops are behind them, and behind those in turn, at a safe distance from the German fire, are NKVD soldiers, the dreaded *zagradotryady* armed with brand-new assault rifles and machine guns. They are the well-fed and well-taken-care-of elite units whose job is to shoot their own if they turn tail.

They are wailing in unison now, all the soldiers of the *shtrafbat*, like wolves at the winter moon, the single voice of rage, fear and patriotism that turns men into cannon fodder. They're all as one now, the career criminals sprung from jails, the deserters, the marauders, the malingerers, the would-be fraggers, the former POWs who escaped the German camps and crossed the lines to rejoin the Red Army, the politicals and the innocents. They can't turn back, they can only push forward, and all their accumulated collective hatred is now focused on the tiny grey figures crouching in the trenches in front of them.

Shtrafbat are not armed. They are not trusted with guns and besides they are not there to do any fighting.

At its highest note, this collective Hooray will lift the *shtrafbat* off the ground and onto their feet. They will begin to hobble toward the German lines, short skinny figures in shabby mismatched uniforms and labor camp jackets, bending low and weaving left and right as the German machine gunners open up. Some will be hit and drop on the snow, but others will reach the mine field. The mines will go off like red teeth, erupting from the red-brown soil mixed with grey snow. The grey figures will become airborne, limbs and heads coming off in mid-flight, but the second wave of *shtrafbat* will be through the minefield quickly and again, into the thickening fire of machine guns. The third wave will be running over torn off limbs and maimed bodies, some motionless and others still squirming, their screams of pain and anguish co-opted into the unceasing Hooray. The third wave will advance only a few paces beyond the second before being mowed down in turn, and the mounds of the dead and dying will grow waist-high in front of each machine gun emplacement. But by then the main force will be scrambling over the top, urged on by junior officers in long grey coats waving their pistols and screaming obscenities. The junior officers are the juiciest targets for German snipers, but they will have gotten the job done before being felled back into the trench. A human wall will have grown out of the white steppe and will move relentlessly on the German positions, cutting through the coils of barbed wire or climbing over the bodies of the *shtrafbat*, engaging the Germans in brutal hand-to-hand combat.

And, through it all, pulsating, ebbing and flowing and never breaking off, will be the thunderous, debilitating, heart-stopping Hooraaaaaaaay, Hooraaaaay-aaaaaay, Hooraaaaay-aaaaay-aaaaaaay.

TWENTY-THREE

"All rise. Court is in session."

When the rustle of clothing and the scraping of shoe soles against the floor died down, we remained standing, as though commemorating the dead with a moment of silence.

I stared at the three massive, empty chairs that had the hammer-and-sickle emblem carved into the dark oak of their high backs. The chairs stood on a high platform behind a long table, which formed a kind of barrier against the public. A bottle of Borjomi mineral water from Georgia, a ubiquitous accompaniment at all official proceedings, was in front of each chair, topped with a glass. On the wall behind the chairs a white-on-red banner in Russian and English proclaimed "Socialist Justice Is True Justice!" Above that was the obligatory portrait of Lenin. In this rendition – which was by no means rare – Lenin wore a cap and was pictured with an impish squint, as though he knew that the folks gathered in this pompous courtroom were up to no good.

Joseph Kofunda's trial was a high visibility event, and that was no doubt why it had been decided to hold it in a courtroom of the Supreme Court of the Soviet Union on Povarskaya Street. Furnished in the style preferred by our officialdom, with plenty of red velvet and workers' and peasants' heraldry, it offered the added advantage of having a pair of earphones attached to each chair, in order to provide simultaneous translation for foreign attendees. Attending the trial was a sizable delegation from the Central African Republic, as well as a handful of newspaper reporters from what the press referred to as the Dark Continent.

Kofunda's countrymen were middle-aged men and women in colorful national dress. They had arrived with their national flag, which was also colorful. They looked like a gathering of village elders filmed for the popular television program *Cinema Travelers' Club.*

The African reporters wore suits and ties and sat with their white colleagues from former colonial powers, behind a row of desks in the back of the courtroom. The black reporters patiently waited for the trial to commence, whereas the white ones exchanged snappy remarks in rapid-fire English and French, guffawed and behaved themselves in the extremely boisterous manner which distinguishes all Westerners from Soviet citizens. Unlike us, Westerners don't mind attracting attention to themselves. But other than that, in their shabby, ill-fitting suits, the reporters looked a great deal like regular Soviet citizens. The similarity was enhanced by their puffy faces, bloodshot eyes, and unkempt hair in need of shampooing. Apparently Western newspaper reporters were the same sorry lot as their Russian colleagues, and only African ones were dignified human beings.

To my surprise, I observed that Malvina Kotova and little Oleg were also present, sitting as far away from Kofunda and his lawyer as the courtroom would permit. They were already there when I arrived. I tried to hide behind the backs of other spectators, in order to be less conspicuous in light of the warning I had received from the Ministry of Foreign Affairs, but Oleg spotted me and began waving enthusiastically. He looked nervous and ill at ease in suit and tie, and seeing a familiar face cheered him up.

"How's Sevka?" he shouted across the room.

I put a finger to my lips while his mother grabbed him by the forearm and pulled him back into his seat.

The Rector of Lumumba University sat in the front row, flanked by his two female secretaries. The typist in a mini skirt was nowhere to be seen, but several Lumumba students from Africa and Asia were on hand. A group of four black students had found seats close to Kofunda. I assumed they were his roommates.

The courtroom had the stifling, oppressive atmosphere that is a distinguishing feature of courtrooms everywhere.

Kofunda had lost a lot of weight. Or else the suit they dressed him in for the trial was at least three sizes too big. His tall frame had somehow shrunk during the weeks at Butyrka, and his dark face had acquired the ashen tint that, like a layer of dust, covers the faces of everyone who spends any length of time in jail. He was still tall, however, a full head taller than his *advocat*, next to whom he was standing, staring straight ahead.

The seats behind the accused were empty, except for two uniformed guards, armed with pistols. They remained standing after the judge and the two members of the people's jury, or assessors, finally entered into the courtroom and we were instructed to take our seats.

But by the time the judge arrived, the moment of silence had stretched on too long, and the foreign reporters had started to chat again. Their prattle got quite loud and unruly, so that it took the judge a few moments to restore the silence.

The judge was a handsome woman who bore an uncanny resemblance to Valentina Tereshkova, the first woman in space. It was a deliberately cultivated resemblance, since she sported the same hair style and wore the same blouse-and-two-piece-suit ensemble our cosmonaut favored while presiding at international women's congresses, peace conferences and other high visibility events.

If the judge was picture-perfect, as if supplied by Mosfilm's casting bureau, the two people's assessors, the ordinary citizens elected to assist the judge in reaching the verdict, were even more true to type. The use of people's assessors in criminal trials is what makes "socialist justice" so exemplary. And in this case, they were the veritable salt of the earth. The man was tall, blond, and broad-shouldered. His face was not handsome but manly, with high Slavic cheekbones, a square jaw, and rather long hair. Not a particularly intellectual face, but then again, he wasn't called upon to play the role of a Moscow State University professor. He was meant to be a perfectly ordinary working-class guy, someone good with his hands and with an abundance of common sense. Biceps bulged through the soft fabric of his elegant suit.

You'd expect the second people's assessor to represent the heroic Soviet peasantry, but that would have been overkill. The producers of this show were more sophisticated than that. She was a woman, of course, but not an ethnic Russian. Rather, she was from the Siberian ethnic region of Yakutia. She had a round face, narrow black eyes, and black hair. Perhaps our leading legal minds had taken the phrase "jury of his peers" to heart and, not being able to produce a citizen of African descent, had settled for an Asian.

Judge Tereshkova and her two helpers took their seats. The judge poured herself some Borjomi to wet her throat, while the two assessors sat woodenly in their chairs neither smiling nor looking around. The trial was declared open. The judge introduced all the participants, and the state prosecutor began by reading the indictment.

I had come to the trial to see what Major Yegorov's men, working in partnership with the Ministry of Foreign Affairs, would produce as further evidence of Kofunda's guilt, aside from his fake confession. After all, it was an international event attended by members of the diplomatic corps and covered by the international press.

The choice of the courtroom was a good sign. You wouldn't choose such surroundings to hold a sham trial, I told myself.

The prosecutor, wearing a black uniform with the two silver stars of a State Justice Counsellor Second Class on his lapels, droned on. A State Justice Counsellor Second Class is not yet a general, but definitely a highly positioned prosecutor, another sign that Kofunda might get a fair trial after all.

He began by describing Comrade Kotov as a famous poet and war hero, showing the court several books of Kotov's poetry, a diploma certifying his membership in the Writers' Union of the USSR, and another confirming that he served for three years as the head of the poets' section. A pretty assistant brought out a red sateen cushion on which Kotov's military decorations were arrayed. She demonstrated them to the judge and the assessors. While the judge took an active interest in the exhibits, leafing through the poetry books and examining the medals closely, the worker and the young woman from Yakutia continued to sit impassively, as if whatever was happening in the courtroom had nothing whatsoever to do with them. Perhaps they thought they were merely props – which most likely they were.

The prosecutor then talked about the poetry reading that took place at Lumumba to mark Victory Day. He digressed a bit to describe Nazism as the most inhumane and murderous ideology in history, specifically noting how Hitler considered black Africans subhuman. Then he digressed even further, and at greater length, in order to describe Lumumba University and the generosity of the Soviet people, who were extending a friendly hand to citizens of nations who had only recently thrown off the yoke of colonialism.

This portion of his speech was apparently directed at the French and English reporters in the back, who sat through it with their heads bowed. Or perhaps they were merely hung over and bored.

Throughout the prosecutor's lengthy digressions, which had little if anything to do with the substance of the case, Judge Tereshkova kept nodding encouragingly. The worker on her right seemed to have dozed off.

Finally, the prosecutor got to the actual murder. After explaining that, following the reading, Comrade Kotov kindly agreed to stay on in order to meet with Lumumba students and to answer their questions about the war, his poetry, and the heroism of Soviet soldiers, one of the students, apparently becoming upset by something he had heard or thought he had heard during the reading, went in and murdered Comrade Kotov.

"I will now show the court photographs taken at the scene of the crime between forty minutes and an hour after the murder had been committed."

He began to reach into his scuffed leather briefcase.

"I did not," came a hoarse, heavily accented voice from the front row.

The prosecutor turned to Kofunda as swiftly as his thick girth would allow. He was a corpulent man of about fifty with a double chin that bulged over the starched collar of his white shirt.

Judge Tereshkova gave Kofunda a look of infinite disdain. "The accused will be given an opportunity to speak," she remarked coldly. "Socialist justice is nothing if not fair. But the accused will not speak out of turn."

The prosecutor smiled: "Well," he said, "if the accused for some reason has changed his mind and decided to deny his guilt, I'll be glad to read to the court his own description of what happened in that room."

He rifled through his files and produced a single sheet of paper.

"'Having listened to Comrade Kotov's poems, I was upset by all the war imagery the poems had so vividly brought to life. The poems had a very unsettling effect upon me. I decided to have a personal conversation with Comrade Kotov. I did not initially have the intention of killing him. But I was very angry, and I became angrier when we started to talk. That was when I stabbed him with a knife that I always carry in my pocket."

"This is not true," Kofunda said firmly.

The prosecutor shrugged as though he was dealing with an unreasonable child.

"It is a signed statement," he said. "Is this your signature?"

"I don't know." Kofunda was getting excited now. "I didn't kill him, I'm telling you. It wasn't me."

His lawyer tugged at his sleeve, but the judge made a sign to allow Kofunda to talk.

"Is this your signature?" the prosecutor repeated. "Were you in some way coerced to make this confession?"

"It wasn't me," Kofunda insisted.

"If it wasn't you, who was it?" the judge asked.

"I don't know. I don't remember. I passed out. All I know is that he was dead. Like my brother Junior, who was murdered by the people who now govern my country."

This time there was a stir in the row in front of me, in the seats filled with Kofunda's compatriots.

"It's a lie," shouted a small man seated in the middle of the group, whom other members of the delegation treated with considerable respect. His Russian was heavily accented, and he was even more difficult to understand that Kofunda.

"Order," the judge shouted, her voice suddenly shrill. She struck her gavel on the table. The thick fabric made the blow almost inaudible. "Please sit down or I'll ask you to leave my courtroom."

"Wait a minute," the small man objected waving his arms at her. "I'm the Ambassador, the Right Honorable Samuel Makuba, and I will not allow this vile murderer to besmirch the reputation of my government. I will have you know, my friends," he turned toward the reporters, "that the Kofunda family are a criminal clan. Felon Kofunda, the father of this murderer, is a fugitive from justice. His son, Junior Kofunda, was murdered by Joseph Kofunda whom you now see before you in this courtroom. That was the ruling of the High Court of the Republic—"

"He was a child," Kofunda's *advocat* shouted, jumping to his feet. "They made him do it."

The ambassador ignored the interruption. "They are a thieving and lying family," he continued, "they are criminals, I tell you. My government is not at all surprised to see a Kofunda in the dock.""

He was quite out of breath when he sat down. Others in his delegation began to clap.

"Order," shrieked the judge. She no longer resembled Tereshkova so much as a consummate communal kitchen warrior.

She turned to the prosecutor, "Please continue."

Instead of going back to reading the indictment the prosecutor asked Kofunda another question. "Was the victim dead before you passed out or when you came to?"

"Objection," shouted Kofunda's *advocat*. He was short and pugnacious and resembled a bantam, with a round chest and a comb over. In fact, he and the prosecutor could have been brothers. He had a high, screeching voice.

"Overruled," the judge said coolly. She had regained her composure.

"Was the victim dead before you passed out or when you came to?" the prosecutor repeated.

"Both," replied Kofunda.

"What do you mean both?" the prosecutor asked.

"Both," insisted Kofunda.

All this was highly irregular. A trial is a process, and there are rules that govern how it is supposed to be conducted. The judge is not supposed to allow the prosecutor to question the accused before he had finished reading the indictment.

But wonders were not about to cease.

"And what about the knife?" shouted the *advocat*. "Where is the murder weapon? How come it has not been produced? We assert that my client never carried a knife and was not armed when he went into that room to speak to the victim."

"What do you want?" the prosecutor snarled. "It's right here in the statement provided and signed by the accused. He admits to murdering Comrade Kotov. I didn't invent it. If the knife wasn't found, it doesn't mean that he didn't do it."

"There was too much blood," Kofunda said, his voice suddenly calm and matter-of-fact. "It was dripping with blood."

"What did you mean by that?" the prosecutor asked.

"Soil alone cleanses blood."

That was the title of one of Kotov's poems. Even I knew that.

Silence fell over the courtroom. The prosecutor and the judge exchanged glances. Everyone's nerves were stretched to the limit.

Then it exploded. Everyone began shouting at once: the judge, the prosecutor, the *advocat*. Kofunda's countrymen and the Right Honorable Samuel Makuba were closest to me, and they shouted something about ancient tribal ritual and children's blood used by

Kofunda's tribe in their religious ceremonies. Behind me, reporters shouted in their various languages. No one was listening to anyone else. It was complete pandemonium. Joseph Kofunda alone was silent and stiff, staring ahead.

But after that tempers cooled as if the nervous energy that had accumulated in that courtroom had been vented. The reading of the indictment resumed. Suddenly, the trial started to move forward properly and briskly. Judge Tereshkova was not just another pretty face; she could control the courtroom when she wanted to.

There wasn't much more to add to what the prosecutor had said. The court was told that the State intended to call witnesses, and a list of witnesses was provided. There was no one who sounded like the Argentinian student, but I hadn't expected to see her there, whoever she was.

There was a break for lunch, during which I went outside to smoke. That was where Oleg found me.

"Are you a detective?" Oleg asked. "Do you work for Moscow Criminal Investigations?"

"How do you know that?"

"Sevka told me. He said it's a big secret. He didn't tell me why. It's not a bad thing to be a detective."

I had warned Sevka not to tell Oleg or his mother where I worked, and he had given me his word that he wouldn't.

"Don't worry," Oleg said. "I won't tell anyone. Especially my Mom. Isn't it her that you're mostly concerned about? That's what Sevka said. I gave him my word that I wouldn't tell her."

I sighed. All their words were useless. I just hoped that Sevka hadn't wagged his tongue to Tosya. He probably hadn't, because if he had, I would have been dead already.

"Yes, I am a detective," I admitted.

"Then you won't take me to the pool? You just said it so that you could meet us?"

I hadn't yet made up my mind about that, but yes, Oleg was right. I probably wasn't going to take them swimming, since this case was speedily coming to an end. I felt myself blushing.

"I'll tell you what," I said. "How about next Sunday?"

I was glad to see that Oleg was more concerned about swimming lessons than the trial of his father's murderer. It was a good sign. Kids are resilient.

I didn't stay much longer after the break. The prosecutor called his first witness, someone named Irina Semyonovna, the cleaning woman at Lumumba University. Except she wasn't. I wasn't crazy. I had met the real cleaning woman at Lumumba and she was a different person, named Klava.

This cleaning woman looked more like a schoolteacher. Central casting had failed. On the other hand, unlike the real cleaning woman, she had all her ducks in a row. She didn't hesitate. She identified Kofunda as someone who had been waiting for Comrade Kotov in the hallway outside the office, and then identified little Oleg as the boy with whom Kofunda had conversed while waiting. It was, strictly speaking, true. But she was not the person who had witnessed it.

I had seen enough of our Socialist Justice. As they say, Socialist Justice differs from ordinary justice the way an electric chair differs from an ordinary chair.

I got up and started to make my way toward the exit. Suddenly I stopped. Sitting behind me was Major Yegorov and two young wags from the Ministry of Foreign Affairs. They must have come in after the break and sat quietly behind me. Yegorov caught my eye and gave me a wink. It wasn't a particularly friendly one.

I had a strong impression that something that had been said during the trial was important and relevant to the case. Maybe when I get outside, and the fresh air clears my head, I will be better able to put my finger on it?

It was a futile hope. What it was and how it connected to the case continued to elude me.

TWENTY-FOUR

The trial moved swiftly, and by the end of the week the judge, presumably assisted by the two somnolent people's assessors, ruled that Joseph Kofunda was guilty of premeditated murder.

I wasn't there to hear the verdict. Judge Tereshkova had formed her opinion of what happened to Kotov, and I had formed mine. Or rather, she knew what happened in that room next to the auditorium and I had no idea. I knew what didn't happen: whatever Kofunda did there, he didn't kill Kotov. He was a sensitive young man traumatized by a horrible childhood experience. I felt that the elusive Argentinian held the key to the mystery. She probably knew what happened and if I got hold of her, I would too.

But I wasn't going to spend any more time on Kofunda. Especially since the Danilov Market case was still hanging over our heads. For all of Lenny's achievements, we had made little progress. Our research into everyone's background had yielded no new leads, and it was starting to look like we were not going to solve the case. The Boss was giving us dirty looks, and we both felt that a storm was brewing.

The verdict and the sentence on Kofunda were pronounced simultaneously. There were several different types of crimes classified as premeditated murder in the Criminal Code of the Russian Soviet Federated Socialist Republic, as updated in 1960. There was ordinary premeditated murder (Article 103). Then there was aggravated premeditated murder, committed for reasons of racial or national hatred (Article 102M). That was what Kofunda had originally been charged with. The evidence that Kofunda bore resentment against Kotov because he was a white man was flimsy and consisted of the fact that his father had fought against French colonial rule and had been held in prison for a couple of years by the colonial government. The prosecution had probably used that charge to keep Kofunda in line, since Article 102, with its complement of letters ranging from A to N, carried penalties of eight to fifteen years of imprisonment, or even death in particularly egregious circumstances.

Later, his charges were reduced to Article 103 – premeditated murder punishable by imprisonment of three to ten years.

But the judge found Kofunda guilty of yet another type of premeditated murder, one covered by Article 104 – premeditated murder committed in a state of violent emotional excitement. It is defined as "premeditated murder committed in a state of sudden violent emotional excitement caused by violence or serious insult on the part of the victim, as well as caused by other unlawful actions of the victim, if those actions entailed or could potentially entail grave consequences for the perpetrator or the perpetrator's relatives."

It was a convoluted article. The charge carried a milder penalty, namely imprisonment of up to two years or correctional labor of the same duration. Two years was the sentence the judge gave Kofunda, even though it somehow implicated Kotov in activities that could potentially have harmed or insulted Joseph Kofunda or members of his family. But it was a nice compromise. Either the judge was kinder than she looked, or the Ministry of Foreign Affairs had instructed her to go easy on the African. Perhaps Comrade Sumarokov had one of his brief, businesslike conversations with Judge Tereshkova before the sentencing, laying out the big picture for her as he had done for me.

I wondered what the representatives of Kofunda's government made of it. They seemed keen to see the young man put away for a good long time and were probably disappointed. On the other hand, my boss,

Budyonny, was pleased. He didn't care one bit about Kofunda's guilt or innocence and wasn't interested in his sentence. He was relieved that the case had concluded smoothly, without it blowing up in anyone's face.

On the day I found out about the sentence, I had a conversation about it with Lenny and Tosya.

Lenny stopped by after work, which he sometimes did to talk things over. There were subjects we didn't have time or inclination to discuss at the office. Besides, sitting in Tosya's room, with a bottle of vodka and a bowl of boiled potatoes between us (the latter mixed with a generous helping of sliced scallions and parsley, and dressed with sunflower oil – about the only dish Tosya had learned to make during her years at the orphanage), Lenny felt his mind worked better than in the airless cage that served as our office.

Lenny also liked to pay court to Tosya. To be sure, he liked to pay court to every woman he encountered, both in and out of uniform, but he was especially partial to my girlfriend. I might have been nervous, because Lenny, despite his chubby physique and balding pate, was quite a Don Juan. However, my Tosya maintained an ironic and even gently condescending attitude toward my partner.

Tosya prepared her usual dish of boiled potatoes and I bought a half-liter bottle of Moskovskaya. Lenny's contribution consisted of a variety of hard-to-find *zakuski* – delicacies to chase down a glass of vodka with. Lenny lived on his salary, which was no higher than mine, and, by any standard, quite low, but if you came to dinner at his house, you'd assume that he was on the take. That was entirely due to his wife Raisa, who somehow managed to procure things you couldn't find on ordinary store shelves, and when she couldn't get anything special she prepared delicious dishes using whatever she had on hand. She managed to conjure up these wonders in a communal kitchen, and do it almost as an afterthought, while plying you with homemade meat dumplings, asking you about Tosya's work and Sevka's grades and slipping out now and again to keep an eye on her cooking.

They had two daughters who were the spitting image of their mother. That was unfortunate when it came to their looks, since Raisa's features were on the heavy side and she wasn't considered a conventional beauty, but a very good thing in all other respects. They were the best groomed and the most neatly dressed little girls I have ever seen, not to mention that their grades were at the top of their class, and they also drew, danced and played musical instruments.

"That's why Jews are so successful," Lenny would say proudly. "It's because our women are so extraordinary. Did you know that you're only a Jew if your mother is?"

I didn't know that, but in Lenny's case it made a lot of sense. Lenny had an extraordinary number of love affairs, and who knows how many chubby balding men and women there would be in the next generation. They didn't necessarily all have to be Jewish.

That evening our conversation started with the Jews – because Arkady Brunevsky was one. Tosya told us about a coworker at the Tryokhgorka plant who insisted that the Jews didn't fight in the war, but spent all four years in the safety of Tashkent and that she, the coworker, had Jewish neighbors who had been evacuated to Tashkent.

"Only the Russians really fought and died in the war to save them from Hitler," the coworker explained to Tosya.

"So what if they were evacuated?" I said. "My mother and I were also evacuated. Not to Tashkent, but to the Urals. It doesn't matter. It wasn't an easy life. We shared a room with other evacuees – all kinds of people, of all different nationalities. Jews, Armenians, Ukrainians. When your plant or office was evacuated, they told you to go with it, and you didn't have any choice."

"Sure," Lenny said angrily. "My Dad fought, and Raisa's Dad also fought and was wounded twice. People like that don't care. They will keep repeating the same lie over and over again, regardless of the facts."

"That's what I told her," Tosya said. "I said I know of a Jewish guy who lost both legs in the war. The guy you're investigating. I used him as an example."

Lenny turned to me.

"I thought we're not supposed to discuss ongoing investigation with our girlfriends," he said.

What Tosya had said about her coworker and her anti-Semitism had made Lenny angry, and when he was angry, he got nasty and could turn even on his friends. Tosya looked lost, as though she had said something she wasn't supposed to say.

"I didn't tell her anything," I said. "I said we'd met a Jewish man who lost both legs in the war."

"Still, you are not supposed to say anything about an ongoing investigation," Lenny grumbled.

"I didn't. Had I told Tosya more about our guy, she probably wouldn't have used him as an example of a war hero. No need to get so hot under the collar."

"There you go, babbling away about an ongoing investigation again."

I poured us more vodka and made him a sandwich of black bread and smoked salmon. Lenny always mellowed a bit if you put food in his mouth.

It was a warm evening. Tosya had the window wide open, to make sure our cigarette smoke would at least partly dissipate by the time she and Sevka went to sleep, and so as to keep an eye on Sevka, who was playing in the courtyard. He had been told to stay in the front yard and not to go behind the apartment building, where older, tougher kid hung out. Naturally, the prohibition made him eager to transgress. Whenever Tosya couldn't see him out the window, she would lean over the windowsill and shout, "Sevka, get back where I can see you."

"Maybe this is happening because people don't know each other very well," I suggested.

"How do you mean?" Lenny asked.

"I mean, look. Sevka is growing up with all kinds of kids. He knows that you can be a Jew or an Uzbek and be a good kid and a friend. He is not going to grow up to be a bigot. But let's take that African student, Joseph Kofunda. He's as black as they come, and we in Moscow are not used to seeing people like him. We're kind of scared of them, we don't know what to make of them, and we are ready to believe all kinds of stupid things about them. I've talked to a lot of people who had come into contact with him, and they all think he's a savage who would kill another human being like a wild animal."

"And your point is?" Tosya asked.

"My point is that prejudice comes from ignorance. If we had many more Africans living among us, nobody would be a racist. Everybody would see that Africans are people just like us. They look different, but they're not savages or brutal murders."

"Nonsense," Lenny said. "We've lived in this country for two hundred years, if not more. It's the same thing all the time. What do you think, that girl Tosya works with, she doesn't know that plenty of Jews fought in the war?"

"Maybe she doesn't."

Lenny sneered loudly, which almost caused him to lose the piece of salmon he was chewing on.

"Sure," he declared derisively. "It's not that, by some strange coincidence, she managed never to meet Jews who fought at the front. Her problem is that she doesn't have eyes for such Jews. She hates all Jews, and her hatred defines what she's able to see. She meets a Jew who lost both legs in the war, for example, and she immediately forgets about him, because he doesn't fit into her picture of the world. Then she meets another Jew, who didn't fight, and he becomes a typical example."

"But if she happened to have a neighbor like your father-in-law—" I suggested.

Lenny had just taken a bite of the salmon sandwich and, with his mouth full, he waved both his short arms in protest. We waited until he finished chewing.

"It doesn't matter, I'm telling you," he mumbled, still swallowing his food. "For her, he'll become an exception that confirms the rule."

"You're both right," Tosya said. "It's true what Pavel said about living side by side with someone, but it is also not true. We had a Korean kid at the orphanage. Wherever he was born, he grew up with us. Even though he looked like his people, he was as Russian as they come. He didn't speak a word of Korean. He was one of us, no questions asked. If the teachers or town kids tried to pick on him because he was different, we would all stand up for him and defend him to the death. But whenever we had a fight amongst ourselves, it was always us against him. And if something went missing in the dorm, he was the one everyone suspected. We never caught him stealing, but we accused him all the same."

"That's exactly what I'm saying," Lenny said, having finished chewing while Tosya talked. "I'm a cop upholding the law, but to most people I'll always be a scheming Jew. And your black African will never get justice here. Unless somebody powerful sticks up for him. But even if it turns out that someone else killed that Kotov character, and the African is let go, they'll still be convinced that he's guilty. If not of that crime, then of some other one."

"He's not going to have such an easy time in jail," Tosya added. "Everyone will be picking on him – the guards, the labor camp personnel, the other inmates. I don't envy him."

Tosya had never been in jail but growing up at an orphanage was pretty close. Maybe not the same as an adult *zona*, but not unlike a juvenile facility.

The two of them got the better of me in the argument, but I didn't come away convinced that they were right.

TWENTY-FIVE

Our little party broke up. Lenny climbed into his precious Moskvich. He should have left the car in our courtyard and gone home by public transport, considering the vodka he and I had drunk, but he never liked leaving it outside other people's buildings overnight. He didn't trust others to check on it properly.

Since he had berated me about breaking the rules and mentioning Brunevsky to Tosya, I could have asked him about driving under the influence. His response would have been that he was merely tipsy, and that he would never in his life drive drunk – not so much out of respect for the law, but because he didn't want to risk smashing his car.

Lenny was a cop, but deep down he was an anarchist who didn't recognize the validity of any laws.

After Lenny was gone, I stood outside for a few minutes enjoying the warm evening. It was still light out. The sky was a phosphorescent blue, and only now starting to tinge orange behind the brick wall enclosing the western end of our courtyard. It was getting late. Moscow doesn't' have white nights the way Leningrad does, but the daylight lingers late. The sun barely dips below the horizon, and the sunset flows seamlessly, almost unnoticeably, into dawn. I was watching the sky and listening to the first five measures of "Moscow Nights" that flowed from an open window, where someone was learning to play the accordion.

Sevka was nowhere to be seen. There was a narrow arch in the midriff of the building leading to the rarely used back stairways of our apartments. This part of the courtyard is isolated and usually deserted, which is why older boys gather there to do things they don't want their parents and other adults to see, like smoke cigarettes, drink cheap sugary wine, pitch pennies, and settle arguments with their fists.

Sure enough, Sevka was there with a group of boys his age. They crowded around some older kids, looking excitedly over their shoulders. Whatever they had been doing remained a mystery, because they stopped the moment they spotted me, hiding their hands behind their backs. Their alarm increased when they recognized me, since it was no secret in my building that I was a cop.

"Come, Sevka, it's getting late," I said pretending to have noticed nothing. Even if they were doing something dangerous and illegal, busting them would have destroyed Sevka's reputation forever. He had already complained to me that some of the older kids had become more careful talking around him since his mother and I began seeing each other.

As I looked over, I couldn't help noticing that all the kids were a mixture of nationalities. There were Slavic faces, round and fleshy Finnish ones, kids who looked like Tartars or Georgians. And one or two were Asians.

It was as if I was continuing the conversation that I had been having with Tosya and Lenny, and I felt the satisfaction of being proven right: if people live together and mix, they can lose their racial and ethnic prejudices.

I walked Sevka to the front entrance and said goodbye. Tosya and I pretended in front of him that we were not doing anything as embarrassing as sleeping together. She would slip out of their room once Sevka had fallen asleep and cross the courtyard under the cover of darkness. We would set the alarm for an unconscionable hour the next morning, so that she had time to get dressed, go back, undress, and slip into her own bed.

I headed home, and as I grabbed the handle of the front door of my building, I spotted a shadow moving away from the wall.

My heart skipped a beat.

"Very well," I said to myself. "I'm being followed."

Giving no indication that I had noticed anything, I opened the front door and headed to the elevator. The door slammed shut on its extension spring, but a second or two later than usual. That gave me pause. My tail had apparently slipped into the building behind me. Surely they knew where I lived and didn't need to make sure I would reach my apartment safely.

I waited for the elevator to descend, which it did with its usual hemming and hawing, as if protesting that it still had to keep ferrying tenants up and down at its advanced age. Since the elevator cage, built into the air shaft in the old-style spiral staircase, shielded me from view, my plan was to open and then slam the elevator door, press the button of my floor and then conceal myself, to see what my tail would do. However, before I could put my plan into operation, I heard hurried footsteps and a hoarse, conspiratorial whisper: "Wait a minute, sonny, I want to talk to you."

Turning around I saw Comrade Klava, my cleaning woman friend from Lumumba University, climbing up to the landing.

"I've been waiting for you for five hours," she grumbled after catching her breath. "Where the hell have you been? Most people go home after work. Don't you have a wife and kids?"

I didn't feel like I needed to account for my movements, or for that matter provide information on my marital status.

"What can I do for you, Comrade Klava?"

"I want to show you something I found," she said after a slight hesitation.

She handed me a bundle wrapped in a soiled cloth.

"What is it?"

"Take a look, sonny. You might find it interesting."

Her hand, as she passed it to me, was shaking slightly. The wrapping was thick, the cloth had been folded over several times.

"What is it?" I asked again.

She said nothing. I continued to unwrap the bundle and soon was holding in my hand a long, thin, crudely made shank. I had seen many such shanks before. No two of them are ever exactly alike, but they're all of a certain kind. They are fashioned from carpentry tools or utensils – usually files or screwdrivers or dull cafeteria knives, with removable handles made of a compressed tin can. They are compact, so that they can be hidden during a search in the cell, but extremely sharp and deadly.

The one I was holding was covered with caked blood.

While I was examining it, Klava had backed away from me and begun to scurry out of the building. Trying not to touch it, I rewrapped the dagger and ran after her.

"Where did you get it?" I asked once I caught up with her. Suddenly, I too was out of breath.

She looked away.

"Where did you get it?" I repeated.

"I found it."

"Do you have any idea what it is?"

"It's a bundle of some kind, sonny. Let me go, please. You're hurting me."

I had not realized how hard I was squeezing her forearm.

"Did you look inside?"

She didn't answer and avoided my eyes.

"Let's assume you did. Do you know what it is?"

She nodded.

"Do you know when it may have been used?"

She nodded again.

"Where did you find it?"

"Keep your voice down, sonny," she said. "I don't want anyone to know I've been to see you."

I repeated the question, softer this time: "Where did you find it?"

She shrugged, avoiding my eyes: "In the gents' on the same floor. It was stuck behind the water tank."

"Is this how you found it? Or did you wrap it yourself?"

Suddenly, she was her talkative self again, running her mouth in a nervous sort of way.

"That's how I found it. I was cleaning the gents this morning, I started to mop the floor and that thing tumbled right out. I said to myself: 'Klava, this thing must be important. I should take it straight to that nice cop who came to investigate.'"

"Did you clean that bathroom before? I mean, after the murder?"

"I sure did, sonny. That's my job. That's what I'm paid to do, to clean up after all the infidels."

"Do you think it was there before?" I asked. "Or did it just appear this morning?"

"Where else would it have been? That's what that poor man was murdered with. I've got to go. I start work early. I've got to get some sleep."

She slipped out the door and was gone.

I came out. There was still daylight outside, but the street lamp in the courtyard had gone on. Klava was scurrying toward the Kirov Street exit. She was limping slightly but moving fast for her age. I shook my head. I wondered what it was all about.

TWENTY-SIX

"There are two kinds of mines; one is the personnel mine, and the other is the vehicular mine. When we come to a minefield, our infantry attacks exactly as if it were not there. The losses we get from personnel mines we consider only equal to those we would have gotten from machine guns and artillery if the Germans had chosen to defend that particular area with strong bodies of troops, instead of with mine fields. The attacking infantry does not set off the vehicular mines, so after they have penetrated to the far side of the field, they form a bridgehead, after which the engineers come up and dig out channels through which our vehicles can go."

– Marshal Georgy K. Zhukov
Quoted by Dwight D. Eisenhower,
Crusade in Europe (1948)

He's having a recurrent dream. He's at his grandma's town outside the city of Vinnitsa. Zayde, grandma's husband, is still alive. The town is small, very poor and full of Jews, almost all his distant cousins. They speak Yiddish among themselves and he strains to understand them. They sometimes address him in a mixture of broken Russian and Ukrainian.

Grandma's house is next to the synagogue. It used to be a prestigious place to own a house, except the synagogue was shut down and turned into a literacy center for collective farm peasants. The house was taken away from Zayde, along with all the rest of his property. Many other families, related to them and not – and not even Jewish – now share the house with grandma and Zayde.

He's playing with the kids, as he used to do when visiting grandma, except in his dream he's the only grown-up among them. His sister is there too. She's older – and she's dead in real life – but in his dream she's still alive and still a little girl.

They're playing on the green pasture at the edge of town. It lies on the banks of a slow-flowing brook that has no name. On one side, there's a pond spreading into the copse of weeping willows from a dam on which men and older boys are fishing. On the other side, on the crest of a hill, wooden houses hide behind wattle fences in the deep shadows of fruit trees. A brick Orthodox Church stands among the homes. The top of its bell tower was knocked off by an artillery shell during the Civil War. The church is a scary place, illuminated by daylight trickling in through holes in the roof. The faded visages of the saints painted on the walls level their zealots' narrow eyes at intruders.

The pasture is thick with juicy grass. Hidden in the grass are huge cow pies. He's running through the pasture. The other kids, his distant cousins, have crossed it already. They huddle together at the far end of the field and shout encouragements to him in their throaty Yiddish accents, mispronouncing their r's: "Be careful, Arkasha, don't step in a pie!"

His feet are getting tangled in the grass, impeding his progress. And he must watch where he places his bare feet, avoiding cow pies hidden in the grass.

It is summer, but he's cold. He's trying to run faster to warm up and suddenly he's hot and sweating and thirsty.

"Run, Arkasha, Run! Faster! Faster!"

And then it happens. His toes feel something thick and warm and his sole sinks into it. There is a sudden silence which lasts for what seems like an eternity and then something huge and red-hot grows out of the grass at his feet, like the Biblical burning bush.

It's a scary, sticky dream. He wants to wake up from it, but it keeps returning. In the dream, he wants to stop running. He doesn't want to get to the far side of the field. And he wants to get away from all the kids, from his first and second and third cousins once and twice removed, because he knows that just like his older sister, in real life they're all dead, exterminated by the Germans in the first two months of the war, after Hitler overran Vinnitsa.

He keeps running through the pasture, and the kids keep shouting and everyone knows what comes next, the conflagration, the fiery opening of the earth that should swallow him up but doesn't, sending him running again and again on the same tall, viscous grass.

There is the familiar smell of chloroform when he finally wakes up. And of blood and excrement, iodine, and human suffering. So it was all a dream. He's awake now and he's back at his field hospital at long last, with his two nurses, one of whom is Nadezhda, whose young body manages to stay sweet even through the stench of the hospital, sweat and filthy clothes. He's slept too long and he needs to get up and play god again, separating the living from the dying and operating on the wounded.

He reaches next to him to feel for Nadezhda. His hand gropes about the bed, not finding her, just a crumpled bed sheet and a rough military blanket. He vaguely recalls something unpleasant connected to Nadezhda, but can't think of what it is.

He's going to open his eyes and get up, but he can't bring himself to do it just yet. His head is throbbing and his body aches all over, as if he has been in a fight or at a wild party at which he drank far too much, mixing vodka with beer and wine. Maybe the latter. He's hung over and that's why he's so thirsty. Licking his lips, he feels them dry and cracked. His mouth feels as if he has been chewing sand. Passing his tongue over his teeth, he feels some missing and others broken and sticking out like shards. It's an unfamiliar, foreign mouth. Maybe he was in a fight after all.

Worst of all, his feet are itching badly – exactly where he dreamt of the fire erupting from cow pies.

He frowns. What a stupid, heavy dream.

He opens his eyes and looks up. The ceiling above him is rough wooden boards with grey hemp hanging through the cracks, tattered like an old man's pubic hair. It isn't a familiar ceiling, but he's used to being on the move and waking up in a new place every few weeks.

He eases his hand from under the blanket. It's heavily bandaged, with brown spots where blood has soaked through the gauze. What a strange situation he has gotten himself into. Worst of all, he remembers nothing of what happened the night before.

He reaches under the blanket to scratch his leg. His hand hits an empty space where his legs are supposed to be. Nothing. Nothing but empty spaces. He doesn't get it at first – what the hell happened? What happened to his legs? To his feet? He tries again, with the other hand this time, and raising his left foot higher. It's a very strange sensation because his foot both lifts and doesn't – at the same time. And there is still nothing there, where his foot itches.

"Goddamnit," he mutters.

He reaches down again, and again there is nothing but empty space.

Horrified, finally starting to realize what happened and recalling everything in a flash – the arrest, the torture, the *shtrafbat*, the cattle car and the cold, the glass of vodka thrust into his hand, which he swallows in one go, cheap spirits leaving a bitter taste in his mouth, the shove of an NKVD soldier, pushing the barrel of a submachine gun into his back, the run through the snow, the flash at his feet—

He rips off the stiff army blanket and sees what he, a military surgeon, already knows he's going to see: the bandaged lower end of his torso, the brown stains of dried blood, the yellow stains of urine on the bedsheet, and nothing below that. A crumpled bedsheet with brown stains on that too.

His broken teeth grinding hard, he groans. And then he laughs. Physician heal thyself. He amputated so many arms and legs, it is really a strange, almost comical turn of events to have had his legs amputated.

He passes out again and is unconscious for another day or maybe more. Then he comes to for good. The itching stops and the excruciating phantom pains begin. As a doctor, he knows all about that, but now he learns it at first hand. His feet and ankles start to ache in his sleep and the suffering is unbearable, as if he's being cut with a dull saw. And there is nothing that can be done for it. His mood is dark, and his thoughts are even darker.

He has plenty of time to think during the next several weeks, an eternity. In fact, he has nothing else to do but think. His mind wanders and he is afraid that he has gone mad from pain and despair, but at other times his thoughts are as sharp and lucid as ever. It will not be hard to get his hands on something to make his end swift and relatively painless, he tells himself.

What good is he to anyone anymore? Going back to his medical profession, back to being a throat specialist? A doctor in a wheelchair? It is perhaps an option, but even the thought of it makes him sick. He cannot bear spending one more day inside a hospital or a clinic. If he ever gets out of this one.

Going back to his wife? He has no doubt she will take him back. He's heard stories of wives turning away their invalid husbands who return from the front without arms and legs. You almost can't blame them – they can barely scrape together enough food for themselves and their kids. Having a burden like that might be the last straw. His wife is different. She loves him.

But he loves her too. He always loved her, even when he slept with the nurses, and now he loves her so much his chest is bursting with the love that fills him. She's so young and beautiful and so full of life. They have a baby daughter and she wants to have more kids. Lots of kids, almost as many as he had cousins in the town outside Vinnitsa. He will not allow himself to ruin her life, take away her dreams. It would have been better if he had been killed. But he is alive, more or less, which is not his fault. It was not even his intention. But he'll stay alive, he'll try to live. He wasn't killed, and there must have been a reason for that, even if he cannot figure it out.

He's only half a man. Less than that. A decimal fraction. But he has a huge amount of self-confidence, enough for two men. He is smart, too, and his mind has not been damaged. And he has courage. It's a secret he learned by being a frontline surgeon: courage is a rare gift and most men are cowards. But he has plenty of courage, also enough for two men. Courage is even more important than brains. He'll survive.

But he will never go back to Serafima. He'll have to banish her name and face from his memory. From his life. For good. Let her think he's dead.

TWENTY-SEVEN

Daria Filippovna stuck her head out into the hallway:

"A man has calling you all evening long," she said. "I got blisters on my feet running to the phone."

Daria Filippovna makes a point of knowing everyone's business, which she achieves by being the first to answer the phone. Her room is the closest to it, which certainly helps. Since most of the calls to our number are for me, and almost all of them are work-related, it is my business that Daria Filippovna knows best. Even though she often sounds annoyed at being disturbed all hours of day and night, she doesn't mind it. She is retired and has little else to do except feed breadcrumbs to pigeons on the ledge outside her window and listen to the radio.

"Who was it, Daria Filippovna?"

She shrugged, her shoulders twitching inside her loose house dress.

"How would I know?"

That meant that it wasn't the Boss or Lenny or any of my colleagues, whose voices she would recognize.

"A *nachalnik* or an ordinary guy?"

"A *nachalnik*. Most definitely a *nachalnik*."

In Daria Filippovna's book, a *nachalnik*, an official or a bureaucrat of some high standing, was the highest, scariest rank a man could attain.

But she's not unique in this regard. Every Soviet citizen can recognize a *nachalnik* not only by appearance, but by the way he speaks.

"Any message?"

Daria Filippovna shook her head.

"If they need me, they'll call again," I concluded.

"That's what I'm worried about," she said. "Because I'm about to go to sleep."

But I could see that she wouldn't mind answering the phone again if it rang. It's a great honor to speak to a *nachalnik*, even if briefly.

The call came two hours later. I had thought some more about the Kotov murder before going to bed and I was asleep when Daria Filippovna knocked on my door.

"I'm sorry to be calling so late, Lieutenant," a deep baritone came on over the line. Its owner didn't sound especially sorry. "You may remember me. We spoke at the Ministry of Foreign Affairs a couple of weeks ago."

Sure. I remembered him. Eduard Vasilyevich Sumarokov, who could ever forget you?

"It's a matter of some urgency, Lieutenant. I know you attended Joseph Kofunda's trial and I assume you're familiar with the verdict."

He didn't wait for my reply.

"The trial was covered by Western correspondents accredited in Moscow. Kofunda's country is of major strategic importance, and for some time now it has been the object of intense rivalry between us and our imperialist enemies. For this reason, the coverage of the trial in the West has been tendentious to the extreme. They are claiming that it was politically motivated, because the convicted man is the son of an ousted former leader, and that we are basically currying favor with the new president."

"I understand," I said. He had explained it all before.

"Worse, an American newspaper has insinuated that Comrade Kotov was killed in order to frame young Kofunda. Can you believe how low they have stooped?"

He paused. I said nothing.

"We have drafted a response to these defamatory accusations which has been signed by your boss, Lieutenant Colonel Matirosyan. The reason I'm calling you is to reiterate in no uncertain terms that you are not to meddle in this highly sensitive case. I hope you understand this."

"Yes, Sir."

I stood there for a few moments, gripping the receiver and listening to the succession of short beeps that meant Sumarokov had rung off.

Why would a big *nachalnik* at the Foreign Ministry keep calling me all evening and then late at night just to repeat his previous warning to stay away from the Kofunda case? Was it a coincidence that he had been calling me at precisely the time when Klava was handing off to me what was most likely the weapon used to eviscerate Comrade Kotov?

"All good?"

Daria Filippovna was standing in her doorway, staring at me. Deep concern for my well-being was written all over her face.

"Was it a big *nachalnik*?" she asked.

I nodded absently as I replaced the receiver.

Were they tailing me? No, impossible. Even if they were, how would Sumarokov know what was in that bundle? And, just at the time when I got it?

"A very big *nachalnik*?"

"*Da*, Daria Filippovna. As big as they come."

I had a plan now. I returned to my room and got dressed. I went down to the courtyard where my Zundapp was parked, revved up the engine, and thrust the four hundred kilo monster forward, reaching the speed of hundred kilometers an hour within a few seconds. I raced along Boulevard Ring, made a left on Chernyshevsky Street to the next circular avenue of the city, the impossibly wide Garden Ring, and headed past Kursk Railway Station toward Taganka.

The city was asleep. The multitude of its apartment windows had gone dark and the roar of my engine bounced off the somber facades of the tall building. It was a pleasure to ride fast in the sparse nighttime traffic, except I nearly hit a line of trucks crawling along, watering the asphalt after a hot, dusty day.

Visitors to the Urumovs were supposed to ring the doorbell four times. I pressed the bell as briefly as I could. Lenny's neighbors were all asleep and receiving a nighttime visitor was a good way to cause a nasty squabble in the morning.

Despite my efforts, the bell resonated loudly beyond the door. I pulled my head in and waited.

The stairwell was dimly lit, the lightbulb attached to the ceiling was weak and braided with cobwebs. The air smelled of cats, cigarette smoke, and sour cooking – the smell of every stairwell of this grotesquely overcrowded city. And yet, at one time it had been a quality building. It had a brass banister with an intricate floral design, now half-hidden under the thick layers of oil paint, as well as ornate floor tiles. These were now chipped, cracked and breaking loose, with large sections missing. The windows on the landings between the floors had once held stained glass.

Despite the lateness of the hour, a steamy gypsy romance was heard somewhere on a higher floor. The record kept skipping. Each time the needle was nudged ahead by an unsteady hand, it slid across several grooves at a time with a nasty scratchy sound

At last I heard the shuffling of feet and Lenny's voice, irritated and hoarse.

"Who's there?"

"It's me, Lenny," I whispered through the door.

"What do you want?" he asked as he opened the door. "Do you have any idea what time it is?"

"I need to talk to you."

Lenny moved to the side to let me pass and pulled the door shut behind me carefully. He was wearing a sleeveless shirt and a pair of long boxer shorts, once blue but now quite faded – the standard sleepwear of a Soviet cop.

"Everyone is asleep," he whispered. "Let's go to the kitchen. But keep your voice down, for god's sake."

We walked down the long hallway in complete darkness. Lenny led the way, deftly maneuvering between boxes, trunks and pieces of furniture stored there by his neighbors. He had an intimate knowledge of the apartment, but I wasn't as lucky. When I hit one of the invisible sharp corners and tried to stifle a cry of pain, Lenny turned and hissed, "Stop making so much noise."

The sounds of heavy snoring, in a variety of tonalities and registers, reached us through the closed doors.

After walking what seemed like a nautical mile, we reached the kitchen, where Lenny finally turned on the light once he had securely shut the door.

"What's going on?" he asked, turning to me.

Instead of replying, I took out the bundle I had gotten from Klava, put it on the table in front of him and carefully unwrapped the object it contained, avoiding touching any part of it.

The communal kitchen had lots of shelves and cabinets filled with chipped, Chinese-made enamel pots and Russian cast iron pans. Various surfaces were also covered with kitchen implements and utensils. There were two industrial-sized gas ranges with eight burners each. A blue-and-yellow pilot light flickered in the gas pipe of the water heater.

"What is this?" Lenny asked.

"I think this is what Kotov was killed with," I replied. "Forensics could confirm it easily enough, except that tonight I got another call from the Ministry of Foreign Affairs, warning me again to stay away from this case."

Lenny made a face.

"You're getting obsessed with this murder," he said. "Even though you should be working with me on the Danilov Market case, which has completely stalled. In the next day or two the Boss is going to bring out the knout."

But I could see his interest was piqued, because even as he spoke, his eyes remained glued to the crudely fashioned blade on the kitchen table.

"How did you get it?" he asked.

"Klava, the Lumumba cleaning woman, brought it to me this evening in great secrecy. She says she found it this morning. She seemed quite nervous and evasive. But if this is the real murder weapon in the Kotov case—"

"Why did she give it to you as opposed to those guys from the Southwest District?"

I shrugged.

"It's a good question. Let's suppose for now that it's because I had taken her testimony more seriously. Major Yegorov's guys didn't pay much attention to her. Perhaps she was offended."

"Yes, but how did she know where to find you?"

"I was going to ask her about that but she was too much in a hurry to get away."

"Curious," Lenny said. "And the moment she gives you the murder weapon you get a fresh warning from the Ministry of Foreign Affairs?"

"Not even. The guy was calling me *while* Klava was waiting for me by the entrance to my building."

I then related to him the call I had received from Comrade Sumarokov.

"What do you think?" I asked in conclusion.

I didn't have to explain to Lenny that if that shank was the murder weapon, it completely changed the complexion of the case against Kofunda. Because there was no way an African student would be able to lay his hands on a prison-made knife. Plus, using it required considerable skill and practice. It was not an easy thing to do, to eviscerate a person with a blade like that, and it was therefore a strange choice of weapon to use on the outside, where you could lay your hands on other knives if you wanted to kill a man.

Lenny leaned over, almost touching the shank with his nose.

"An unusual specimen," he observed. "It's bigger and better made than other weapons of this kind. I'd say whoever made it didn't have to hide it as much. The workmanship is better, more care was taken with it, which suggests that whoever made it had time on his hands. Most likely it was done at a shop where prisoners work unsupervised. Or else it was made by someone on the outside. This also answers the question of why take the risk of smuggling something like this out. Most likely it has never been inside."

I nodded in agreement.

"Judging by how ardently the Ministry of Foreign Affairs is denying the fact that Kofunda was framed," Lenny continued, "I would think that he definitely was framed. And the murder weapon confirms it."

Now Lenny was speaking in an even softer whisper. I had to lean close to him to make out his words. Lenny had a much better grasp of international affairs.

"What I wonder about is whether they got Kotov, a prominent poet, killed in order to do get Kofunda?" he continued. "Let's say they hire some thug to kill Kotov and then Kofunda walks into that office unawares and gets arrested?"

Lenny pondered the question.

"No," he said at last. "I don't think so. It's too convoluted, too risky and involves a prominent poet. There are plenty of simpler ways to frame an African student, even for murder. If you need to sacrifice someone, stick to one of the girls who come to the Lumumba dorm to party. Throw her out the dorm room window, for example. Nothing easier. And easier to tie all the loose ends, because this case is both messy and unconvincing."

He shook his head.

"I'd say someone else killed Kotov," he concluded. "Kofunda happened to be on the scene and the Ministry jumped on the opportunity.

"But it had to be a Russian who killed him," I said.

"No doubt," Lenny agreed. "Which means that whoever did hide this thing in the men's bathroom – and we assume it was the murderer – did our government a huge favor. Otherwise they'd have to suppress the evidence, which is against the law."

He chuckled at his own joke.

"So, if we want to find the murderer, we should look for a career criminal," I said. "Maybe even a thief in the law. We need to look into Kotov's connections more closely. Something to do with money?"

"It's a possibility," Lenny agreed. "If you actually want to find this murderer. But if I were you, I'd give it a pass. I'd pay a little more attention to our friends at Danilov Market."

"Yes, Lenny, but Kofunda has clearly been framed," I objected.

"You're not listening to me. And in your eagerness to catch the real murderer you're ignoring the facts."

"What do you mean?"

Lenny shrugged, annoyed.

"Did you hear what I just said about the murderer doing the government a favor? Think of it. Put yourself in his place. You've just murdered a man in a crowded place. You're running away. Why hide the murder weapon?"

"It's pretty big object. It's dripping blood. You don't want to be caught with it."

"Then just drop it at the scene."

"There might have been a reason why the murderer needed to remove it. He might be tied to it in some way. Or he thought he might have to threaten someone with it as he is getting away. Plenty of possibilities."

Lenny shook his head.

"And now look at Klava delivering it to you. Unless we find Kofunda's prints all over it – and I don't believe we will, since Foreign Ministry guys are too smart to plant a shank like this on a foreign student – then it proves the opposite of what the Ministry wants to prove. Is there someone else who's deliberately sabotaging the case against Kofunda? And why did the Ministry's big boss, Sumarokov, call you at the precisely the time when you were being handed the murder weapon? Think it over, Matyushkin, and once you do, stay as far away from this case as you possibly can. You may end up out of the job, and even sharing a jail cell with Kofunda."

TWENTY-EIGHT

It was no doubt good advice. I didn't really need it. I knew that it was prudent to do nothing. There were national interests at stake, and that was no joking matter. And even though Lenny later decided that the timing of Sumarokov's call was a mere coincidence – after all, Kofunda had been sentenced two days before and foreign newspapers would have come out a day later – I could not be sure that I was not being followed. The Ministry of Foreign Affairs had close links to the KGB through its Foreign Intelligence Directorate, which handled our spies abroad, and you should never underestimate that agency's ability to spy on you.

I also had a conversation with Tosya when she came to my bed late the following night. I had hardly slept the night before, but Tosya's visits were not so frequent that I would pass one up in order to catch up on sleep.

I still could not get Joseph Kofunda out of my head.

"You know," I said. "I'm pretty sure that the African was not the killer. Someone else murdered Kotov. It had to be a Russian, and possibly a career criminal. He must have had a reason for murdering Kotov which has escaped everyone's attention."

"But the African was found guilty," she said. "And he confessed, too."

"That's the thing," I said. "I think he was convicted wrongly."

"Is there anything you can do? Can you prove that he didn't do it?"

"Maybe I can. If I find the person who did it."

"Look for him then. Isn't it your job to find killers?"

I reached out to the night table and lit a cigarette.

"I can't. An official at the Ministry of Foreign Affairs told me that sending Kofunda to jail was a matter of national interest. There is foreign policy involved there, even though I don't know much about that sort of thing."

Tosya didn't like cigarette smoke. She slipped out from under the blanket, went barefoot to the window and opened it wide. Morning air filled the room, letting in the smell of lilacs which grew wild around the bust of Lenin in our courtyard.

"What are you going to do then?" she asked when she got back into bed and lay next to me. She was shivering lightly. Her body, touching mine under the blanket, felt cold.

"I don't know," I said.

Swiftly, she turned toward me. I could see her silhouette imprinted sharply against the grey of the morning sky. She was leaning on an elbow, looking at me in the half-light.

"Don't even think about it," she said. "They'll destroy you. They'll squash you like a bedbug. Don't you know the saying: You can't break an ax head with a whip?"

Letting it go was common sense, but I could not resist taking the shank to Sasha Grigoriev's office and asking our forensics expert to do me a favor: to provide me with the results promptly, and in secret. It was perhaps not necessary to stipulate the latter. Sasha was taciturn by nature and it was hell trying to get information out of him at any time.

I was going to keep it a secret from Lenny, too, since he didn't approve of my continued meddling in this case, but the results, when they were returned two days later, were so astonishing that I had to share them with someone. Plus, I needed Lenny's advice. I certainly wasn't clever enough to figure it out on my own.

I placed the sheets with Grigoriev's conclusions on Lenny's desk and waited while he read them. Reading didn't take long, but he took his time to process the information – as I had, too, a couple of hours before that.

"So," Lenny said at last. "Did Major Yegorov provide all that information to Grigoriev? Everything, the fingerprints, the blood work?"

I hadn't even thought about that. It wasn't the most surprising thing in Grigoriev's report, but it was another piece of the puzzle that fitted in.

Our forensics expert had found that the blood on the shank was of the same group as Kotov's – a fairly rare A-negative – which meant that in all likelihood it was the murder weapon. That was not unexpected. What was unexpected were the fingerprints on its metal handle. There were two sets of them. One belonged to persons unknown – even though a search of a wider database might have resulted in a match. The other was, unmistakably, that of Joseph Kofunda.

When Lenny read that, he gave me a look that said: "I told you so, buddy."

But Grigoriev's report contained three parts. One addressed the blood type, the other identified the fingerprints, and then there was a third part. That one described the dried substance also clinging to the blade as "garden soil".

"Garden soil?" Lenny shook his head dubiously. "Where did that come from?"

"Certainly not from behind the water tank at the men's room," I said.

That part, at least, I had figured out. I recalled something that Kofunda had said during the trial, which escaped my notice at the time but now came rushing back:

"Soil alone cleanses blood."

"What does it mean?" Lenny asked.

"It's the title of one of Kotov's poems," I said.

"Uh?"

"Think of Joseph Kofunda, an impressionable young man traumatized by a terrible experience in his childhood, when he was made to murder his own brother. He enters a room at Lumumba and comes upon a scene which looks very much like that of the murder he committed. Blood is everywhere and there is a dead body slumped in an armchair. He is in shock. He is not aware of what he's doing. He spots the murder weapon lying on the floor, abandoned there by the killer. It reminds him of the dagger they made him use to kill his brother. He picks it up, carries it to the window. He wants to get rid of it. He opens the window but then he remembers that soil alone cleanses blood, as Kotov's has just read from the podium. That's his most famous poem, and it must have been the one that impressed Kofunda. He sees a flowerpot on the windowsill, and he sticks the blade in."

"Isn't it a little contrived?" Lenny suggested.

"Believe it or not, I saw it when I went to inspect the room in which Kotov died. I didn't realize what it was. Klava must have found it."

"And then decided to bring it to your attention, but lie that she had found it in the men's room? Obviously, someone told her to get it to you. Which explains why Major Yegorov decided to cooperate with us all of a sudden, by promptly providing the information to Grigoriev."

"Fair enough," I said. "But why?"

Lenny pondered the question for a few minutes.

"I'll tell you what. It's the Ministry of Foreign Affair and your contact there, whatever his name. They're orchestrating this case from behind the scenes. They were obviously unable – or unwilling – to use the shank at the trial, even though it had Kofunda's fingertips on it. Everyone would have readily seen that it was not the kind of weapon an African student could have gotten his hands on. In fact, his fingerprints on it could have been used by foreign journalists as proof that Kofunda had been set up. On the other hand, they may not have wanted to provide evidence that was too damning for Kofunda. Think of the shortest possible sentence that he got. I'm sure the Ministry had a hand in it, too."

"Maybe," I said, unconvinced.

"In any case, I'd steer clear of this mess for now," Lenny said and then added. "Sit tight and expect more developments in this case. It is far from closed."

FROM ALL THIS I could draw two important conclusions. First, that Joseph Kofunda was definitely innocent. The Ministry of Foreign Affairs evidently know that he is, but for now they're keeping him in jail for reasons of their own. Second, Kotov was killed by a Russian, possibly a career criminal. Whoever he is, however, should not be any of my business. The case is too complicated, there are various considerations involved which I no longer understand, and so I should sit tight, just as Lenny had advised me.

But I could not stay away from the Kotovs entirely. I had promised Oleg that I would take him to the pool and teach him to swim. When I saw him at the Kofunda trial, he made me feel guilty, since I had been cynically using him.

I mentioned to Tosya that I had promised Oleg to take him swimming and asked her whether I still should.

"Of course you should," she cried out. "You absolutely have to. You promised it to the poor boy. He has no one else, now that his father is gone."

"But what about the Foreign Ministry?" I objected. "They'll be sure to suspect that I'm still meddling in that Kotov case."

Tosya shrugged contemptuously: "Who cares about the Foreign Ministry. You've got to keep your promises to kids because they trust you. And if you keep betraying their trust, they'll grow up to be cynics."

Women are not logical. They are ruled by emotions. I had no doubt that if the Foreign Ministry caught me and I got in trouble, Tosya would blame me for that, too.

Be that as it may, at exactly nine o'clock in the morning the following Sunday Sevka and I appeared at Oleg's doorstep with a bundle of towels and our swimming trunks packed into my knapsack. Tosya had even made sure we had an extra towel for Oleg, and put Sevka's extra pair of trunks in too, in case Oleg didn't own any.

Oleg was especially excited to be going in my Zundapp, declaring motorcycles to be the best mode of transportation ever, better even than Tu-104, the supersonic passenger airliner. He wanted to ride in the passenger seat behind me, and kept insisting until I put my foot down. He was too small and too skinny to ride in the back, I ruled, telling him to get into the sidecar instead.

"Next year, if you're as big as Sevka, you might be able to ride there. And the following year, I'll teach you and Sevka to handle the bike if your legs are long enough."

I caught myself making another promise to the kid. Would I have to make good on that one too, I wondered.

After that, we took off in the direction of the Moskva pool.

The pool is the city's pride. It stays open year-round. When you pass it late on a freezing January night, when the thermometer has dropped to twenty below zero and two-meter high snowdrifts abound, it is a sight to behold, the steam rising from the heated water in the green neon light, and kids and grown-ups splashing about in their bathing suits.

The pool is an afterthought. Before the revolution, a large Orthodox church, the Cathedral of Christ the Savior, stood on that spot. After the revolution, the government decided that there was no god and churches were a waste of perfectly good living space. They blew up a bunch of them, including the Cathedral. My mother, then still a young girl, used to live in the neighborhood. She saw it being blown up. It was winter, the middle of the night. The government had kept the preparations secret, but everyone knew it was about to happen. Her father woke her up and took her to the roof of their house. They saw the first explosion, which failed to knock down the massive structure. The second charge was even more powerful. It did the job, but it also shook the earth for miles around and shattered the windows in a bunch of houses.

The church was supposed to be replaced with the tallest skyscraper in the world. It was going to be called the Palace of the Soviets. It was going to have offices for government bureaucrats but also giant auditoriums for Party congresses and theaters for holding pageants and providing entertainment for the masses. Ours is an enormous country, with more land and empty spaces than any other place on earth, but the government wanted to reach upward, to the stars, and to concentrate all power in a single very tall building.

The Palace of the Soviets had to be taller than the tallest skyscraper in New York, and it was going to be topped with a colossal statue of Lenin – so high that it would practically be seen from Paris, it was said. Construction went on for many years, a deep pit was dug up and tons of concrete were poured into it, but in the end the project was abandoned. And then the war began.

After a while, the giant hole in the city center became an eyesore and the government, making a virtue of necessity, announced that it was building a year-round pool instead. If they could not have the world's tallest building, they would build the largest and deepest open-air pool. It is round because it follows the contours of that misbegotten skyscraper, and the pool is exactly the size and shape of the biggest auditorium of the skyscraper's ghost.

Swimming is not my sport. I'm a decent skater, like every Moscow kid who grows up chasing an empty tin with a homemade hockey stick on a frozen pond six months out of every year. I also like soccer, even though I'm not particularly good at it. After spending ten minutes in the lukewarm, chlorinated water, which made my eyes tear up and turn red, I left the two of them in the capable hands of their instructor and got out. There was a bench on the side of the pool from which I could watch their beginners' group hopelessly flop about at the shallow end.

It felt good not to be thinking about the Kotov murder. I was glad that I was taking Oleg to the pool. His evident excitement was gratifying to see. It was also nice not to be thinking what kind of information I could draw out of him, about his late father and his possible connections with the underworld. I hoped I would not have to go back to that case ever again.

Flushed with excitement, and squeaky clean after the shower, Sevka and Oleg ran out to greet me. Oleg's joy was slightly diminished now because the swimming instructor had told him that he would need at least five more lessons just to stay afloat. Sevka, on the other hand, was a much more talented pupil and by the end of the session could swim a few meters doggie style.

"Don't gloat," I warned him. "You're a year older and it's natural you would do better."

"He's not gloating," Oleg replied, sticking up for Sevka like a real friend. "The instructor was very impressed with him and said so at the end of the class."

"Very well then," I said. "What now?"

We still had three hours to kill, because Tosya was doing a bit of spring cleaning and had warned me not to bring Sevka back until five.

"I want to go for a ride in your motorcycle," Oleg said.

We held a brief council of war and picked the Exhibition of Economic Achievements as our next destination. Not because they were interested in the economic achievements of our country, but because it was relatively far and Oleg would enjoy a long ride in the Zundapp. An added attraction was the Space and Aeronautics Pavilion and a cafe which carried a very special kind of ice cream. They were badly in need of ice cream, or at least something sweet, having swallowed a good deal of chlorine.

The pleasantly warm May day was turning into a hot afternoon. You could feel that summer was just around the corner. Riding a bike you always feel cool, but by the time we dismounted and passed through the tall gates topped with the statues of Worker and Peasant, the three of us were sweating profusely. We got the famous ice cream and ate it alongside the Friendship of Nationalities Fountain, which had sixteen gilded figures representing the sixteen republics of the Soviet Union. Sevka and Oleg kept up an animated discussion centered on whether Sevka, with his newly acquired skill, would be able to swim the width of the fountain had its bowl been a bit deeper and had a patrolman in a white uniform not been stationed nearby to make sure no one attempted such a stunt.

Having finished our ice cream and cooled off, we were about to go in to check out the Space and Aeronautics Pavilion when I spotted a man in a wheelchair being rolled by a young woman along the central avenue of the Exhibition Park. As I caught up with them – I had started to walk faster, telling the boys not to fall behind because the place was crowded, and we could easily get separated – I recognized Brunevsky and his housekeeper Gulya. What a touching scene – an older invalid being taken for a walk by a pretty young woman who could have been his daughter.

"Good afternoon," I said and began to walk alongside them.

Brunevsky gave me a cold look. He didn't remember me – or perhaps pretended not to – and I introduced myself again.

"Senior Lieutenant Pavel Matyushkin, from Moscow Criminal Investigations," I said. "My partner and I came over to talk to you a few days ago. We were investigating an attack at Danilov Market in which the daughter of your friend Stepan Maltsev was injured."

I turned to Gulya.

"And, incidentally, your housekeeper was the only witness," I added innocently.

Brunevsky's thick lips spread in a smile. The bright sunlight reflected off two even rows of gold teeth. His smile was not necessarily very sincere, since his dark eyes remained watchful, but it was cheerful enough. The kids caught up with us and Brunevsky flashed his glittering teeth at them.

"Very nice to see you, Lieutenant. Sorry I didn't recognize you right away." He winked at Sevka and Oleg. "Yours?"

As I started to answer, I noticed out of the corner of my eye that Gulya let go of the handle of the wheelchair and made a momentary motion as though she was about to walk away. That jolted the wheelchair and Brunevsky grumbled: "Easy please, my dear. Steady as she goes."

She got hold of herself and continued to push the wheelchair but turned away and didn't take part in our conversation. She clearly wasn't glad to see me and was not going to pretend otherwise.

"We're taking a walk," Brunevsky kept saying, oblivious to his housekeeper's discomfort. "We're enjoying this beautiful spring day. It almost seems like summer is already here. You know, in my condition, I have to be mostly confined indoors during winter months."

Underpinning Brunevsky bonhomie was a mocking acknowledgement that we at Moscow Criminal Investigations are trying to figure out how he is connected to the Danilov Market incident, but also a complete certainty on his part that we are never going to get to the bottom of it.

Gulya was another matter. We had not talked to her since that first visit to Brunevsky's apartment in Mazilov, and since then something had clearly spooked her. I made a mental note to tell Lenny that we needed to go to see her again.

Meanwhile, Gulya had slowed their progress to a crawl, prompting Brunevsky to turn around once again and give her a questioning look. The conversation flagged. We had nothing further to say to each other. It was time for us to say our goodbyes and pick up the pace. Once again, Brunevsky was overly polite and cheerful, while Gulya was still sulking, turning her face away.

But as we started to walk a little faster and separate ourselves from Brunevsky and Gulya, I realized that Oleg kept falling behind and turning to look over his shoulder.

"What's the matter, Oleg?" I finally asked. "Can you just keep walking and not stop every two meters?"

"It's just—" Oleg's voice trailed off.

"Yes?"

The boy frowned, still looking back. I saw how pale he had grown, and he was about to start crying.

"It's that woman," he said, sounding puzzled. "I've seen her before."

"Where?" I asked even as the truth was starting to dawn on me. It was a simple truth, even though it was totally unexpected. And yet somehow, on some strange level, all was falling into place. Lots of loose ends still had to be tied, all those whys and hows, but the overall picture was beginning to form in my head.

"At the university where Dad was killed," Oleg said. "She was waiting to see him. She's that Argentinian student I told them about."

TWENTY-NINE

"It's time you came clean," Lenny said.

We were standing in Brunevsky's house, in the same room where he talked to us on our first visit.

We had been let in through the gate by the young thug Shamil the moment we arrived – once again immediately upon ringing the bell, as though we had been expected. There was no dog in the front yard – just an empty doghouse and a length of heavy chain lying on the ground. The dog was inside, sitting next to Brunevsky's wheelchair, as alert and vicious as ever. It was breathing hard through its mouth and scowling.

Brunevsky was once again sitting at the table, but now a glass of white wine and a half empty bottle stood on the table in front of him. The bottle was foggy with condensation on that hot, humid morning.

Dry wine is a women's drink; men drink vodka or settle for cheap plonk with high alcohol content if they don't have enough money to buy vodka. A big man like Brunevsky was ridiculous with a wine glass in hand, and its dainty crystal stem looked fragile in his thick hairy fingers. It didn't seem to bother him in the least, and he was thoroughly enjoying the women's drink. His stumps, clothed in folded pant legs, were enough to vouch for his masculinity.

"Cheers, boys," he saluted, raising his glass. "To your very good health. To the success of all your investigations."

He was clowning. Whether or not half a bottle of dry white wine could get a big man like him drunk, he looked like he had had enough.

"We've just seen each other," he addressed me. "And yet we meet again. You must really enjoy my company. I wish I could say the same about yours."

He didn't offer us a seat and, in fact, aside from his wheelchair, there was no place for us to sit this time. Other chairs had been removed.

As before, Shamil remained standing behind our backs, propping up the locked door as though he expected someone to try to bust their way in.

When Lenny opened his mouth, Brunevsky placed a finger over his full lips.

"Hush, my friends. I'm listening."

Only then did I become aware of the soft sounds of classical music filling the room. An LP was playing on a turntable set on top of one of the bookcases.

We stood like idiots while Brunevsky sat in his wheelchair with his eyes half-closed, swaying slightly and taking small sips from his glass. Lenny and I were so thrown off by the scene that we didn't utter a word even after the music stopped.

The needle went on spinning and making a crackling sound. A moment later, Shamil peeled off from the door, picked up the lever and replaced it on its stand.

"Verdi's *Requiem*," Brunevsky said, breaking the silence. "So underappreciated. So dramatic. I would even say tragic. Beautiful. Do you like Verdi? No? It's a pity. What can I do for you, Comrades?"

I saw Lenny's face flash with rage. He would have liked to go over to the turntable and swipe it off the bookshelf. He was certain that the entire show, including Verdi's *Requiem* and the wine, had been put on for our benefit. If Brunevsky was trying to get us angry, he was succeeding only too well – at least as far as my partner was concerned.

"To start with, you can perhaps tell us what sort of connection there was between you and Valentin Kotov," Lenny croaked, his voice constrained in his throat.

"Valentin Kotov the war hero and famous poet? None whatsoever of course. I don't read war poetry, and I don't believe modern poets are any match for the great Russian classics. Pushkin remains unmatched as a writer of both poetry and prose, wouldn't you agree?"

He raised his eyes to the ceiling, then raised his glass and toasted the imaginary Pushkin.

"You're lying, you son of a bitch," Lenny shouted.

I felt a slight movement in the room, like a soft breeze on the back of my neck. It was Shamil taking a few quick steps forward. The dog, too, pricked up its ears.

Almost imperceptibly, the invalid shook his head and patted the dog's head. Shamil's wiry frame, taut as a compressed spring, now relaxed, but he had stopped an arm's length behind Lenny, ready to move in. The scene made me glad I had my service Makarov in my shoulder holster. I took a couple of steps back, to be a step behind Shamil and at a greater distance from the dog.

Brunevsky didn't seem to be offended.

"Watch your language, Lieutenant," he said amiably. "Let's be reasonable. What kind of connection could there be between us? Comrade Kotov, may he rest in peace, was up there" – he raised a hand high above his head – "and where am I, a humble night watchman?"

He was still taunting us, and he wasn't even trying to hide it.

Lenny by now had serious difficulty breathing and his angry outbursts were not doing us any good. The man had thrown us off balance and it was making Lenny furious. We needed a different approach to get the questioning back on track.

"You two are definitely on the opposite ends of the social ladder," I said calmly. "Or rather you were, before somebody murdered Comrade Kotov. Nevertheless, there had to be a connection between you two. Judging by your lavish lifestyle, it had to be money. Am I hitting the mark?"

Brunevsky grinned.

"Was Comrade Kotov a wealthy man?"

"No, he wasn't," I admitted.

"I didn't think so," the invalid agreed. "Then money couldn't have been the reason he was murdered. Anyway, what makes you think there was any connection between us?"

Lenny appeared to want to put in a word. I preempted him. I was going to carry the conversation from now on, and I didn't need his unrehearsed bad cop routine.

"More to the point," I said, "what is the connection between you and Gulya Aliyeva?"

"Why, you know that very well. You visited her and questioned her at length only a couple of weeks ago. And you saw us just yesterday at the Exhibition of Economic Achievements. She's a poor girl from Azerbaijan and I have hired her to do some housekeeping. In my condition I need someone to help me. Shamil here—"

I interrupted him.

"So she cleans things for you?".

"I suppose that's what housekeepers generally do. Keep houses clean. Shop. Cook. Wash dishes. Do laundry. Take me for a walk when I need fresh air. That's the job description. Not easy to work for an invalid, but she's a strong wench. She manages."

Brunevsky poured himself some more wine, but I noticed that he had stopped sipping it since the record ended. He was perfectly sober and only pretended to be tipsy.

"Does she do your dirty work for you too?" I asked. "Along with Shamil?"

Brunevsky grinned: "It very much depends on what you mean by dirty work. Look at me. There's a limit on how dirty you can get with me."

Lenny was chomping on the bit. Once again, I spoke up before he could intervene: "I mean dirty work like seducing Kotov and starting to make love to him in that office so that he would be taken unawares when the killer struck."

Lenny and I had reconstructed the scene of the murder to the best of our abilities before coming to see Brunevsky. Our reconstruction rang true. Gulya must have come into the office, getting Kotov alone. She probably started kissing him, pulled down his jacket over his forearms as if in play. The only question was how the killer got in. He may have been hiding in the auditorium or even in that same office. It had been left unattended while Kotov was reading his poems.

"What an interesting idea," Brunevsky said pretending to think it over.

"It fits," Lenny croaked.

"And who are you suggesting was this killer who stabbed Comrade Kotov as he was being kissed and hugged by my housekeeper?"

"Why not him?"

Lenny turned sharply on his heels and pointed at Shamil, who was standing so close, Lenny nearly stuck his finger in the kid's right eye. "He looks the type. And he is sure to be familiar with this sort of thing."

Lenny pulled out the shank which was now professionally packaged in plastic.

"What is this?" Brunevsky asked, squinting at the knife.

"It's the murder weapon. And it had a set of finger prints on the handle which I would dearly like to compare with his."

"I see." Brunevsky waved his hand dismissively. "Shamil couldn't have done it. He has an alibi for the time the murder was committed."

"Ah," Lenny exclaimed triumphantly. "So you do know when the murder was committed."

"*Net.* I don't have any idea. It's that Shamil has an alibi for entire days because he stays with me. He didn't kill Comrade Kotov, I give you my word."

"We'll see about that alibi," Lenny grumbled darkly. "And your word, too."

"Oh, yes," Brunevsky said. "I remember now. It was four days before Victory Day celebration. Shamil and I were at a reception at the War Veterans' Association. There would be any number of highly respected war veterans, decorated heroes, who will be able to confirm his presence there. And ,anyway, Comrades, why would Shamil or me or anyone else associated with us want to kill an upstanding citizen like Comrade Kotov?"

"Rest assured, Brunevsky," Lenny hissed. "We'll find out."

"No, you won't."

Brunevsky sat up in his wheelchair and he was no longer pretending to be friendly. His voice was cold, threatening. More threatening than Shamil standing close behind Lenny.

"Valentin Kotov was killed by an African, who stabbed him in a state of extreme emotional excitement. The African has been tried, convicted and sentenced. What's more, it will take me two or three phone calls, and when a certain highly placed Foreign Ministry official hears that you two clowns have been coming here with some harebrained theory about my housekeeper and Shamil having been involved in Kotov's murder, you will lose your jobs and will consider yourselves lucky if they let you walk the beat somewhere east of Khabarovsk. The only reason I haven't done this yet is because it suits me to have morons like you working as detectives. Imagine if in your place they got someone competent? Did I make myself clear, Comrades?"

He did. And he was right. What Lenny and I were doing was freelancing, not conducting a bona fide official investigation. The case was closed, and we should have absolutely left it alone. There was the Danilov Market case that had to be addressed, but the weird thing was that it featured the exact same cast of characters. Moreover, Lenny and I were now convinced that Gulya and Shamil were the ones who attacked Oksana. The question that remained unresolved was why.

THIRTY

Stepan Sergeyich Maltsev sat on a tabouret in his kitchen. His empty left sleeve was carefully folded, showing ironing creases. In his right hand, which was missing two fingers and a phalanx of a third, he held a glass of tea, taking sips with his disfigured mouth. The tea was burning hot, and the kitchen was hot too, despite the wide-open window. The air outside was heavy, the sky low and grey. A line of violent spring thunderstorms was passing over the city, drenching the streets and creating rivers on the sidewalks, but bringing no relief.

Maltsev's smooth, featureless face was red and shiny. Drops of sweat formed on top of his bald head and rolled down along the sides, while the skin on his face, burned off by an explosion, was leathery and dry.

Lenny had spent plenty of time talking to the man, whereas I hardly knew him. In this case, it was better if my partner carried on the conversation. I sat on my stool, blowing into my glass, which was too hot even to touch.

"We have reasons to believe that Arkady Brunevsky was behind the attack on your daughter," Lenny was saying. "We strongly suspect that he ordered it and that Gulya Aliyeva, who claims to have been a witness to the attack, was a participant."

"Did he now?" Maltsev asked.

"Yes, he did," Lenny insisted. "Even though you seem to be good friends. Why would he do that?"

There was a long silence. Maltsev took another sip of his tea. He seemed to be impervious to its scalding temperature. The cuckoo clock on the wall behind his back was ticking loudly.

"We also suspect that your daughter knows the identity of her attackers and has always known who ordered it. In other words, she knows it was Brunevsky, but she is covering up for both Aliyeva and him. Do you know why she would do that?"

Oksana was out. Maltsev's wife was at home, but she had left the kitchen after serving us the tea.

Maltsev remained silent. You could not read anything on his impassive disfigured face. I could not even tell whether he had heard Lenny at all.

"We know that Brunevsky is connected with the black market," Lenny continued. "He was found guilty of speculation years ago. The fact that we haven't caught him again doesn't mean that he has mended his ways. He lives well above his means, in a way no night watcher or disabled veteran would be able to afford to live. To us, that indicates that he is still engaged in illegal activities. We will get to the bottom of it. And you can help us – and save yourself a great deal of trouble into the bargain."

Lenny's voice got harder and had some steel in it by the time he finished, but at that moment the cuckoo clock struck quarter of an hour. It sounded as if it was making fun of him.

Maltsev grinned. A crooked smile twisted his small, lipless mouth, which looked a bit like a five-kopek slot on a metro turnstile.

"Let me tell you a story, my friend," the blind man said at last. "You guys are young and healthy. You're probably good-looking. I can't tell, but let's assume you are, and girls fall head over heels in love with you. You don't know what it is like, to wake up in a hospital bed blind and missing an arm – and you're all of twenty-one. You have not yet started to live and your life is already over. You have no idea what it is like crying all night long, night after night, and wishing you were dead.

You don't know what it is like, coming home the way you are and being greeted by a wife whose face you cannot see, but who you can sense would rather you were dead. Because she has to feed your daughter who's just two years old, not even, and she can barely make ends meet without you hanging like a millstone around her neck, a useless hunk of meat as you have become. You don't know what it is like, and I don't wish it on you to find out.

His voice was soft, hoarse, intimate. He was speaking just to the two of us, but I was wondering whether his wife could hear him.

"So, you get together with a couple of other war cripples. One is also blind, like you, another is missing an arm and a leg. A right arm and a left leg. And along the way, out of the goodness of your heart, you pick up a Samovar. You know what I'm talking about? Ever seen a real Samovar? It's a useless torso with a head stuck on top of it. The torso can't move, it can't even crawl, just roll on the ground. It can't wipe itself after it's done shitting, and it can't hold its dick when it has to piss. The Good Lord didn't make any creatures like that. Even the most despised, the snake, can move around and defend itself. It's man who created Samovars, because man is the most vile of the Good Lord's creations.

"Your blind buddy is from Belarus, his whole family was wiped out by the Germans and his house burned down. He has no home to return to. He is older than the rest of you. He'll die soon, hit by a freight train which he couldn't see, and for some reason decided not to hear. The other cripple went home, but his wife kicked him out. My wife didn't kick me out, I left on my own, but it was a relief to her, I could tell. She didn't ask me to stay. That cripple, the one missing an arm and a leg, will die too, of pneumonia in the first winter after the war, when we were still celebrating the victory over the Fritz. Living under the bridge is not a good thing for your health.

"So, you get together with three other losers and make a pact, like the four musketeers – one for all and all for one. You'll either live, all four of you together, or die – also together. You beg at markets and on train platforms, because you have developed an act – one plays the accordion, the Samovar sings – he has a nice voice, a tenor they call it, and he is musical, the Good Lord has granted him at least that talent – the other amputee provides a chorus, and you walk around with an officer's peaked hat in your mouth, collecting change. It's a freak show, comic relief for the masses and amusement for the kids. They throw you copper change – three, five kopeks, who has what. Except for war profiteers and party officials, no one has a lot of money, and none to spare. You'd steal, of course, but if you happen to be a cripple it's hard to get away.

"Pensions you say? Did we have pensions? First the war had to be won, then the country had to be rebuilt – the factories, the roads, the houses. The state needed the money, and there were so many of us freeloaders. Millions of cripples crawling all over the country. Paying us pensions was a waste. We weren't going to get better, were we?

"What would we have done with our money, anyway? Whatever we collected, we would use to buy vodka. All we were doing was drinking. Drinking ourselves to death. The sooner the better. It's a more pleasant way to go than jumping in front of a moving train, and if I've earned anything in this life, it's a pleasant death."

He paused, took a sip of his tea. I attempted to do the same, but mine was still too hot.

"Is this story too grim for you?" he asked. "Be patient, it is about to get far more cheerful.

"Then the other two are gone within three months of each other and you're left with the Samovar. He has a little platform on wheels that a carpenter in Tambov had made for him out of the goodness of his heart, with wooden boards on it so that he wouldn't roll off. He still has his arms, at least up to their elbows, but it's not easy for him to push himself with those. The Samovar tells you where to pull him in his pleasant tenor voice, and you pull him with your one remaining hand. That's how you get around.

"So, you decide to head south, to Central Asia, to Tashkent. It's warm down there, and there is food because it was never ravaged by the war the way the rest of the country was, and people have money to spare. But even in Tashkent you know that the two of you won't last long.

"You go by freight trains, and it takes forever, because you can't easily hop on and off trains, a blind man and a Samovar. One day on the way there, you're drinking behind the warehouses in some city you don't even know the name of, and this Jew comes along. Or rather rolls along, since he's one of you. He's missing both legs. But he's not getting around on some platform with wheels, he's travelling in comfort, in a war-booty German wheelchair. And he has a healthy young guy pushing him who treats him like he is a Party committee chairman or something. You can't see them, of course, because you're blind, but the Samovar gives you a running account of everything that's going on around you, describing the landscape and telling you what the Jew and the young guy look like. That's his payment for what you're doing for him. He's your speaking eyes.

""Let's have a drink, boys,' the Jew says.

"You're not happy with the intrusion, because you never know what to expect of people, even of your own kind, and you have learned from experience to keep to yourselves. But he's one of you, so you've got to share with him what you got. Except he doesn't want your crappy cheap *samogon*, the illegal moonshine you buy on the black market. He treats you to his, and it's real Armenian cognac. You haven't tasted anything that good since before the war, if ever. He pours each of you a full glass. And then he starts asking questions. He wants to know everything: who you are and what you do and how you got your injuries and what the story is with your family. So, you tell him everything, once the cognac has warmed you up to the core and loosened your tongue.

"You even tell him what you don't tell anyone else. That you were *shtrafbat* and were blinded clearing minefields. You can't see him, but you feel his firm handshake. He says that he admires you because you didn't give up on each other. And that is the first time in a very long time that anyone tells you they admire you. Because when you're *shtrafbat*, it's your fucking duty to clear landmines and they don't expect anything less of you than to march and be blown to pieces.

"And then he puts you to work. Really, I'm not bullshitting you. He puts you to work. All kinds of work, not all of it above board. Actually, very little of it is. Don't expect me to say any more about that.

"And then you start having some money in your pockets. Not much, but enough to put food in your stomach. And soon you realize that the Jew has a network all over the country, and all of them are guys like you. Many fewer limbs among them than in the general population. Thing is, they've all been begging at markets all over the country and traveling between train stations ,and the smarter ones eventually made friends with war profiteers and black market operators and underground sweatshop owners and common thieves and robbers, and they started to figure out how to make a little money for themselves. And then a whole lot of money and in many different ways. As I said, very little of it was above board.

"It's like a spider web spanning the entire Soviet Union and the Jew is in the middle of it, pulling strings right and left. He finds things to do for everyone, no matter how useless. Even for your buddy the Samovar. And there's loyalty among your kind, no snitches or spies.

"This goes on for a while and you start to put on weight and enjoy life. You even get women. True, some dregs from among train station prostitutes, but what chose do you have?

And then the day comes when they start rounding your kind up. Your kind meaning war cripples, who else? They stage surprise raids at the markets, not the usual police raids against beggars and speculators, when they keep you at the station for a day or two and put you on a freight train somewhere, telling you never to set foot in their town. This is different and it's serious. They hunt down the amputees, the blind, the cripples. They load cattle cars with you like you are prisoners of war and take you way north, north of Leningrad. The trains are guarded by State Security troops, so you know it's not going to be a walk in the woods at the other end.

"They take you to the edge of a northern lake, unload you and put you on a barge. The barge takes you to an island in the middle of the lake and they dump you there. It's like a leper colony, or like a concentration camp for cripples.

"You want to swim ashore? Go ahead, be my guest. How will you swim with no limbs? Ha-ha-ha. Sure, you can walk ashore in winter, when the lake freezes over, but what will you do when you get there? You'll just freeze, that's all. At least they feed you on the island, and if you're a Samovar, the nurses take you out in one of those big wicker basket and hang you on a branch, to let you breathe some fresh air.

"Why are they doing this? Because with your arms and legs missing, and your faces disfigured, you don't look half as heroic as the nation wants its victorious soldiers to look. You're filthy, dressed in rags, and perpetually drunk. You've got homemade wheelchairs and crutches. You don't fit the picture of Victory. Something has got to give, and of course it's you.

"A week or so before the raids begin the Jew comes to you. He wants to talk to you alone, without your buddy the Samovar being present.

"'I've spoken to your wife,' he says. 'You must go back to your family.'

"He knows about your family situation. You have been passing money to them using his contacts.

"You say nothing. You shake your head.

"'They'll be rounding up everyone who's not living with a family and sending them to Valaam. Go back. Your wife is waiting for you.'

"'What about the Samovar?' you ask.

"He ignores your question and looks away. But you know that if he could have protected him, he would."

Maltsev groped for his cigarettes. While he was speaking, he had inadvertently pushed his pack on the floor. Lenny picked it up and handed it to him.

"How did you like my story?" Maltsev asked.

I didn't think he was expecting an answer, and so said nothing. Lenny too was silent. The invalid lit a cigarette, adroitly striking a match on the side of a matchbox with his one hand.

"You can draw your own conclusions," he said, exhaling.

The cuckoo clock struck three. There was the sound of a key turning in the lock, and of the front door opening and then closing softly. Then some whispering in the foyer.

"I hope Oksana has recovered from her injuries," Lenny said.

It was now Maltsev's turn to be silent. He used a mutilated finger to locate the ashtray and stubbed his cigarette into it.

"By the way," Maltsev said. "He eventually got the Samovar out of there, too."

"He's at the oncology ward at Botkin," Lenny said.

"Not anymore, he isn't. Andryukha Samovar is dead. He died two days ago, may he rest in peace."

Maltsev made a sign of the cross.

"I'm sorry," I said.

"Don't be. This world wasn't particularly nice to him. When you're an invalid you learn not to linger in places where they're not nice to you. Andryukha gave it too much slack as it is. It was time for him to go. Arkady will take care of the funeral arrangements."

He sighed.

"If it wasn't Brunevsky, who could have attacked your daughter?" Lenny asked.

Maltsev lit another cigarette.

"I didn't say it wasn't him," Maltsev said. "You listened to my story but you didn't understand what it was about. What I was trying to tell you is that Arkady Brunevsky doesn't do anything at random. He may not be a good guy, but he always does what needs to be done. Even when he doesn't always like what he is doing."

He exhaled the smoke toward the open window and the heavy raindrops falling on the ledge.

"It's not always an easy thing, doing what needs to be done."

THIRTY-ONE

Maltsev's last sentence didn't make much sense to us, and the next day brought no clarification when Lenny and I stopped by Vagankovo Cemetery in the northwestern part of the city, where Andryukha Samovar was being buried.

The arrangements Brunevsky had made for the funeral were modest to the extreme. It was more like a pauper's funeral. A plain pine casket stood by the side of a freshly dug grave. There were no wreaths with ribbons and inscriptions that are customary at most funerals. Certainly, no brass band playing Chopin's Funeral March. A few bunches of flowers lay on the lid, surrounding an enlarged black and white photograph with a black ribbon crossing the lower right corner. Andrei Nikolin was pictured on it as a young man, still whole and healthy. The photograph must have been taken right after his high school graduation and before he was drafted. He wore his hair short on the sides, with a long forelock over his forehead in a style of the early 1940s. He had small, light-colored, unsmiling eyes. The eyes of someone who works hard and doesn't reach for the stars. Not tall and rather skinny, and probably not a great athlete, he was an ordinary Russian kid. Yet, he was somehow memorable in his ordinariness.

A handful of mourners stood by the graveside. Their entire group had fit into the mortuary bus that brought the casket over, with room to spare. The full cast of characters of the Danilov Market drama were on hand. Stepan Maltsev came, leaning on Oksana's shoulder, and trailed by his wife. Brunevsky's wheelchair was pushed by Shamil. Gulya arrived late, having not ridden in the bus with the rest of them. She came running down the central avenue of the cemetery, holding a large bunch of lilacs she had purchased by the main gate.

Lenny and I stood on the opposite side of the open grave. Gulya and Shamil cast hostile glances at us while the others paid us no attention. Two gravediggers, unshaven and already half-drunk, stood at either end, shovels at the ready.

Cemeteries are supposed to be melancholy places, but to me they are a place of work. We visit them often and are too busy to contemplate the evanescence of human existence. Besides, being interred at a cemetery, in peace and surrounded by friends and family, is preferable to the way we sometimes find buried bodies.

Vagankovo is an old cemetery and a pretty crowded one. It gets more and more crowded with each passing year. I don't think much of dying, but if I were an old man of, say, sixty or sixty-five, I would probably derive a least some satisfaction from seeing all the crosses and headstones carefully arranged in the Russian tradition, inside fenced-in enclosures. If so many people have already died, dying can't be such a dreadful thing.

I was looking around, to see whether someone else would show up for the funeral at the last moment or would linger unobtrusively behind other graves, but my eyes kept being drawn to Andrei's portrait. It reminded me of someone – or of something.

The ceremony was short and to the point – to match Brunevsky's austere funeral arrangements. Maltsev said: "Rest in peace, Andryukha." His wife added: "May the earth be soft like down to you." Others pronounced similar banalities. Unexpectedly, Gulya started to sob and Brunevsky patted her gently on the shoulder.

The casket was lowered into the grave and they all tossed clumps of reddish clay onto the lid. Most of the bouquets followed, including Gulya's lilacs, which exuded an overpowering, artificial smell, as if they had been bathed in cheap perfume. The gravediggers, working so fast their shovels sent sunbeams into the crowns of surrounding trees, quickly piled up a fresh orange mound. Shamil placed Andrei's photograph on top, along with the remaining flowers.

"Let's drink to his memory," Maltsev proposed. His wife pulled out a bottle of vodka from a shopping bag. A couple of shot glasses appeared out of nowhere. Brunevsky poured. One glass went on top of the grave, for the deceased, and the mourners drank silently from the other glass, taking turns. The gravediggers joined in. When they were done, Maltsev said, "Poor me one more."

His wife stared at him and, since Brunevsky didn't move, poured vodka into the shot glass and placed it into his hand. Maltsev raised it.

"God bless" he declared before tossing the contents into his mouth.

I don't know why, it seemed like an awkward moment, but it lasted only a few seconds before Brunevsky called out to us, "You boys want to join in?"

"We're on duty," Lenny responded grimly.

It was rude, to refuse to drink to the memory of the deceased, but Lenny still couldn't forgive Brunevsky for the way he had treated us.

As we turned to leave, I suddenly noticed that Oksana had her eyes glued to Brunevsky. Was it love? Hatred? I couldn't tell and I couldn't make out her expression.

WHEN WE WERE at the cemetery, Lenny had no idea how close he was to exacting his revenge on Brunevsky. Yet it was the question of days.

Of two days, to be exact. Two days later, we were sitting in our office under an electric fan, gasping for air and waiting for our shirts to come unglued from our backs, when Della, the Boss's secretary, rushed in.

"Matyushkin," she shouted from the threshold. "To the Boss. On the double."

She was gone before I could open my mouth to ask why I was being summoned with such urgency. I saw her tight-fitting skirt disappear around the corner as I wiped my face with a drenched handkerchief and trotted obediently after her.

"What's the matter with you," she asked when I finally caught up with her near the Boss's office. "Were you taking a swim with your clothes on? The Boss won't appreciate this look."

But Budyonny took little interest in my appearance.

"How is the case going, Lieutenant?" he asked when I got to his office.

His office was even hotter than Lenny's car, and there was even less air. Yet, the Boss sat behind his desk in his full winter uniform – a wool jacket, a blue shirt, and a tie hanging on an elastic band around his neck at a crooked angle. Regulations prescribed summer uniforms to be worn only from the start of June, regardless of the weather. The heat didn't seem to bother him – except for the dark half-moons of sweat spreading under the arms of his jacket.

"We're close to solving it," I said, trying to imbue my answer with plenty of confidence. "We have identified the perpetrators and we know who ordered the attack, but we still need to be sure about the motive."

I was wondering why the Boss wanted to hear this from me, and to hear it immediately, without delay.

"I don't know what you're talking about, Lieutenant," Budyonny said coldly. He gave up leafing through the files on his desk and raised his eyes at me, which was never a good sign.

"We think we know who attacked and robbed the used clothing stall at Danilov Market," I said.

"What used clothing stall?" the Boss roared. "Why the devil should I care about a case in which one gang of speculators decided to rob another? I don't give a damn about it, do you hear? I never want to hear this case mentioned again in this office. You wasted enough time on it. What I want to know is where you stand on the Kotov murder."

Budyonny, whose native language was Armenian, spoke Russian well, but his accent became almost impenetrable whenever he was angry or excited.

"The Kotov murder?"

I could hardly believe my ears.

"Yes, Lieutenant. The Kotov murder. Isn't that what you were supposed to be looking into?"

Now I really needed time to think. How I was supposed to answer that?

"I'm sorry, sir, I've been told—"

"Never mind what you have been told," the Boss exploded. "The African's conviction has been overturned on appeal. He has been acquitted of all charges and released. He's on his way home to Africa. Or wherever the hell he's from. And because I was worried about such an eventuality, I specifically asked you to look into this case. For your sake, Lieutenant, I sure as hell hope you have."

It took a few moments for this to sink in.

"Acquitted?" I repeated in amazement. "Why? How?"

"Never mind how. As to why – don't you ever read the papers? Didn't you see what happened in the Central African Republic?"

I stood at attention, saying nothing. It's useless to explain to the Boss that I knew nothing about international affairs and cared even less. He'd bawl me out for that just as on a different occasion he could bawl me out for trying to be smarter than I was and sticking my nose into things that didn't concern me, such as international affairs.

"There was a military coup, that's what happened. The president was shot, the government arrested. The coup leaders are bringing back Joseph Kofunda's father."

Well, now that made perfect sense, even to me. You didn't have to be a hot-shot diplomat to figure out the connection. The Soviet Union couldn't have good relations with Kofunda's father if it was still holding his son in prison.

"I did have a gut feeling something like this was going to happen sooner or later," the Boss added bitterly. "Those African devils have a way of getting you into trouble. Now they want us to find the murderer – on the double. I mean the Ministry of Foreign Affairs does. But they want it to be the real murderer this time, so that it makes sense to everyone why they let the African go."

The Boss sighed. For obvious reasons, I didn't share his dejection. On the contrary, I could have hopped and skipped for joy as I hurried back to my office down the long hallway. They needed the real murderer and – presto – I was going to produce him. Actually, a whole bunch of them – not just Shamil and his accomplice Gulya Aliyeva, but also the guy who ordered the killing, the gangster Arkady Brunevsky.

The first monumental thunderclap shook the building as I entered my office. I had slowed down to make my entry weightier. The flash of lightening, the deafening thunderclap, and the blackening of the daylight outside our window made my entry even a little too dramatic, like that of the Stone Guest in the last act of Pushkin's play about Don Juan.

I did feel a bit like an implacable avenger.

"Guess what," I announced once I was in. "Kofunda has been acquitted and released. And now it is our job to find Kotov's real killers. I mean the *real* ones."

Lenny's brains must have melted in the heat. It took him more than a minute to grasp the meaning of what I had said and to work out the implications. Then he jumped up from under the fan and performed some sort of a war dance in the narrow space between our desks. When the first raindrops began to drum a tattoo on the ledge outside our window and a gust of wind slammed it shut nearly smashing its panes, he stopped, unlocked the bottom drawer of his desk and pulled out the shank that had killed Kotov.

"You'll get your day in the son, my baby," he told the shank before placing it carefully back in the drawer.

THIRTY-TWO

We were on the brink of the greatest success of our careers—not just because we were going to bring the murderers to justice but because we were going to do it swiftly, almost as soon as the Boss had put us back on the job.

Only a few details remained to be worked out.

Lenny and I were in a great mood and in a state of unbridled elation, rubbing our hands in anticipation. Especially Lenny. A fatuous smile filled his face and his eyes glazed over dreamily now and again when he imagined how we would arrive to Brunevsky's house with an arrest warrant for Shamil.

Lenny's dreams notwithstanding, I thought we should start by checking the unidentified fingerprints on the handle of the shank. We would be on firmer ground if we found that they had belonged to Shamil – rather than to Klava, for example.

But Lenny, in his current state of excitement, had no patience for that kind of scrupulous desk work. He felt triumphant, he was eager to act. Trying to get him to sit still even for a moment was hopeless.

The question was where to start. I believed that we should start in Mazilov and to have a heart-to-heart with Gulya Aliyeva first. I was no longer laboring under the illusion that she was a weak link in their chain, but I was still convinced that we could get more out of her than out of Brunevsky, based on our two visits to his place of residence. Using what we now knew, we should be able to get her to finger Shamil as Kotov's killer and to tell us why he was killed in the first place. She might also identify her boss as the one who ordered the killing. She was an accomplice and unless she cooperated, she was looking at a lengthy jail term.

And, into the bargain, we may finally find out what exactly happened that day at Danilov Market, who really attacked Oksana and why.

But Lenny had his dreams of revenge and he would not let go of them. He was itching to get back at Brunevsky. He wanted to start with him and there was nothing I could say to make him change his mind.

In the end I gave in. The case was coming to an end – both cases, in fact. Did it really matter so much in what order we finished it? It wasn't worth haggling over.

We were about to leave when the office phone rang. Lenny, who had gone ahead of me into the hallway, returned and picked up the receiver. He listened intently for a few seconds, then said:

"Calm down. Speak slowly. I can't understand a word you're saying."

This time he listened for a much longer stretch, repeating "Yes" and "I see" a few times and concluding: "Please, get hold of yourself. I'm sure he'll turn up. Eh? What? You don't think so? Well, let's see what we can do."

He replaced the receiver.

"It's Oksana," he said. "She says her father has disappeared."

I shook my head: "When? How?"

"Might have been kidnapped. Nothing is known yet. Yesterday morning Maltsev was home alone. When his wife got back from the food store, she discovered him gone. He sometimes goes out for a walk – and may go out to buy cigarettes by himself when he runs out. There are a couple of other routes around the neighborhood he's familiar with, on which he sometimes ventures out by himself. But this time he left without his cane. That has never happened before."

"I'd say."

"He didn't come back, and after a while they started to get worried. And then a neighbor told them that he was seen walking downstairs with two men and the three of them got into a car."

"Did she call Brunevsky? Maybe Maltsev was distraught by the death of his friend, Brunevsky sent a car for him and they drank themselves silly?" I suggested.

"I don't know," Lenny said. "But we'll find out soon enough. Let's go pay Brunevsky a visit."

But now I put my foot down. Sure, Maltsev might turn up at Brunevsky's place or at one of his other friends' once he sobered up. But what if he had been kidnapped? That would surely be tied in with the Danilov Market case.

I was convinced it was serious. Otherwise, Oksana would not have called Lenny.

"We need to go to Mazilov," I said.

"Are you kidding?" Lenny cried out.

"*Nyet*," I said. "We need to move fast and start with Gulya Aliyeva. We stand a much better chance cracking her than getting anywhere with Brunevsky."

In the end, having stood at the threshold of our office for about fifteen minutes arguing fruitless, Lenny said:

"I'll tell you what. Why don't you go to see Gulya and I go to see Brunevsky? It will be more efficient and, in any case, you're investigating Kotov's murder, while I'm working on the Danilov Market attack. We have lumped the two cases together, but they can remain separate, too."

My memories of Lenny's overheated Moskvich were still fresh and I was glad to get on my Zundapp. While Lenny and I were arguing, the sky had cleared, and the day felt freshly washed of the heat, humidity and stickiness of the past several days.

I headed out of town. The road was nearly empty. My engine was making its usual amount of noise and spewing its quota of bluish smoke as I sped past the factories and warehouses and the villages that began once I crossed the outer boundary of the city. Brunevsky's apartment building was easier to find in daylight. The whole trip took just over an hour.

Gulya answered the doorbell almost immediately. She greeted me quietly, looking down as she let me in, and stood aside while I walked past her to the living room.

A surprise awaited me there. Sitting at the glass-top table was Arkady Matveyich Brunevsky. Even though it was mid-afternoon, he was dressed in a pair of checkered flannel pajamas.

Seeing him made me think of Lenny. I had killed both birds with one stone while he drew a blank. Unless of course he was having a productive discussion with Shamil. I wondered about that.

"Oh, it's you," Brunevsky said. "I was afraid it was going to be Oksana. She's been chasing after me lately."

I stared at him. On my way to Mazilov, I had given considerable thought to how I was going to handle Gulya, but I was unprepared to face Brunevsky.

"Do you know why she's trying to get in touch with you?" I asked.

Brunevsky nodded.

"And do you know why I'm here?"

Brunevsky nodded again.

"Let's have a talk," he said. Then, turning to Gulya, he commanded: "Go take a walk."

"Oh, no," I interposed quickly. "I may end up charging her. She can't leave the apartment."

"She's not going to run away," Brunevsky said wearily. "But, if you insist, she will wait in the kitchen."

There was a sadness in his face. He looked older, smaller, hunched over. His infirmity, his helplessness, which had until now been camouflaged by his energy, his powerful forearms, and the mocking expression on his face, was suddenly starkly evident.

THIRTY-THREE

Brunevsky was hoarse by the end, but so was I, even though I had done very little talking. The sun had set and the room with its fancy modern furniture and rare antique objects, and all the books on the bookshelves, had lost its contours in the weak evening light. Brunevsky had not turned on the light and I could see his curly head silhouetting against the window and the whiteness of the tulle curtains.

While we were talking, Gulya had been in the kitchen, and she too stayed in the darkness, with the door shut. I don't know whether she could hear what Brunevsky had told me, but it probably didn't matter.

"I have to decide what I'm going to do," I said when he was done. "I'll let you know, but I don't want you to leave town. Neither of you," I gestured toward the kitchen.

"Where do you think we're going to go, Lieutenant?" Brunevsky asked.

"I don't know," I said. "But if you try to run, you'll force my hand."

"Run?"

He guffawed loudly. There was bitterness in his voice.

I got back to the city in the middle of the night. I was riding slowly; I was not in a rush. I needed to think.

Tosya came to me when May's early dawn was brightening the sky outside my window.

"Do you want me to leave?" she asked in an anxious whisper when she saw the look on my face.

"No, please stay," I said.

We put our arms around each other and lay like that for a long time. Her breath became soft and even and she began to snore lightly. I was wide awake, sorting out what I had learned.

When the sun peeked over the metal roofs and lit up the edge of the floor in my room, I gently shook Tosya by the shoulder. She wanted to be back in her room by the time Sevka's alarm went off, to get him up and ready for school. They went out together on most days, he to go to his first class, and she to take the metro to the Tryokhgorka plant.

The phone rang in the hallway the moment she got out of bed. Barefoot and wearing only a pair of underwear I rushed out to answer it, since the call was almost certainly for me. I had not yet heard from Lenny, and it was only natural he would be eager to talk to me now.

But instead of my partner's voice, the receiver greeted me with Sumarokov's aristocratic baritone. As usual, he got right to the point – which I didn't mind. I was not in the mood to exchange pleasantries.

"Lieutenant, I assume I don't need to explain to you the circumstances surrounding the Kotov murder case," he said. "Your Boss should have put you in the picture. It's unfortunate the way it turned out, but there's nothing that can be done about it now. Naturally, we have issued an official apology to Mr. Kofunda. Judicial mistakes are a reality of life and our African friends understand that."

I listened in silence, waiting to see where he was going. There had to be a reason why he was telling me all this.

"However, there is a slight problem. Quite unreasonably, Mr. Kofunda, Senior, who is once again the leader of his country, believes the vile lies spread by French newspapers that Comrade Kotov's murder was a political assassination, and that his son was framed for it by our government in order to curry favor with his predecessor. Needless to say, it is complete nonsense, but Mr. Kofunda persists in his accusations. To prove that it was an ordinary crime, he wants the culprit to be found – and the motive for the killing presented to his government. He wants to make sure the Soviet government has had no hand in it. How do you like that?"

Sumarokov suddenly sounded peevish, self-pitying, completely out of character. It was as if the man's professional skin had been peeled off and I was being treated to a glimpse of the real person beneath the polished, diplomatic veneer.

"We could of course make use of the services of Major Yegorov and his ilk," the man went on. "But I have a feeling they're going to screw it up yet again – the way they screwed up with Kofunda, inveigling him into signing a confession—"

I see, I said to myself, it is now all Major Yegorov's fault. He's been appointed chief scapegoat for this mess. A transfer or early retirement now surely loomed for the poor sod.

Tosya came out of my room and waved to me from the other end of the long corridor. I made frantic signs to her, meant to indicate that I was almost finished talking and that she should wait for me, but she went out, shutting the front door carefully behind her.

"We need a real professional on the job," Sumarokov was droning into my ear. "We rely on you, Lieutenant, to find the culprit. And please, no tricks this time. Just do solid detective work and find the murderer. It's all that is required of you. If you need assistance – anything at all – call us. We have very impressive resources which I will personally place at your disposal. And trust me, if you're successful, your efforts will not go unrewarded."

How easy it could have been. I have to admit, I was tempted to tell Comrade Sumarokov right there and then that the case had been solved and the murderer had been found. But all I said was "Yes, Sir, I'll do my best."

"Hm," Sumarokov said on the other end before hanging up.

I went back to my room, made my bed and got dressed. Then I went outside. It was a beautiful morning. The birds were singing. No traffic noise reached our courtyard from Kirov Street. Curtains started to be drawn in the windows as my neighbors were waking up and getting ready to go to work.

A jogger came out of the building across the courtyard, did a couple of stretching exercises and started toward Frolov Lane and the boulevards. I envied him. A couple of years ago I had resolved to get up early and jog every morning in order to get back in shape. I even quit smoking for an entire week. I did it exactly twice before laziness took its toll.

I lit a cigarette. If I had been in the least paranoid, I would have been convinced that the Ministry of Foreign Affairs was not only tailing me but had penetrated my thoughts, as well. It was the second time that Eduard Vasilyevich Sumarokov had called me at a pivotal moment, as if prompting me to do the right thing – from their point of view – just as I had been planning to do the exact opposite.

Damn it. It would have been so easy, I repeated to myself. I knew exactly what happened at Lumumba University, who killed Kotov and why. I could just arrest the killer, write up a report, and make a hole on my epaulets for a captain's fourth star. And all I would be doing is performing my professional duty. Telling the truth. Punishing the guilty.

While at it, I could also charge Klava the cleaning woman with obstruction of justice.

I stood there for a long time. I watched from afar as Tosya and Sevka came out of their front door. She bent down and Sevka gave her a quick smooch on the cheek after casting a furtive glance left and right to make sure none of his buddies was around to see him. Then he broke free of her hug and ran off.

I got to the office at twenty minutes to nine. Lenny wasn't there yet. All the offices on our hallway were empty, which was unusual but not extraordinary, since the workday didn't officially start until nine. But when it got to be nine thirty and then quarter to ten and Lenny still didn't up, and none of other detectives were there either, I began to be concerned. Lenny's absence was especially galling. He is never late for work and yet he had decided to be on the one day I badly needed his advice.

Della, Budyonny's secretary, was at her desk, her blonde beehive sticking out from behind a pile of papers and a typewriter.

"Where is everybody?" I asked in a conspiratorial whisper. I didn't want to attract the Boss's attention. It might have been an unnecessary precaution because, even if he were in his office, his door was soundproof.

"You don't know?" Della arched an eyebrow disapprovingly. "Your partner is in the hospital and you have no idea?"

My heart sank. I must admit I had not given much thought to Lenny's visit to Brunevsky. The image of Shamil standing behind Lenny, literally breathing down his neck and looking daggers, flashed before my eyes.

"I don't know where you've been, Pavel. He's been attacked by a dog. He should've shot the damn thing, but you know how he is. He has a soft spot for women, children and animals."

So that what it was, Brunevsky's German shepherd. At least he wasn't shot or stabbed, and that was a relief.

"Where is he? Which hospital?"

"The Sklif. The guys went to see him this morning. I don't know why you didn't."

"I didn't know," I said as I turned to leave.

Budyonny was the last person I wanted to see just then, but as I was walking out of his reception area, he stuck his head out to ask something of Della. Most of the time, he would call her on the internal line, but now luck would have it that he needed something in person.

"Aha, Matyushkin," he exclaimed. "I've been wanting to talk to you. Step into my office, will you?"

Reluctantly, I went in, with the Boss holding the door open to let me through.

"I hope you're working on the Kotov murder," he said, hauling himself up into the chair behind his desk. His desk loomed over the room and sitting at it made him seem seven feet tall.

"Yes, Comrade Colonel," I responded. "I'm going to have results fairly soon."

"I'm glad to hear that," Budyonny said. "Because your partner is doing very strange things. He has contrived to get himself attacked by a dog and he needs to get a whole slew of shots to make sure he's not going to get rabies. I've had plenty of cops under my command injured, but none who was mauled by a rabid dog."

He fell silent, as was his want, then leafed through a file for a few minutes while I was chomping on the bit, desperate to get out.

"I'm sure you thought me a fool telling you to go poke your nose in the Kotov murder," the Boss said when he finally came back to reality. "Don't deny it, I know you did." He waved his hand, seeing that I was about to protest. "But you should have trusted me. I know that when you get involved with foreigners, especially Africans, there will be nothing but trouble. Now Major Yegorov will be cashiered. And what did he do wrong I ask you? He got the guy to confess, just as those smart alecks from the Foreign Ministry demanded he do. Anyway, I won't miss him, to be honest with you. He has always been bad news, that Yegorov."

He sighed.

"In any case, the sooner you produce the culprit – any culprit – the better. But the charges had better stick, d'you hear?"

Having started on a friendly note, the Boss ended with a threat, even raising his voice and nearly shouting at me at the end.

SKLIFOSOVSKY HOSPITAL, KNOWN simply as Sklif, is the best in the city. It was built at the turn of the nineteenth century and some of the babushka patients sitting in the park in front of it, breathing the exhaust wafting in from traffic-clogged Garden Ring, look like they've been there for at least that long.

The clerk at the information window had a plump round face with full lips and red cheeks, as though she had been placed there to torment the ailing and the infirm with a vision of robust good health.

Instead of directing me where I needed to go, he pointed to a sign that stated that visiting hours were from five to six in the evening daily and from five to seven on Sundays. I pulled out my Criminal

Investigations ID. She ignored it and continued to copy from one ledger to another. I waved the document in front of her face, to no avail. Apparently, good health went with the enviable ability to ignore those who were seeking information at the information window.

Fortunately, at that moment I spotted a group of our guys descending the imposing main staircase. They assured me that Lenny was out of danger and explained where to find him, thus taking over the functions of the information desk.

The hospital building was designed by one of those Italian architects who made Leningrad such an elegant city, but it's an old building and old buildings tend to be confusing. It took me a few more minutes to locate the trauma unit in the labyrinth of corridors, and then to find Lenny's room.

He was in a pretty bad shape. His hands and feet were bandaged, and gauze covered his right cheek. His face was pale and drawn. He could speak, albeit uncharacteristically softly. He still looked like the old Lenny, my best friend and partner, except somewhat deflated.

The walls of his room were painted obnoxious yellow. Five other beds, empty and unmade, stood in two rows in the middle of the room. The place smelled of antiseptic and stale bedding. Staying there in and of itself seemed detrimental to convalescence.

"It was a ferocious battle," Lenny said. "But I won."

He was embarrassed by what had happened and tried to make light of his condition. He was eager to hear about my trip to Mazilov, but I insisted he told me first what happened to him.

He had no one but himself to blame. He rang the bell at Brunevsky's front gate, got no answer and, after ringing it a few more times, gave the gate a push. It turned out to be unlocked. He shouted Brunevsky's name and went in, forgetting that there was that German shepherd guarding the house.

At first it went well. The dog showed no hostility toward Lenny. It waited for him to approach the house and only then got to its feet, cutting off his retreat. The length of its chain allowed the dog to reach everywhere except the remote corner of the yard.

"It's a weird animal," Lenny said. "It neither barked nor growled. Just fought silently and doggedly. Like a contract killer."

After standing in the corner pinned to the wall for a while, Lenny made several attempts to break for the gate, each of which was cut short by the ferocious beast. Shooting it was out of the question, Lenny claimed. The reason he wasn't killed was the chain, which he could grab and keep the monster off him for short periods.

After an hour of this, exhausted and bleeding, Lenny finally hit upon a solution. He got his gun out and fired it in the air. Whether the dog was genuinely frightened or regarded a man with a gun as its master, it slunk into the doghouse and let Lenny leave.

The last thing he remembered before passing out in the street was asking a passerby to call an ambulance.

"I wouldn't be surprised if that bastard Brunevsky was at home all along, watching us out the window," Lenny concluded. "I'm going to kill him when I get a little better."

Recounting the story tired him out. He fell silent, catching his breath.

"Now what about you?" he asked after a while. "How did you do with Gulya? Not nearly as much excitement, I bet."

I was about to tell him what I had found out and share with him what I was planning to do, but I was interrupted by the arrival of a nurse.

"You have no shame," she announced from the threshold. "You beg to be allowed a half-hour visit by your coworkers and then they stick around for the entire day. Didn't I just kick out the whole bunch of you?"

"It wasn't him," Lenny objected. "The others left, just as you said they should. By the way, this is Nurse Zoya. And this is my partner Senior Lieutenant Matyushkin. He is not married, but he is in a relationship. I wouldn't tangle with his girlfriend if I were you, Zoyechka."

Nurse Zoya snorted contemptuously.

"Either way, he's got to go. I need to take your temperature and change the bandages. On your way, Lieutenant. Give my best to your girlfriend."

In the end, I was glad she stopped me. My mind was made up. I should not get Lenny involved in the kind of thing I was about to do.

THIRTY-FOUR

My next stop was Kotov's apartment. Oleg was at school, and I was sure to catch Malvina Kotova alone. I wanted to know more about something she had mentioned in passing, on the day we met at the zoo. It involved the transaction between her late husband and Rubashkin, the black-market car dealer and the murderer of my friend Nastya.

"Let's go out," the widow suggested. "The neighbors are so nosey, they eavesdrop on everything I say. It has got worse now that Valentin Viktorovich is no more, because they were afraid of him."

Living at a communal apartment is an art. You share everything – the kitchen, the bathtub, the toilet – and then split the bills and keep to the cleaning schedule. There are two ways of doing it: you can either live in peace or wage a perpetual war. Some people thrive on good relations with their neighbors, others relish a good fight. The worst-case scenario is when you crave peace but get constant squabbles. Then your life becomes hell, you're permanently harassed and unhappy.

But I didn't mind being overheard by Kotova's neighbors. They could corroborate my account if a corroboration was needed.

As Malvina had suggested to me, Kotov's purchase of the car had not gone smoothly. Deals between private citizens and professional crooks rarely do. The former get swindled—and that's in the nature of the game. Crooks have a term for their victims – *frayers*. A *frayer* is pretty much everyone who doesn't belong to the community of thieves and is therefore fair game. It would have been a blow to Rubashkin's professional reputation if he hadn't taken advantage of an inexperienced *frayer* such as Kotov.

The question I needed answered was whether Kotov had been aware that he had been had, and if so, what he had intended to do about it.

It turned out that soon after buying the car, Kotov complained to his wife that he might have overpaid for it – by as much as one thousand rubles. He had a talk with Rubashkin and threatened to go to the cops, at which point Rubashkin laughed in his face. Naturally, black-market dealers enjoy high level protection, which is the main reason we can never put them out of business.

"Eventually Valentin Viktorovich decided to drop it," Malvina concluded. "Even though his fists were itching to teach the scoundrel a lesson."

That was very good news.

Malvina kept a black and white photograph on the bookshelf, a wartime snapshot of a group of soldiers and a lieutenant. She had given a copy of it to Lenny and I had seen it before, but I gave it another look just to make sure. The lieutenant was Kotov – younger, with jet-black hair and a dashing mustache, still easily recognizable. Next to him was a skinny private at the end of the middle row on the right – a very typical Russian kid, very ordinary looking but somehow memorable in his ordinariness. A couple of days ago I had seen his enlarged portrait on a freshly made orange mound at Vagankovo Cemetery.

I was glad to see that picture in the Kotovs' room. Not that I doubted what Brunevsky had told me, but it was nice to get a confirmation.

Now I was ready to turn my attention to Rubashkin.

Rubashkin is a cautious type. To see him, you have to go through friends of friends and intermediaries and make an appointment a few weeks in advance. But I had been keeping track of him ever since Nastya's death and I knew where to find him.

Perovo is located a couple of kilometers inside the new Ring Road. The town had only recently been incorporated into Greater Moscow.

It still had odd structures with no clear function standing along the grandly named Enthusiasts Highway and awaiting their turn to be bulldozed – to make room for new high-rise apartments.

Before going to see him, I checked back at the headquarters. Everyone except Lenny was back. The customary hum of voices and bluish cigarette smoke were seeping out of the smoking room and spreading down the hallways.

I opened the bottom drawer of Lenny's desk and took out the shank. I removed the plastic that now enclosed it and carefully separated the blade from the handle. I put the blade aside and wiped the handle clean. I was fully conscious that I was tampering with evidence and that was severe dereliction of duty. I placed the hand in a plastic bag and dropped it in my pocket. I replaced the blade in the drawer and locked the desk.

The old name of Enthusiasts Highway was Vladimir Tract, and it was the road that connected Moscow to the nearby town of Vladimir. From there it ran further east, through the swamps and forests beyond the Urals. It was the starting point for convicts as they were transported to Siberia. There are songs about the Vladimir Tract, mostly melancholy and sentimental. In the old days, the journey was made on foot, with convicts clapped in irons and guarded by soldiers.

I grinned as I got onto Enthusiasts Highway, because it seemed so appropriate for what I was about to do.

Rubashkin's headquarters was marked by a bent and rusty shingle proclaiming it to be a Perovo truck maintenance facility. The gate that gave onto the road was padlocked, and the driveway was overgrown with weeds. To a cursory observer, the place looked abandoned. You had to go in from the back, and there, once you got behind the tall fence topped with barbed wire, you would see that the workshops over the garage had been converted into a kind of cozy private social club with pool tables, card tables, couches, and a fully stocked bar.

The place also housed Rubashkin's inventory – not too many humble Moskvich subcompacts or even upscale Volgas and Pobedas, but mostly luxurious ZIL and ZIS limousines, in which party and government officials were typically driven around.

A rarity – a Volkswagen bug, light green and with a patch of rust running along the passenger door – had been give the place of honor.

What you wouldn't see in this truck maintenance shop were trucks. Nor were there any mechanics in dirty overalls, with grease up to their elbows. This was a showroom for hand-picked, thoroughly vetted customers.

A muscular young man looking like a rugby player finally deigned to answer my persistent knocking. He looked over my Zundapp, made a face and left me standing outside, on the dusty driveway.

"You planning to trade your pile of junk for a vehicle?" he asked when I told him I wanted to see Rubashkin.

"Not right away," I replied, adapting his smart aleck tone. "I'm with Moscow Criminal Investigations. I want to ask your boss a few questions."

The man left and was gone for a long time. Finally, the gate opened again. Rubashkin come out to greet me. The rugby player's round head was bobbing over his shoulder.

"What do you want?"

"You sold a car that was defective," I said.

Rubashkin shrugged.

"It's of no concern to me," he said coldly. "I sell vehicles as is, my customers know that. It's a buyer-beware kind of world, the Moscow used car market."

"Not when the person who bought a car from you is killed," I said. "The car appears to have been rigged in order to kill the driver. If that was done on purpose you'll be charged with murder."

Rubashkin was a tall, gaunt man of about forty, dressed in a checkered cowboy shirt and in need of a shave. I had seen him once before, when Nastya was alive.

"Wait a second," he said. "What car are you talking about. What did you say was the name of the client?"

He wasn't worried yet but starting to get concerned.

"The name is Ivan Mikhaylovich Petrov," I replied. "But it wasn't him who died. It was his young wife. Naturally, Comrade Petrov is extremely upset, and he has very good connections at the very top."

Rubashkin shrugged, relieved.

"I don't know what you're talking about. I have never heard the name."

"Don't try to deny it," I said. "All the papers are in order and your signature are all over them."

"Nonsense," Rubashkin said. "I never sign anything myself."

"You will have to explain this to the judge," I said, pulling out the handle of the knife that killed Kotov. "Look at what had been placed in the engine."

"Let me see," he said.

He took it, brought it close to his eyes, frowned. For a moment, it made no sense to him. All that strange talk about a guy whom he didn't know buying a car from him, the accident, the rigging of the car. He stared at the handle for a minute, then back at me when he realized what it was. And then he recognized me. He was not dumb. He knew who I was and what I was doing. Not in detail, but in general terms. He got the picture.

He tossed the handle to the ground, but it was too late. I retrieved it from the dust and replaced it in the plastic bag.

My next stop was Major Yegorov's office at the Southwestern District headquarters. My visit was very brief. Major Yegorov came out to greet me personally, and to usher me into his office. I placed the blade, now once more connected to its handle and sealed in plastic, on his desk.

"What is it?" Yegorov asked, eyeing me suspiciously.

"It's a murder weapon in the Kotov case," I said. "Be careful with it, the killer's fingerprints may still be on the handle. Check them against your files. If you don't get a match, check with the Eastern District. There is a black-market car dealer to whom they may belong."

Major Yegorov stared. His lips were still stretched in an obsequious smile, but his eyes were full of distrust. What on earth this fancy Criminal Investigations detective is playing at, they seemed to wonder.

"Why are you giving it to me?" he finally thought of asking.

I leaned over his desk. At close range he smelled of sweat, cheap tobacco, and aftershave.

"The Ministry of Foreign Affairs," I said softly. "Secret orders. From the very top."

He nodded. I leaned back.

"You see," I explained in my normal voice, "it turns out that Comrade Kotov bought a car from that character and they had an argument about the transaction. Comrade Kotov was threatening to go to the cops and get them to shut down the guy's business."

Major Yegorov kept staring at me. His mind was working feverishly, I could almost hear the cogs turning. He couldn't understand what had just happened, except that, with his highly developed instinct for self-preservation, he could grasp that it could save him from being cashiered. Yet, it could also turn out to be a trap that would land him in even greater trouble. He didn't trust me for a minute.

I left him to sort out all those possibilities.

THIRTY-FIVE

Friday of that week was an eventful day. First came the good news: Lenny was released from the hospital. I went to visit him at his house, and he gave me the second piece of good news: Anton Rubashkin, a notorious car thief and dealer who controlled the black market for cars in Moscow, had been arrested and charged with the murder of poet Valentin Kotov.

Except Lenny didn't think that was good news at all.

"They're now saying Rubashkin sold him a shoddy car, Kotov threatened to go to the cops and Rubashkin did him in," Lenny said, looking puzzled. "What about Gulya? What about Brunevsky? What happened?"

I did my best to look puzzled, too.

"They who?" I asked.

"Major Yegorov. The Southwestern District. He's the one who arrested Rubashkin."

I shook my head in amazement.

"How do you know that?"

"Gromkovsky came to see me. He just left five minutes ago. What about that shank that we have? What about Gulya?"

Gromkovsky was another member of the Boss's team. Lenny, who tended to fight with most other detectives, was friendly with Gromkovsky.

"Damn it," I said. "I got another call from Sumarokov. Somehow, he knew I had the shank. He told me to take it to Yegorov."

"You see," Lenny declared triumphantly. "I told you it was a plant. There had to be a reason why Klava passed it on to you."

"But why?" I asked. "For what purpose?"

I felt bad about lying to my partner and making a fool of him, but having started, I had to carry on.

"I have no idea," Lenny shrugged. "Maybe they had a plan, but it got changed once they had to let Kofunda go. Now of course you're in hot water. Gromkovsky says Budyonny has been in a rage all morning, screaming that we missed a great opportunity. He's singled you out, too. You know how mad it makes him, when someone gets the better of us."

My dismay was almost genuine.

"This is some kind of a joke," I said, shaking my head. "It's the second time they have screwed up, I mean Major Yegorov and his crew. Two times out of two they have nabbed the wrong man."

"So you're sue that Rubashkin is not the real killer?"

"He is not."

"Why are you so sure?"

"Because. Brunevsky told me who killed Kotov."

Lenny stared.

"Was it Shamil?"

"No, Lenny," I said. "It was Brunevsky's daughter."

"That's a new one. You knew even that he had a daughter. Who is she?"

I paused for effect. "Gulya Aliyeva," I said.

Lenny shook his head. The information was coming in too thick and fast for him.

"She started an affair with Kotov about a month before the murder," I continued. "Remember one of his students told you that a young woman was waiting for him while he was teaching a class at the Literary Institute? I'm pretty sure it was she."

"Did she pretend to be from Argentina?" Lenny asked.

"No. Not to him. He knew who she was. I mean he knew she was a young woman from Azerbaijan. He invited her to come to his reading at Lumumba and she jokingly suggested she'd pretend to be an Argentinian student. After the reading she went into that room and stabbed him."

"With a weapon that had been made in prison?"

Lenny shook his head. None of it made sense to him. I would have been the same way had I been in his place.

"Her real name is Anya Kerimova. But even that is not the name she was born with. The name she was born with was Brunevskaya."

Lenny shook his head again.

"If you say so."

"Had we known to look up Kerimova in our files, we would have discovered that she had done a year and a half at a juvenile offenders' facility and another two at a labor camp. The reason she lives in Mazilov is because as a convicted felon she can't live in Moscow."

"And she is Brunevsky's daughter?"

"She is," I said. "During the war Brunevsky was a frontline surgeon. At one point, he punched a SMERSH officer. He was arrested and sent to a *shtrafbat*. When he lost his legs clearing land mines, he decided not to go back to his wife and daughter. He thought it would make her life easier. But he was wrong. The SMERSH officer was a vengeful son of a bitch. They arrested Brunevsky's wife, too, and his daughter was taken to an orphanage for the kids of the enemies of the people. Brunevsky's wife died in a labor camp before the war was over, and all the traces of their daughter were erased."

Lenny frowned. He was the father of two little girls. Any mention of kids' suffering filled him with outrage.

I went on: "Brunevsky kept looking for her. But the problem was that she had been too little when she was taken away from her mother to even remember her own name. They called her Anya Kerimova at an orphanage in Azerbaijan, where she grew up, and she thought it was her real name. Eventually, like many other kids growing up in those places, she fell in with a wrong crowd, began to steal, was arrested and put away. It was only after her second jail term that Brunevsky finally found her."

"And Gulya, where did that name come from?" Lenny asked.

"Just some fake passport they were using to conceal her real identity."

"Why would she want kill Kotov? A crime of passion?"

"That's all he thinks about, passion. Even after a dog had nearly unmanned him."

Lenny's wife Raisa had walked into the room, in time to hear his last words.

"Joking aside, we were worried about him, the girls and I," she said. "He should have shot that dog. It was legitimate self-defense. You should tell him, Pavel. He's got a wife and two daughters to think about. We should be his first priority, not some stupid German shepherd. How are you, by the way?"

She took off her coat, changed into a house dress behind a screen, and departed to the kitchen to make chicken broth. She was a strong believer in the healing power of chicken broth.

Lenny was eager for me to continue and resented the interruption. He was starting to believe my story.

"There was no passion," I said. "It was strictly business."

"Money?"

"*Nyet*, my friend. Revenge."

"Revenge for what?"

"Remember you told me that during the war Kotov had been with an NKVD unit? You brought a photograph of him that Malvina Kotova had given to you? When we attended Andrei Nikolin's funeral, I kind of thought that the dead man, or rather his picture as a young guy, looked familiar. I checked it: he was in that same wartime photograph in the Kotovs room."

"He and Kotov knew each other?"

"Only too well. Kotov was his commanding officer. Their unit was on rearguard duty. Their job was to machine gun frontline infantrymen if they refused to advance or turned tail. Basically, if you're on the front line you had a good chance of being killed or maimed by German fire or an absolute certainty of being mowed down by your own. And then, in addition to being killed, your family would be punished because you were a coward and a deserter.

"Andrei at one point refused to fire on his own men. He had a nervous breakdown and told Kotov that he was tired of murdering Russian soldiers and getting medals for it. Kotov got him court-martialed and sent to a *shtrafbat*. You don't want to send others to clear minefields? Very well then, try doing it yourself."

"Natural selection," Lenny muttered darkly.

"A few years ago, Andrei heard Kotov on the radio, reading his war poems. That was soon after Brunevsky got him off the death trap that was Valaam Island. Hearing Kotov being lauded as a war hero got to him. He became obsessed with the man. He couldn't do the man any harm himself, but he got Brunevsky to give him his word that he would get Kotov killed. The Samovar lived for it in his last years, but Brunevsky kept finding excuses why he had to postpone the killing. I think he was hoping that Andrei would eventually get over his fixation.

"But then the Samovar got terminal cancer. He pressed Brunevsky to keep his promise before he, Andrei, died. Reluctantly, Brunevsky began to plot Kotov's murder. For starters, he sent his daughter to get in good with Kotov."

"Not a very nice thing to do," Lenny interjected.

"They're not very nice guys. Anyway, Andrei's condition deteriorated much faster than anyone had expected. He wasn't going to last long. Brunevsky would never have sent his daughter to do the murder, but she took matters into her own hands. She liked the Samovar, or rather felt sorry for him. I guess his broken life reminded her of hers. Andrei insisted that Kotov be killed with a shank fashioned for him by a buddy on Valaam. He passed it to her in secret, and she stabbed Kotov with it after the reading. It was a reckless thing to do, and Brunevsky was furious with her. Fortunately for her, there had been that African student, Kofunda, on whom the murder was pinned. At least for a time."

"And now she's been lucky a second time," Lenny observed.

Raisa entered the room carrying a pot which exuded an appetizing smell. Chicken broth is not a sophisticated dish, but Raisa had a magic touch. She could make even the most ordinary dish look, smell, and taste like something served at the finest hard currency restaurant in Moscow.

"Sit down to have lunch with us, Pavel," she announced, seeing me stand up.

"*Nyet*, Raisochka, I'm afraid I've got to leave," I said, making a face. "I'm in hot water with the Boss, and if I stay out of the office any longer there will be hell to pay."

"So, what are you going to do about it?" Lenny asked.

I shrugged, pretending to think it over.

"I suppose there is nothing I can do about it," I said.

"I don't think you can," Lenny agreed. "Rubashkin hasn't been tried yet, but the verdict is in. It's clear by this setup that the Ministry of Foreign Affairs is determined to nab him for the murder."

I nodded.

"Rubashkin makes a far better-looking murderer than a disabled war veteran and his young daughter," I said. "No African country on earth would protest if a car thief is sent to jail."

"And you for one are not going to shed any tears for Rubashkin, either, even if he's completely innocent," Lenny added. "Didn't you have a score to settle with—"

He broke off suddenly.

"You guys. I can never figure out what you're talking about," Raisa said. "Come on, Lenny. Get yourself to the table. The chicken broth is getting cold and you should have it while it's hot."

Lenny waved her away. He kept silent for a few more seconds, figuring things out in his head, then burst out laughing. He laughed hard and for a long time, and Raisa was standing there dumbfounded, wondering what she had said that was so funny.

"Oy, you're a smart one, Matyushkin," Lenny said at last, wiping away tears with his bandaged hand. "You almost had me fooled. But I predict you'll outsmart yourself one of these days, you son of a bitch."

I snuck out of their room trying to look as innocent as I could manage.

EPILOGUE

A third thing happened that day, but it happened late at night and we didn't find out about it until next morning.

Stepan Maltsev's body was fished out of the Moscow River a few kilometers downstream from the city. There was no sign of foul play on the body. He had drowned, and the doctors said he had been in the water for several days, which jibed with the date of his disappearance. There was water in his lungs, and it was the river water. The man had drowned. His death was ruled a suicide, which was not a rare thing with men in his condition.

The investigation into the attack on Oksana was eventually dropped. The Boss gave Lenny and me quite a talking to on account of the time we had wasted, with nothing to show for it. I took it lightly. I had grown accustomed to his reprimands and lectures since he had been calling me into his office regularly and dwelling on my professional incompetence as revealed in the Kotov murder case.

I could not tell him what I knew about the murder. Nor could I tell Lenny what I knew about the Danilov Market attack and Maltsev's death.

Stepan Maltsev, Brunevsky told me, had been stealing money for years while he was deputy director of the Danilov Market, a position which Brunevsky had arranged for him.

That he was stealing from the state no one gave a damn about. But he was stealing from his friends, too. From Brunevsky and his associates, some of whom were men of respect, the big bosses of the criminal underworld. It didn't come out until Maltsev had retired, but when it did, the sentence passed on the blind man by the thieves' community was restitution and death.

First restitution, then death.

Brunevsky had a talk with his old friend and put the cards on the table. Maltsev explained that he had started to steal in order to support the Samovar, to whom he was bound by a pact they made when they were both beggars in the early years after the war. It didn't matter. The matter was out of Brunevsky's hands.

He and Brunevsky put together the required sum – the full amount Maltsev had stolen from the *obshchag*, or the common pot of the criminal fraternity, plus a stiff penalty – but the moment the money was paid out, the contract on Maltsev would go out. Brunevsky held on to the money as long as he could. He didn't want Andrei to see Maltsev lose his life on his account.

The criminals knew nothing about this arrangement and cared even less. They kept telling Brunevsky to turn up the heat under Maltsev. Otherwise they'd do it themselves, they warned him. Brunevsky finally decided to stage an attack on Oksana. Shamil and Gulya carried it out. It had to look convincing, so Oksana had to sustain a real injury and the attack had to be reported to the cops, so that Brunevsky's associates would know that it was real.

Oksana was in on it, she knew it had to be done to protect her father. What she didn't know was that the attack merely put off her father's execution. She guessed eventually that a more serious game was being played. She thought Brunevsky could still save Stepan Sergeyich. That was when Lenny saw her go to Brunevsky's house.

Brunevsky was telling her the truth. He couldn't do anything about it. Nor could he delay it any longer. The day Andrei was buried, he paid the money out and the next night Maltsev was killed.

That was how it ended. I had no regrets about putting away Rubashkin. Sure, he didn't murder Kotov, but he had committed various other crimes. And, even though they did commit a murder, I felt that sending Brunevsky and Gulya to jail after what she had lived through would have been a crime, too.

But sometimes I wondered whether by associating with criminals for so long I had become one of them. It was not a pleasant thought.

There was one more thing. Returning home one night a couple of months later, after Rubashkin had been tried and convicted, I found a note on my dining table. It had three words written in a fussy, effeminate hand medical doctors often have. It read "I owe you." There was no signature.

To this day I have no idea how it got into my locked room.

HISTORICAL NOTE

Valaam, an island in Lake Ladoga north of St. Petersburg, is located on one of those fault lines between Russia and the West, between the Eastern Orthodox faith and Western Christianity.

Founded by the Novgorod Republic, the Valaam Orthodox monastery on the island was one of Imperial Russia's most holy sites, visited by both tsars and prominent citizens.

After the 1917 revolution, Valaam became part of independent Finland, as a result of which the monastery avoided desecration and destruction by the militantly atheist Bolsheviks. Until 1940.

During the Soviet-Finnish Winter War, Finland evacuated some 140 monks to the mainland and the island was occupied by the Red Army. The monks decamped to Northern Finland, to New Valaam, where even now a small Orthodox monastery continues to function.

After a few years of neglect, in the late 1940s the Soviet government found a new use for the empty monastic cells and other religious structures. Another Great War between the USSR and its western neighbors had been fought, leaving 20 million Soviets dead. The dead didn't cause the government any problems. To quote Stalin, "when there's no person, there's no problem." The problem was the two and a half million disabled veterans discharged by the Red Army during the war. Nearly half a million were amputees. Many had lost their families in the war and had nowhere to go, but some were turned out by their wives, who were unable to care for their "useless" husbands in the harsh postwar economic environment. Still others decided not to return home at all, preferring to let their loved ones think that they were missing in action.

Those men – many of them still kids – begged in flea markets, on trains and out front of movie theaters. They moved on homemade carts and leaned on crutches; they were homeless, filthy and often drunk. They were not the image of Victory Stalin wanted to present.

After a while, the police began rounding them up by the tens of thousands and sending them to special camps for cripples, far from the public eye. One of the largest, housing the worst cases, was established on Valaam Island in 1948.

No one knows how many war veterans lived and died on Valaam. In the early 1950s there were close to one thousand. Mortality was probably fairly high, but since some of them were still in their twenties, even as late as in 1971 Valaam housed over 500 inmates.

The facility was relocated in 1984. Today Valaam is once again a place of worship, visited by Russian officialdom and even by Vladimir Putin, known for his interest in the Russian Orthodox faith.

ABOUT THE AUTHOR

Alexei Bayer is a New York-based author, translator and, by economic necessity, an economist. He writes in English and in Russian, his native tongue, and translates into both languages.

His first novel, *Murder at the Dacha*, was published in 2013. The second, *The Latchkey Murders*, followed in 2015, and the third, *Murder and the Muse*, was published in 2016.

Bayer's short stories have been published in *New England Review*, *Kenyon Review*, and *Chtenia*. His translations have appeared in *Chtenia* and *Words Without Borders*, as well as in such collections as *The Wall in My Head*, a book dedicated to the twentieth anniversary of the fall of the Berlin Wall, and *Life Stories*, a bilingual literary anthology to benefit hospice care in Russia.